Female Voices and Egyptian Independence

Female Voices and Egyptian Independence

Marginalized Women in Egyptian and British Fiction

Rania M. Mahmoud

I.B.TAURIS
LONDON • NEW YORK • OXFORD • NEW DELHI • SYDNEY

I.B. TAURIS
Bloomsbury Publishing Plc, 50 Bedford Square, London, WC1B 3DP, UK
Bloomsbury Publishing Inc, 1385 Broadway, New York, NY 10018, USA
Bloomsbury Publishing Ireland, 29 Earlsfort Terrace, Dublin 2, D02 AY28, Ireland

BLOOMSBURY, I.B. TAURIS and the I.B. Tauris logo are trademarks
of Bloomsbury Publishing Plc

First published in Great Britain 2024
This paperback edition published 2025

Cover design: Adriana Brioso
Cover image: 'Egypt - Native Women', c1918-c1939 © The Print Collector /
Alamy Stock Photo

A catalogue record for this book is available from the British Library.
Library of Congress Cataloging-in-Publication Data
Names: Mahmoud, Rania M., author.
Title: Female voices and Egyptian independence : marginalized women in
Egyptian and British fiction / Rania M. Mahmoud.
Description: London ; New York : I.B Tauris, 2024. |
Includes bibliographical references and index.
Identifiers: LCCN 2023024180 (print) | LCCN 2023024181 (ebook) |
ISBN 9780755651047 (hardback) | ISBN 9780755651009 (paperback) |
ISBN 9780755651030 (pdf) | ISBN 9780755651023 (epub) | ISBN 9780755651016
Subjects: LCSH: Women in literature. | Nationalism in literature. |
Arabic fiction–Egypt–History and criticism. | Arabic fiction–20th
century–History and criticism. | Arabic fiction–21st century–History
and criticism. | English fiction–20th century–History and criticism. |
English fiction–21st century–History and criticism. | Egypt–In literature.
Classification: LCC PJ8212 .M33 2024 (print) | LCC PJ8212 (ebook) |
DDC 892.7/36093522–dc23/eng/20230906
LC record available at https://lccn.loc.gov/2023024180
LC ebook record available at https://lccn.loc.gov/2023024181

ISBN: HB: 978-0-7556-5104-7
PB: 978-0-7556-5100-9
ePDF: 978-0-7556-5103-0
eBook: 978-0-7556-5102-3

Typeset by Newgen KnowledgeWorks Pvt. Ltd., Chennai, India

For product safety related questions contact productsafety@bloomsbury.com.

To find out more about our authors and books visit www.bloomsbury.com
and sign up for our newsletters.

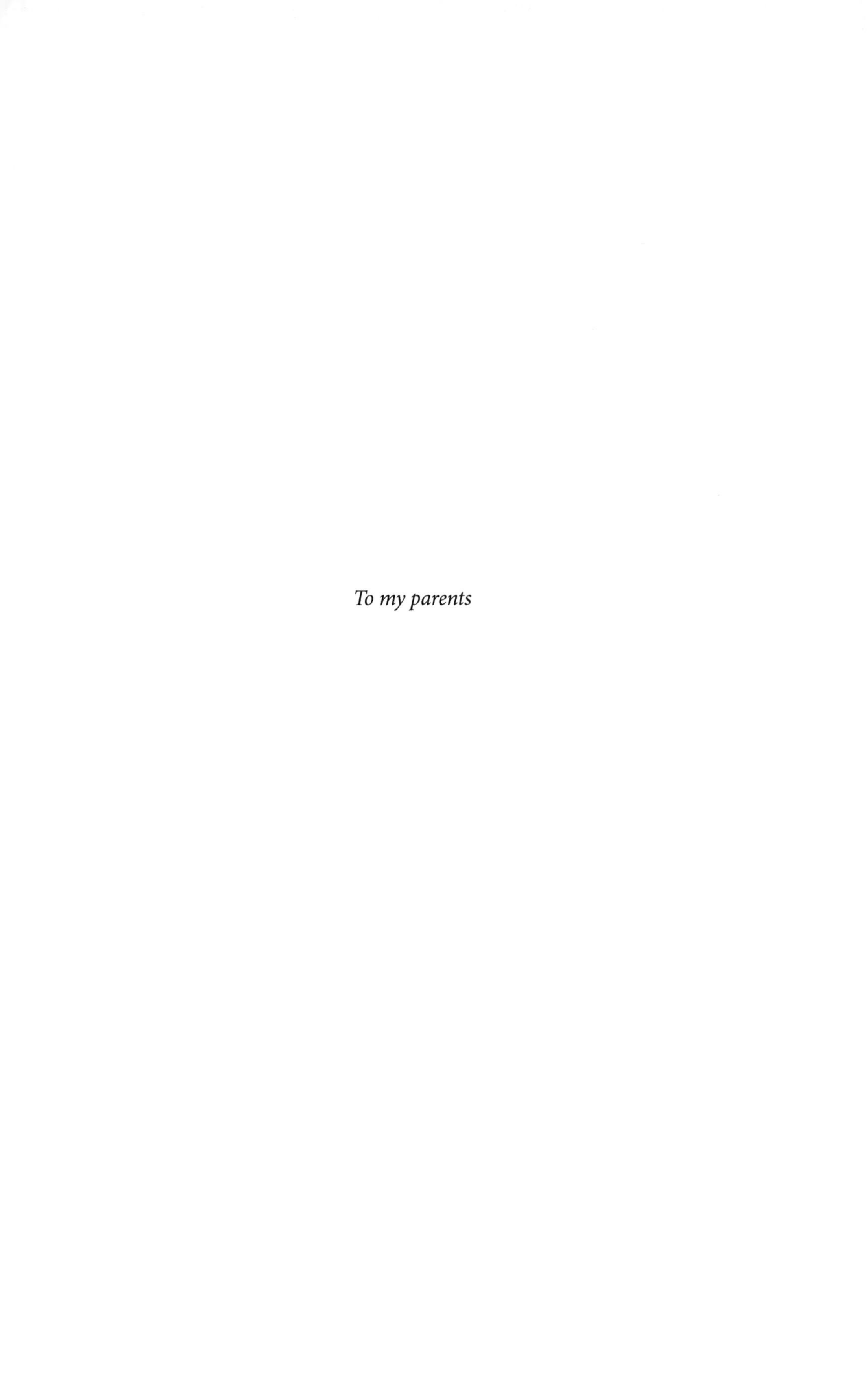

To my parents

Contents

Acknowledgments

I owe a debt of thanks to the many people whose presence in my life made this book possible. Joel Gordon has been an invaluable mentor. His willingness to read my work and the promptness with which he provided feedback helped sharpen my arguments. I thank Hope Christiansen for kindly offering her editorial expertise; Adnan Haydar and Paula Haydar for their support during the writing process; Nancy Arenberg, Kathleen Condray, Jennifer Hoyer, Kathy Sloan, and Ted Swedenburg for their mentorship as I found my way around a new institution; and Mohja Kahf, May Kosba, Reem Kosba, Violeta Lorenzo-Feliciano, and Shirin Saeidi for their friendship and for countless intellectually stimulating conversations. I am grateful to Kate Cummings, Sandy Silberstein, and Elliott Colla for seeing this project through its initial stages as a doctoral dissertation. The King Fahd Center at the University of Arkansas has provided me with the resources to complete my project. I thank the Middle East Studies Association and the American Comparative Literature Association for acting as venues to workshop my work. For their friendship and collegiality, I thank Hawraa Alzouwain, Joy Reeber, and Rhodora Vennarucci. My deep gratitude goes to Pascale Barthe, Greta Bliss, Nandana Bose, Raymond Burt, Amrita Das, Michaela Howells, Lisa Pollard, and Helena Kopchick Spencer for helping me settle into professional life. Hussein Elkhafaifi's tips on work-life balance have served me well. Many thanks to Hidy Basta, Susan Benson, Jim Chin, and Ellie Karapetian for listening to my concerns over the years and for cheering me on. I am grateful to all editors and reviewers. Above all, I thank my mother Aziza Ali Reda Sherif and my father Mohamed Mahmoud for their patience, encouragement, and unfailing support. Their unconditional love and belief in me helped me push through the toughest of times. It is to them that I dedicate this book.

Introduction

When Britain's longest reigning monarch, Queen Elizabeth II (r. 1952–2022), passed away in 2022 at the age of ninety-six, her death sparked varied intense reactions both domestically and abroad, particularly in former British colonies. While many celebrated the life of a strong female monarch, viewing her death as the end of an era, antimonarchists called for an end to the monarchy, the Irish celebrated her death with their videos going viral, and many others remembered the Queen primarily through the legacy of British imperialism.[1] For example, while Kenya's then president-elect William Ruto referred to the cordial ties the Queen had established with his country, praising her leadership of the Commonwealth, South Africa's Economic Freedom Fighters declared that they would not mourn her death. For South Africa and the whole African continent, they explained, her death evoked a painful history, noting how "she never once acknowledged the atrocities her family inflicted on native people that Britain invaded across the world."[2] Many Black Americans, although they recognized her as a human being and a grandmother, indicated that she was "an embodiment of white supremacy and inequality," inspiring voices calling for the return of the crown jewels of former colonies as well as reparations to individuals and lands divested of their natural resources. Whereas a half Jamaican American, half African American female university professor saw this as "an opportunity to question the legacy of the British monarchy and its impact on former colonies, including Jamaica and the Indian subcontinent, and their respective diasporas," another university professor of Nigerian and Trinidadian descent wished the Queen an "excruciating" death, causing an outcry that led Twitter to delete her tweet.[3]

The Queen, who ascended the throne at the age of twenty-five, took over a crumbling empire whose hold on foreign lands was becoming more and more tenuous thanks to decolonization movements, which transformed Britain in the mid- to late 1950s from a far-reaching Empire to a Commonwealth. Not only had Britain lost India, the Jewel in the Crown, in 1947, but five months after Elizabeth's accession to the throne, Egypt, which had gained nominal independence in 1922, cast off continued British control along with remnants of British presence, which had lingered in the Suez Canal zone. Yet, the official narrative of decolonization was, in large part, one of success at teaching inferior natives how to lead a modern life. Although, as Peter Hansen notes, the Queen showed optimism about the Commonwealth, her coronation speech, which coincided with euphoria about British success at climbing Mount Everest, was not free of a condescending tone as the Queen referred to the United Kingdom as an "equal partner with many other proud and independent nations. And she [the United Kingdom] is leading other still backward territories forward for the same goal."[4] Intense reactions to the Queen's life and death reflect conflicted engagements with (de)colonizing narratives. A (de)colonizing project usually poses as a civilizational program; a bildungsroman—a story of education in which underdeveloped peoples are guided by a "modern" nation, in a paternal (and mostly patronizing) relationship. Decolonization is identified as the crowning moment, indicating the relative success of the colonized in reaching a measure of modernity. Yet, this modernity remains incomplete, therefore entailing continued dependence on the former colonial power.[5]

The current project is a comparative study of twentieth- and twenty-first-century Egyptian and British engagements with British civilizational narratives in Egypt through an exploration of the cultural legacy of two of Egypt's modern revolutions (and Egyptian resistance to British hegemony) by the two main rivals involved: Egypt and Britain. In the absence of female-authored texts that discuss these revolutions, and the near absence of works that focus on female protagonists, the project examines four male-authored, male-centered texts that situate themselves either directly during the events of the Urabi Revolution and British occupation or in the aftermath of the 1919 Revolution. More specifically, I examine the use of the bildungsroman as a conduit for evaluating the modern Egyptian national project in the backdrop of both revolutions. Thus, the study shows contending visions of the Egyptian national project. I argue that while the British works evince occasional ambivalence toward Empire, they eventually capitulate, and while the Egyptian side may employ a more nuanced critique of the national project, it marginalizes female minorities. However, it is important to note that this study is not intended to be a panoramic view of the portrayal of the Egyptian national project in Egyptian and British literature. Rather, it is written as a case study of the visions presented in the four novels examined: Lawrence Durrell's *Mountolive* (1958), Naguib Mahfouz's *al-Sukkariyya*, 1957 (*Sugar Street*, 1992), John Wilcox's *The Guns of El Kebir* (2007), and Bahaa Taher's *Wahat al-ghurub*, 2006 (*Sunset Oasis*, 2009).

A literary genre emerging in eighteenth-century Germany, the European bildungsroman became connected with Enlightenment discourse that signified an imperial stance, which normalized Europe and the West as the fount of scientific, rational modernity while pathologizing alternative models. The traditional European bildungsroman focuses on a young character who undergoes a journey of education until they reach an enlightenment that allows for a harmonious coexistence with and acceptance of the social order. For normative white, heterosexual males this entails sacrificing a measure of individual freedom, while for gendered and/or racialized females existing on a spectrum of otherness marked by race, gender, sexuality, and so on, the resolution of a formative journey involves giving up individual freedom with the goal of assimilation into the exclusively domestic role that society prescribes for women. First, this formula centers youth, presupposing the linearity as well as the inevitability of development and, second, views any deviations from such progress as a mark of regression that denotes failure on the part of the protagonist to acclimate to the social order—failure to be educated. Mostly, while this affects some white male characters (as I will clarify further on), nonnormative characters tend to bear the brunt of this restrictive formula.

In both narratives (the civilizational/(de)colonizing as well as the fictional bildungsroman), the education of the subject is given narrative whereby a superior social order or an imperial power assumes the role of mentor professing to train a "different" person or group of people in the values of modernity, often presented as coeval with Westernness/whiteness and promising to leave once subjects demonstrate their maturity by shedding their supposedly outmoded values and assimilating into the European paradigm. At the end of the journey of development, natives will supposedly receive the gift of independence and self-government as a reward for adopting a normative European model. Thus, political maturity is concomitant with personal maturity.

Although scholars of the Arabic novel have increasingly studied the interplay between colonialism, modernity, nation, and identity, studies of the bildungsroman in an Arab sociopolitical context, let alone full-length or comparative studies of the genre, remain sparse. *Female Voices and Egyptian Independence* has three main goals.

First, it addresses this gap by focusing on explorations of the coming-of-age narrative as a blueprint for identity negotiation in four novels published between 1957 and 2007. Second, by retrieving suppressed female narratives of education in these texts, I illustrate the ways in which these marginalized female characters, who challenge the normative model of domesticity and docility, ultimately shape the male protagonists in ways that either challenge or confirm the Anglo-European development narrative and, in turn, subvert or reaffirm the paradigm of individual progress as a yardstick for the nation's political maturity and, therefore, modernity. Third, by adopting a more flexible definition of bildungsroman—one that does not necessarily stress youth—the project decenters the idea of youth and a singular watershed moment signalling maturation. On the contrary, I argue that, first, one may reach enlightenment quite late in life, or reach it at the moment of death, as in my analysis of *Wahat al-ghurub* (*Sunset Oasis*) and, second, that the idea of bildung exists in every story. Consequently, any life-changing experience that one encounters could potentially be seen as a bildungsroman, as is the case with Simon and Alice in *The Guns of El Kebir*. Both *Wahat al-ghurub* and *The Guns of El-Kebir*, which are clearly not bildungsroman narratives in the traditional sense of the term, destabilize definitions of the genre.

The Bildungsroman and Arabic Literature

First emerging in late eighteenth-century Germany at the hands of Goethe whose *Wilhelm Meister* (1795–6) is often upheld as the prototypical bildungsroman and described as a novel outlining the journey of education, development, formation, or coming of age of an individual, the genre was picked up by British and French writers. According to Tobias Boes, many subsequent works diverged from the German model shifting the emphasis from performativity, which highlighted the process/journey of the protagonist, to a prescriptive fixation on the positive end result of the protagonist's teleological movement.[6] Associating growth with modernity, of which the West became paradigmatic, classic Anglo-European narratives portrayed a progression, which culminated in positive closure that marked the protagonist's advent into modernity and history. Self-congratulatory in its affirmation of Western European cultural superiority, the classic European bildungsroman required the European protagonist to give up only a measure of freedom in exchange for a harmonious existence with society. In contrast, by standardizing the European paradigm as the only path toward modernity, the genre became restrictive, compelling minority characters to give up their individuality, identity, and/or history, and submit to the European social order in order to be pronounced modern. Thus, modelling a narrative of acculturation into a superior Western model, the bildungsroman nurtured a European sense of self-worth while marking the Other as inferior.

Recent scholarship points to the genre's complicity in the colonialist imperialist project where the male protagonist's education, paralleled by the nation's final maturity and enlightenment—their entrance into modernity and history as subjects—is predicated on reconciliation to the European paradigm as the only road toward individual and national growth. Jed Esty, for example, examines the modernist bildungsroman's challenge to this developmental template. Recording disillusionment in modernist narratives of formation set in colonial contact zones, he analyzes white, male-centered texts whose protagonists either refuse or fail to mature, existing in a state of eternal youth. Esty concludes that, by replicating the imperialist project as a never-ending endeavor where individual and nation live an eternal adolescence, these narratives emerge as antidevelopmental, showing resolution/adulthood to be an illusion.[7]

Increasingly, critiques of the genre have paid attention to its portrayal of peripheral groups. In a genre that presupposes a European social order, and links personal growth to political maturity, fulfilment for the racialized or gendered Other is requisite upon self-marginalization. In her study of Asian American bildungsromane, Lisa Lowe critiques the genre's assumption of a universal selfhood that excludes alternative modernities and affirms orientalism's binary power structure.[8] Geta LeSeur writes on male and female African American and West Indian coming-of-age narratives that show protagonists subverting the rigid norms of colonial, imperial societies that forestall their development.[9] In a similar vein, feminist scholars study female characters who insist on staying true to their identity. Constricted by male, heteronormative rules, they find madness and/or death synonymous with autonomy—endings that in the traditional, male bildungsroman signify failure to grow. Thus, female protagonists find no fulfilment in a genre where domesticity is the only path available. In the narratives analyzed, suicide and death constitute acts of defiance to genre conventions that, denying women the same paths as their male counterparts, aim to socialize them in the values of domesticity.[10] Such critiques expose the classic Anglo-European bildungsroman as stifling racial, sexual, and gender difference, since resolution is dependent on self-suppression, repudiation of native culture, and submission to a rigid, patriarchal, foreign order.

For Arab intellectuals, as for many subjugated peoples, the genre served as a space for exploring indigenous identities and cultures that, more often than not, were portrayed as lacking in their encounter with Western civilization, sometimes by the colonized subjects themselves. Tawfiq al-Hakim's *'Awdat al-ruh*, 1933 (*Return of the Spirit*, 1984), his *'Usfur min al-sharq*, 1938 (*Bird of the East*, 1966), Yahya Haqqi's *Qindil umm Hashim*, 1940 (*The Saint's Lamp*, 1973), and Tayeb Salih's *Mawsim al-hijra ila al-shamal*, 1966 (*Season of Migration to the North*, 1969) are well-known examples. Nedal al-Mousa finds the bildungsroman narrative integral to the Arabic novel. Often depicting a hero torn between two cultures, judging native culture by the norms of the foreign one, bildungsroman novels sought ways to teach the protagonist how to reconcile two allegedly opposed cultural systems.[11] Despite interest in literary explorations of identity, however, many studies tend to focus more on the Arabic novel in general and less on the bildungsroman. For instance, Jeff Shalan discusses the emergence of the novel as the genre par excellence for nationalist self-expression in early twentieth-century Egypt.[12] In an informative study, Muhsin al-Musawi investigates the genre's engagement with the politics of the postcolonial nation, as well as female writers' subversion of patriarchy through the Scheherazade trope.[13] Further, al-Musawi investigates the interrogation of nation, selfhood, family, and religion in post-1967 Arabic literature.[14] Writing on the socialist romance, Ellen McLarney theorizes romantic love as a socialist antidote to modernity's and the nation's classism and patriarchy.[15]

Bringing more attention to marginalized groups, scholars such as Hoda El Sadda, explore the hegemonic nature of modernity, the nation, and the novel itself, introducing recent works by men and women that break writing codes, while Christine Gilmore finds in Nubian expression of expropriation a demand for inclusion.[16] Mary Youssef analyzes twenty-first-century Egyptian narratives that focus on traditionally marginalized groups, such as Copts, Nubians, Siwans, Bedouins, and non-heteronormative groups.[17] Finally, Dina Heshmat studies fictional, dramatic, and cinematic representations of the 1919 Revolution, recording revisionist voices by contemporary male and female authors. Heshmat explores how the screen adaptation of Mahfouz's classic *Bayn al-qasrayn*, 1956 (*Palace Walk*, 1990) for example, inaccurately inserts in the 1919 Revolution female and underprivileged voices missing from the original work. Such additions align the work with Nasser's discourse (with its ethos of the inclusion of women), portraying the 1952 military coup as a teleological outcome of 1919.[18] However, only few studies of Arabic literature investigate the Arabic bildungsroman, or Arab women's struggle against patriarchy in female narratives of formation, or the creative ways in which Arabic literature merges the bildungsroman with Arabic memoirs to address gender and race in postcolonial Morocco.[19]

Maria Elena Paniconi's 2023 book on the Egyptian Bildungsroman redresses this imbalance. Covering novels from Mohammed Hussein Heikal's *Zaynab* (1913), canonized as the first Arabic novel, all the way up to the contemporary moment, Paniconi sheds light on the ways in which Egyptian male and female authors have utilized the bildungsroman (or some of its tropes) to explore, question, subvert, and revise the coming-of-age narrative. In a similar manner to the current study, the author does not confine herself to texts that adhere to the classic definition of the form, with its emphasis on youth and progress. Her texts extend from classics, such as Taha Hussein's *Adib*, 1935 (*A Man of Letters*, 1994) whose thirty-year-old protagonist, in Paniconi's analysis, emerges as a modernist antihero, to experimental and/or nonlinear plots in the late twentieth century, examples of which are *Al-Khiba'* (*The Tent*, 1996) by the female author Miral al-Tahawi and Sonallah Ibrahim's *Sharaf* (1997). In place of teleological growth, many of the protagonists in Paniconi's study experience stasis, deformation, disintegration, fragmentation, and alienation.[20] The current study adopts a similar approach.

Methodology

Following two major methods, *Female Voices and Egyptian Independence* offers a nuanced analysis of the ways in which four male-authored works evaluate the Egyptian nationalist project in its struggle against British hegemony. First by reading the novels against the grain, the study recovers female voices that are multiply marginalized, due to their gender and/or ethnicity, whether by colonial imperial powers, the nation, their immediate regional community, or, finally, by the works under discussion themselves. Second, using a comparative lens, the study foregrounds the ways in which Egyptian and British authors confirm, critique, rewrite/revise, or reject developmental narratives. In my analysis, I pay particular attention to women who range from the uneducated Black slave (a topic only mildly discussed in Arabic literary studies), to the uneducated rural Siwan woman with artistic talent (*Wahat al-ghurub*), to the wealthy cultured Coptic housewife (*Mountolive*), to the rising late-nineteenth-century British female professional (*The Guns of El Kebir*), and, finally, to the eclipsed twentieth-century Egyptian female national intellectual (*al-Sukkariyya*), all of whom play crucial roles in the journeys of the respective male protagonists.

A representative rather than a comprehensive study, *Female Voices and Egyptian Independence* offers a comparative analysis of two Egyptian and two British novels that evaluate the Egyptian national project while using the bildungsroman as an analytical category that aids in understanding this project. Each chapter begins by shining a spotlight on a marginalized female character whose actions are instrumental to the development of the male protagonist. To this end, this book examines Egyptian sociopolitical life in the aftermath of two revolutions: the 1881–2 Urabi Revolution, known for inaugurating the British occupation of Egypt, and the 1919 Revolution, constructed in Egyptian nationalist discourse as the classic Egyptian revolution par excellence.[21] For their negotiation of the legacy of Egypt's 1919 Revolution almost two decades later, this study pairs two classics whose authors, perhaps unbeknownst to themselves, competed with each other over the Nobel Prize in literature in 1988 until it went to Naguib Mahfouz. Lawrence Durrell's *Mountolive* (1958), the third volume of *The Alexandria Quartet*, is placed in conversation with Mahfouz's *al-Sukkariyya* (1957), the last volume of *The Cairo Trilogy* (1956–7). For twenty-first-century reappraisals of the 1881–2 Urabi Revolution, John Wilcox's *The Guns of El Kebir* (2007) appears alongside Bahaa Taher's *Wahat al-ghurub* (2006).

In showing different perspectives on Egyptian resistance to British domination, I argue that the marginalized women in the narratives are instrumental to the male protagonists' rejection/understanding/critique of the national project. For example, in *Mountolive*, David Mountolive is coached by the Coptic Egyptian Leila Hosnani until he blossoms into a cultured diplomat. His view of Egypt throughout the novel is colored by his view of Leila and the Hosnanis. Impressed by their sophistication at first, he romanticizes both the Hosnanis and Egypt. In the end, following his knowledge of the family's involvement in an anti-British conspiracy, his exoticization of Leila and Egypt turns into rejection of both, and rejection of Egypt as a potential equal or a sovereign state capable of self-government. In *al-Sukkariyya*, I argue that it is the marginalized female journalist Sawsan Hammad who helps the male protagonist define the parameters of the Egyptian national project. In *Guns of El Kebir*, it is the marginalized feminist journalist Alice Covington who, despite her anti-imperialism, eventually pronounces Urabi a villain, thus justifying Empire. Ultimately, both she and the unconventional Simon Fonthill (the male lead) acknowledge the necessity of the British occupation. Finally, in *Wahat al-ghurub*, the two marginalized women (Ne'ma and Maleeka) haunt Mahmoud, forcing him on a journey of introspection that leads him to understand that his rejection of Ne'ma and his treatment of Maleeka mirror Egypt's exclusion of minorities from the national project.

Although the study follows reverse order starting with the 1919 Revolution first before moving to the 1881–2 Urabi Revolution, it progresses in terms of the publication dates of the texts analyzed. Thus, *Female Voices and Egyptian Independence* ends with contemporary views of Egypt's recent past where the authors' reckoning with their respective histories reflects attempts to understand and/or rethink the contemporary moment. John Wilcox's *The Guns of El Kebir* betrays lingering nostalgia despite attempts to see events from the point of view of the "Other." One in a series of fourteen novels that attempt to revive a glorious British imperial past, *Guns* reflects unease with Britain's now much-diminished power on the world stage. The novel's setting in the early 1880s coincides with an already waning Empire. Yet, evocations of the imperial past coupled with assertions of Simon's nonconventional character and Alice's anti-imperialism, although promise a revisionist narrative, portray Britain as an unwilling participant in the imperial project. The British occupation of Egypt poses as an act triggered by altruistic motives whereby Britain bears the burden of colonialism in order to restore order and civilize unruly Egyptians. Thus, *Guns* exposes reluctance to face the exploitative reality of the imperial past.

Bahaa Taher, in his reappraisal of Egyptian national identity, revisits an era rife with nascent *Nahdawi* debates on nation, identity, and modernity—debates in which the minority voices of women, Copts, and Syrian Christians were active.[22] Yet, the mostly elitist contributions to these debates, premised upon access to a Western-style humanistic education, precluded the participation of racial, ethnic, geographic, class, and gendered voices. Thus, Ne'ma's presence as a gendered and racialized member of an enslaved group, and Maleeka's identity as a woman belonging to the periphery of Siwa, whose males are themselves marginalized, signal Taher's recognition of the need to re-draw the contours of Egyptian identity. Additionally, *Sunset Oasis* shows sensitivity to the role played by a native form of Egyptian colonialism (extended to Siwa, Sudan, and enslaved peoples) in the historical definition of Egyptian identity. The text calls for a fresh new start.

Female Voices and Egyptian Independence, therefore, contributes to studies on fictional (re)evaluations of revolutionary moments that, in their engagement with the colonial past, seek to understand the effects of (de) colonizing impulses and the concomitant center-periphery pattern on a global (Britain-Egypt) as well as a local (Cairo/Alexandria-Siwa) scale. The four novels under discussion, each published a year apart from its counterpart, reflect a trajectory in the understanding of Egyptian revolutions and national identity at two different historical moments. In its analysis of textual engagements with the lingering legacy of Empire, the study traces the ways in which, on the one hand, the imperial center continues to struggle to come to terms with its imperial past and, on the other hand, the postcolonial periphery replicates colonialist patterns by acting as a center that marginalizes its local peripheries.

Egypt in the Nineteenth Century

The 1881–2 Urabi Revolution and the 1919 Revolution were born out of the intellectual and cultural ferment sustained since the early nineteenth century by Muhammad Ali's (r. 1805–48) efforts to create a modern Egyptian state to rival the Ottoman Empire. A soldier himself, the Albanian ruler knew that his political ambition depended on centralized power and a strong, modern army with modern state institutions. Thus, the need for an efficiently organized medical practice that ensured soldiers' good health spurred transformation in the study and practice of medicine. This was accompanied by reform in education that was to supply the state with bureaucrats. Rather than institute a complete overhaul, Ali worked with old and new models simultaneously so that folk and modern medicine existed side by side, as did *Katatib* (nongraded religious schools) and Western-style schools. On the international level, state-sponsored students sent on education missions to Europe (mostly France) brought back much-needed expertise in many fields including medicine, engineering, science, and languages.[23] To varying degrees, Ali's successors followed in his footsteps, and the desire to transform Egypt into Paris on the Nile fueled infrastructure projects as well as huge enterprises such as the Suez Canal, inaugurated in 1869. Changes that obtained in the professional and cultural arenas engendered the *Nahda* (intellectual renaissance) so that when the 1919 Revolution occurred, Egypt not only had post offices, a railroad system, and an expanding Western-style education system (despite British efforts to constrain it)[24] but also boasted a vibrant theater culture and an active press, including a women's press, whose ideas circulated both locally and nationally, thanks in large part to the mail service that facilitated the traffic of periodicals from Cairo to villages.[25]

In his fascinating study of Egyptian mass culture and the 1919 Revolution, Ziad Fahmy offers the framework of "media capitalism," to counter Benedict Andersen's concept of print capitalism, as a more useful category in studying Egyptian nationalism. With its beginnings in the 1870s, Egypt's mass culture included newspapers, plays, and *azjal* (sing. *zajal*; poetry written in the vernacular) that mostly used colloquial Egyptian. The pioneers of these cultural productions were 'Uthman Jalal (1828–1898), Ya'qub Sannu' (1839–1912), and 'Abdallah Nadim (1845–1898), the famous orator of the Urabi

Revolution.[26] This mass culture facilitated the flow of written ideas through "oral/aural" means, to use Fahmy's words, reaching the masses in a country with a high illiteracy rate. Fahmy shows that entertainment delivered in colloquial Egyptian (such as satirical newspapers read aloud, vaudeville, political cartoons, *zajal*, and songs) was more popular and more commercially successful than written documents in *fusha* (formal Arabic), arguing that this orality/aurality helped create an imagined Egyptian community.[27]

Hoda Yousef explains that Egypt's rich print culture included newspapers, periodicals, schoolbooks, new editions of traditional Arabic texts, in addition to fiction and nonfiction. Although many newspapers and periodicals did not survive long, there was a sizeable output during the late nineteenth century and into the twentieth century.[28] Despite a low literacy rate in 1897 (0.2 percent for women compared to 8 percent for men, in total 5.8 percent of Egypt's population), there were an estimated 169 periodicals in 1898, not to mention over thirty Arabic-language women's journals available between 1892 and 1919, the circulation of which increased in the twentieth century.[29] For instance, over 200 new Arabic periodicals appeared in Egypt between 1880 and 1900, and by 1910 Egyptian newspapers exceeded 100,000 daily circulation.[30] Additionally, as Beth Baron notes, private printing presses multiplied so that by 1910 there were 130 presses in Egypt, not including those with one or two people.[31] Bahaa Taher, author of *Wahat al-ghurub*, counts ten unofficial newspapers representing different schools of thought under Khedive Ismail (r. 1863–79).[32]

Although literacy was lower among women, between 1892 and 1919 the women's press yielded "more than thirty Arabic-language weeklies and monthlies produced by, for, and about women."[33] Between the start of the twentieth century and after the 1919 Revolution women's journals had an estimated circulation of high hundreds, with some in the few thousands, compared to several thousand daily copies for male-led newspapers. More women's journals surfaced in the 1920s and onwards, with mounting circulation corresponding to growth in education.[34] Fahmy explains that

> by 1915 the total number of schools and *katatib* (religious schools; sing. *kuttab*) reached 9,060, with more than 543,000 students (80,000 of whom were female). This dramatic rise in the number of students not only increased Egypt's literacy rate, which slowly inched to 6.8% by 1917 … but

also simultaneously exposed tens of thousands of students every year to a standardized curriculum, which in most cases included the history and geography of Egypt.[35]

By the early twentieth century reading habits had changed; reading for leisure having become more common and for more than just the most educated.[36] This reformulation of literacy practices happened in tandem with a steady increase in literacy rates—5.8 percent in 1897, 6.8 percent in 1917, 11.8 percent in 1927, and 17.1 percent in 1937—and published material, complemented by other literacy modes such as song, theater performances that supported the nationalist cause, constant renditions of these cultural productions, as well as pieces from the satirical press.[37] By 1937, when 17.1 percent of Egyptians were literate—9.5 percent of women compared to 24.7 percent of men—Egypt had over 250 Arabic-language periodicals, and its top-selling newspaper, *al-Ahram*, sold 50,000 daily copies.[38]

Egyptians' reading ability, though consistently on the rise, was but one form of literacy that was higher among males and in the urban centers of Cairo and Alexandria.[39] *Al-Ahram*'s 20,000 daily copies in 1919,[40] would have been "read" by literate and illiterate alike as the habit of reading newspapers aloud turned into a social activity. As Fahmy puts it, Egyptians consumed culture not only by hearing songs and performances but also by hearing the newspaper read aloud so that "cafés and other urban meeting places became important oral communication centers and were intimately connected with newspapers and, later, newly introduced sound media."[41]

Sustained by as well as inspiring this rich cultural life were two revolutions: the 1881–2 Urabi Revolution and the 1919 Revolution. Debates brewing in the press since well before the British occupation nourished nationalist thought. Chief was the question of how to make Egypt a modern nation, along with the attendant issues of education, governance, and women's role in the nation. Egyptians, especially elites who had been distancing themselves from the Ottoman practices of polygamy and seclusion, agreed that Egypt's modernization lay in the reformation of the family. A microcosm of the nation, a democratically governed family free of the despotism of the father was the blueprint of a democratically governed nation. Intellectuals deemed education essential for women,[42] who were to take on the active task of "nurturing the nation" from home.[43]

The Urabi Revolution comprised a complicated set of events, whose causes and consequences have remained widely contested by historians. What is clear is the economic context: When French, British, and other powers deposed Egypt's ruler, Khedive Ismail, in 1879, he had indebted Egypt by 90 million pounds. In April 1876, Ismail's efforts to modernize Egypt sent the country into bankruptcy. Huge projects, prominent among which was the Suez Canal, heavily financed with money borrowed at exorbitant interest rates from foreign moneylenders, brought the country to ruin. An International Commission for Public Debt was formed, which included British, French, and other European members, with two presiding European controllers general.[44] Under this system, French and British observers in Egypt, who were entitled to attend and participate in all cabinet meetings as counselors, had more power and higher salaries than ministers.[45]

Between 1876 and 1879 the number of European nationals in the Egyptian civil service rose to 534, their large, tax-exempt salaries putting a financial strain on the Egyptian treasury. For example, Captain Evelyn Baring, later Lord Cromer and British high consul in Egypt from 1883 to 1907, earned 3,000 Pounds Sterling a year when he was first appointed to the Commission of Egypt's Public Debt. In the meantime, Egyptian employees' already diminutive salaries were in arrears.[46] To add insult to injury, under the Law of Capitulations over 100,000 foreign residents in Egypt paid no taxes "at a time when the fellahin [peasants] were being flogged to disgorge their last piastre."[47] By 1881 Britain had controlled 70 percent of Egyptian trade and half of Egypt's income was dedicated to the payment of the debt, the burden of which fell to impoverished Egyptian peasants.[48]

Although the Urabi Revolution started in the military, it garnered the support of almost all Egyptians who were affected by increasing European control of the country's political and economic life.[49] The revolution was punctuated by two main demonstrations occurring in February and September of 1881 during the reign of Khedive Tawfiq, Ismail's son and successor. It started as a protest against the Circassian Minister of War, Uthman Rifky, who held Egyptian officers in contempt and favored Turco-Circassian and Albanian officers. Under Khedive Said (r. 1854–63), predecessor of the deposed Ismail, Egyptian officers had finally found an opportunity to advance in the military. While during his reign Ahmed Urabi, the leader of the revolution, received promotions in the military rising to colonel quickly, during Ismail's reign (1863–79) he was tried and imprisoned. Although he was later released and reinstated, his promotion was frozen for nineteen years while Turco-Circassian subordinates bypassed him. Other Egyptian officers suffered similar injustices. The early days of Khedive Tawfiq (r. 1879–92) boded a continuation of the status quo. Under Rifky, inefficient Turco-Circassian officers were promoted ahead of more deserving Egyptians while Egyptian officers were denied the right to a fair trial and demoted or banished to the Sudan based on false charges.[50]

The first event of the revolution, the Qasr al-Nil demonstration on February 1, 1881, was a reaction to Rifky's decision in January 1881 to transfer and dismiss two Egyptian officers and replace them with Circassians. Officers, including the affected ones, elected Urabi their leader, upon which he submitted a petition requesting reforms in the military. Khedive Tawfiq agreed to these demands, promising to institute the constitution drafted under his father and predecessor, Khedive Ismail, whose deposition had prevented its approval.[51] According to twentieth-century Egyptian historian Abd al-Rahman al-Rafi'i, Tawfiq's failure to make good on his promise led to the September 1881 Abdin demonstrations, the second major incident in the Urabi Revolution.[52]

In a manner that anticipates the 1919 Revolution, Egyptians from various parts of Egypt belonging to all strata of society—religious scholars, the elite, village leaders, and Arab sheikhs—who recognized the urgency of reform, signed documents delegating Urabi to represent the nation.[53] With their blessing, he demanded a parliament and an end to the government led by Riyadh Pasha, whose proclivity toward absolute rule was compounded by his support of European Powers.[54] Failing to dissuade the demonstrators, with even his personal guards joining the protesting army, Khedive Tawfiq eventually conceded to their demands. Rafi'i notes that the demonstration, which included around 4,000 officers with their arms and artillery, was a huge event that the public watched from the outskirts of Abdin square and from neighboring houses.[55]

While the British government was not happy with the turn that events had taken after the demonstrations, it was the Alexandria massacre of June 11, 1882, that precipitated, or rather facilitated, Britain's advent into Egypt. The massacre, which *The Guns of El Kebir* vividly details albeit with imperialist tones, broke out after an altercation between an Egyptian donkey-boy and a Maltese national in which the latter stabbed the former. Egyptians sided with the donkey-boy and a fight ensued, upon which Europeans started firing with guns and rifles from upper windows of houses. The result was an "indiscriminate struggle" where many Europeans were killed by Maltese and Greek bullets. Trying to stop the fight the British consul in Alexandria was attacked, and his servants injured while the Italian and Greek consuls sustained some injuries.[56] Up until this point, the British Cabinet had been divided on how to deal with nationalists, its decisions mainly colored by its members' views of Irish nationalists. However, according to twentieth-century-Egypt-historian Afaf Lutfi Sayyid-Marsot, after the Alexandria massacre even radicals were convinced that Urabi was a dictator—a point quite relevant to Alice's assessment of events in *The Guns of El Kebir*.[57]

Britain used the incident to occupy Egypt under the pretext of restoring stability and protecting European residents from a so-called anti-Christian sentiment. The bombardment of Alexandria began in July 1882, and on September 13, 1882, the British won the decisive battle of Tel el Kebir that lasted about forty minutes. Ten thousand Egyptian troops were killed in contrast to only fifty-seven British troops.[58] Twentieth-century Egyptian historian Mahmoud al-Khafif writes that fires went on in Alexandria for several days after the bombardment.[59] The British occupation of Egypt lasted seventy-two years, the British making about 120 declarations and pledges to leave Egypt between 1882 and 1907 even as they introduced actions that tightened Britain's grip over the country.[60] However, the occupation did not go unchallenged. In 1919, Britain would face another revolution.

Saad Zaghloul and the 1919 Revolution are closely intertwined in the Egyptian national memory. To this day, Zaghloul is commemorated in various street, square, and subway station names across Egypt, his figure and the 1919 Revolution invoked, through reappropriation and remobilization of the image of a cross nestled into a crescent during the 2011 Revolution.[61] According to Israel Gershoni, two anti-British nationalist strains dominated Egypt before the 1919 Revolution. The first favored continued alliance with the Ottoman Empire as a means of preserving a Muslim identity, which, for a long time, carried with it military, scientific, commercial, and cultural hegemony. The second stance, which advocated independence from both empires (Ottoman and British), viewed the Ottoman presence as an invasion that caused Egypt's stagnation while enriching the Ottoman metropole.[62]

The 1919 Revolution encapsulates a series of demonstrations that occurred on March 10, 1919, after Britain denied an Egyptian delegation, *wafd* (the seedling of the *Wafd* Party) its request for a hearing at the Versailles Peace Conference. To retaliate the Ottoman Empire's decision to side with Germany, Britain had declared Egypt a protectorate in 1914. During the war, Egypt not only served as a military base for Britain in the Middle East and as a center for British propaganda, eventually aiding Britain's victory, but also endured atrocities committed by soldiers of the British Empire stationed in Egypt, some of whom attacked and sometimes killed Egyptians.[63] Inspired by both the Allies' promises of freedom for smaller nations at the conclusion of the First World War and by President Woodrow Wilson's Fourteen Points Speech, Egyptians saw an opportunity to discuss the country's situation after the First World War.[64]

When the British government refused to grant permission to travel, the *Wafd* Party collected signatures form Egyptians authorizing former Egyptian cabinet minister and vice-president elect of the Egyptian Legislative Assembly, Saad Zaghloul, and his companions to speak for the nation. According to Sayyid-Marsot, the *Wafd* enjoyed such popular support that its Central Committee reached seventeen members, while public membership included almost all Egypt. The party also included members from the Coptic community who, for the first time, allied themselves with the rest of Egyptians.[65] As a means of rallying public support, the *Wafd* delivered speeches around the Egyptian countryside.[66]

Ignoring the petitions, on March 9, 1919, Britain exiled Zaghloul and two other *Wafd* members to Malta. This provoked the six-day demonstrations that came to be known as the 1919 Revolution, transforming Zaghloul (previously seen as servile follower to the British) into a national hero.[67] Demonstrations in the name of the exiled *Wafdists*, but mainly Saad Zaghloul, were initiated by students at the colleges of Law, Medicine, Engineering, and Al-Azhar, who were joined by tram and taxi drivers as well as Cairo shopkeepers who closed their shops in solidarity. Protests grew to include the Syndicate of Lawyers, all government officials, railway workers, and elite women in their veils. Students circulated the news as they traveled back to their hometowns spreading the revolution to other parts of the country. To avoid a repeat of the British crackdown on the 1881–2 Urabi Revolution with troops from India, demonstrating Egyptians tampered with railway lines and carriages and in rural areas even killed British officials.[68]

Although in April Britain released the exiled nationalists giving them permission to go to Paris, unrest continued in Egypt until the end of 1919, and over the period of ten months British forces killed 800 Egyptians and wounded 1,400.[69] The *Wafd*'s negotiations with Britain continued until Britain's unilateral declaration of 1922 granting Egypt independence. However, this independence proved nominal as Britain continued to intervene in Egypt's affairs, objecting in 1935, for instance, to the restoration of the 1923 constitution,[70] or surrounding the King's palace in 1941 ordering him to choose between abdication and the appointment of a pro-British *Wafdist* prime minister.[71] The party was also instrumental in achieving the 1936 treaty, which slackened Britain's grip over Egypt, reducing the foremost British official in Egypt from high commissioner to ambassador, the post that David Mountolive occupies in Durrell's *Moutolive*.[72] The *Wafd* continued to lead the national struggle until 1952 when Gamal Abdel Nasser, second president of Egypt, dissolved it after the 1952 Coup.[73]

Egypt's revolutionary moments, 1919 more so than the Urabi Revolution, have fed literary explorations of nation and identity as writers sought to understand, celebrate, commemorate, or critique the revolution and its iconic figures. For example, in two comic plays that Heshmat analyzes, *al-Intikhabat* (*The Elections*, 1923) and *Imbratur Zifta* (*The Emperor of Zifta*, 1924) Amin Sidqi respectively critiques the constraints of the parliamentary system made possible by the 1919 Revolution and sees as a failure the declaration of independence of Zifta (a town in the Egyptian Delta) during the 1919 events.[74] In his novel *'Awdat al-ruh*, 1933 (*Return of the Spirit*, 1984), Tawfiq al-Hakim's protagonist Muhsin matures as an artist and an intellectual against the backdrop of the 1919 Revolution. In *'Usfur min al-sharq*, 1938 (*Bird of the East*, 1966), by the same author, the protagonist's memory of 1919 evokes unpleasant, bloody scenes, thus betraying an elitist antidemocratic perspective toward 1919.[75] Fikri Abaza's autobiographical novel *al-Dahik al-baki* (*The Weeping Laughter*, 1933), set in Upper Egypt, narrates the events from an elitist point of view.[76] Naguib Mahfouz, who witnessed some of the events as a seven-year-old, was preoccupied by 1919. In *al-Samman wa al-kharif*, 1962 (*Autumn Quail*, 1985), for example, he reflects on the corruption of the *Wafd* Party. *Hiyakat haritna*, 1975 (*The Fountain and the Tomb*, 1988), features eight out of seventy-eight tales that address the 1919 Revolution, while *al-Maraya*, 1972 (*Mirrors*, 1977), briefly hints at it.[77] Even as writers moved on to explore the 1952 Coup/Revolution, fictional characters reflected the cultural and literary ethos of *Nahdawi* thought that accompanied the 1919 Revolution and influenced prominent figures, such as Nasser himself who was deeply moved by Hakim's *Return of the Sprit*.[78] In Latifa al-Zayyat's iconic female bildungsroman *al-Bab al-maftuh*, 1960 (*The Open Door*, 2000), depicting a protagonist coming of age sexually and politically in the context of 1952, Layla and her male cousin grow up reading the influential thinker Salama Musa.

For purposes of scope, this study limits itself to a discussion of the Urabi and 1919 revolutions and only to texts where marginalized women play an active role in the conversation on Egyptian national identity. In its efforts to propose original readings to newer and classic texts by centering women's roles (e.g., Mahfouz's *Sugar Street*), *Female Voices and Egyptian Independence* leaves out works, such as Heikal's *Zaynab*, Hakim's *Return of the Spirit*, and Haqqi's *Qindil umm Hashim*, already extensively discussed by scholars of Arabic literature.

Chapter Overview

Chapter 1 focuses on the third volume of Lawrence Durrell's famous *Alexandria Quartet* (1957–60). Mostly set in 1930s Egypt and engrossed in evaluating British-Egyptian relations in the aftermath of the 1919 Revolution, *Mountolive* (1958) delivers an imperialist evaluation of Egypt's national project. Reading the Coptic Egyptian woman, Leila Hosnani, as an individual, I rescue her from the orientalist image in which she is cast as the young British diplomat's lover whose ugly face toward the end of the novel suddenly awakens him to the true face of Egypt. The chapter starts by unearthing the story of Leila as a modern, elite woman who is better educated than David Mountolive, the British diplomat and protagonist. My reading breaks the Egyptian woman's orientalist shackle by showing that Mountolive blossoms into a cultured individual under her aegis. I argue that despite an exotic representation, Leila, who becomes synonymous with Egypt, is an agent who dictates the terms of her relationship with Mountolive over around two decades and mocks him and the text through sarcasm.

Reading the novel through colonial fantasy, I argue that the novel is ridden with nostalgia such that Mountolive refuses to see the real Leila/Egypt in none other than orientalist terms. First seeing them both as fantastic, that is, unfamiliar and exotically attractive, he falls for the romanticized image of Egypt, only to be rudely awakened by the presumably ugly face of the scheming Leila/Egypt. Mountolive, who returns to Egypt in the mid-1930s as ambassador to a now independent country, discovers that Christians in Egypt have been plotting against the British to establish a Jewish state in Palestine—an event with no basis in history. Ultimately, both Egypt and Leila, whose sons are involved in the conspiracy, are depicted as grotesque. Mountolive's maturity, as the novel depicts it, hinges on his recognition of Egyptians (both Christian and Muslim) as irredeemably corrupt and politically immature, therefore reaffirming colonialist claims stating that Egypt is in constant need of British patronage.

Chapter 2 analyzes the last volume of Naguib Mahfouz's celebrated *Cairo Trilogy* (1956–7). Set in the 1930s and 1940s, *al-Sukkariyya*, 1957 (*Sugar Street*, 1992), is preoccupied with evaluating the legacy of the 1919 Revolution and the Egyptian national project. In this chapter, I bring an original perspective to this classic by centering the minor character Sawsan Hammad, a female journalist who guides the male protagonist through his apprenticeship as journalist and national intellectual. Appearing in six out of fifty-four chapters, Sawsan's story is buried deep in the narrative waiting to be pieced together. I argue that a closer examination of the text reveals her to be the undeclared protagonist and national intellectual of a new kind of female bildungsroman where the new educated Egyptian woman guides and indeed instructs the male protagonist, Ahmad, in his role as national intellectual. She emerges as an adept national intellectual, an active Marxist, and feminist thinker at the forefront of the national struggle in 1930s and 1940s Egypt. An independent thinker, she synthesizes knowledge she has gained, adeptly creating a distinctly Egyptian framework that fits the Egyptian context.

Sawsan's training of Ahmad as journalist and, more importantly, as critical thinker, mirrors her own journey as a female national intellectual. It is, therefore, *her* bildungsroman that we follow as we watch him progress. Thus, *al-Sukkariyya*, wittingly or not, offers a female narrative of education where woman as agent fights textual, on top of social, marginalization. It is thanks to her guidance that Ahmad can formulate a theory of revolution at the end of the whole *Trilogy*. Sawsan creates a new kind of bildungsroman by helping him envision a more flexible conceptualization of governance and national culture. For this, the novel singles him out (not his uncle Kamal) as the protagonist of a new indigenous Egyptian bildungsroman that marries European Enlightenment principles to the cultural specificities of early twentieth-century Egypt.

In Chapter 3, *The Guns of El Kebir* (2007) revisits the 1882 British occupation of Egypt on the heels of the Urabi Revolution. This chapter reads the novel as another deeply nostalgic work in a series of fourteen novels that follow the young British male protagonist, Simon Fonthill, on his assignments for the British military across British dominions. Reviving the genre of the imperial romance à la H. Rider Haggard and G. A. Henty, where a white protagonist's conquest over exotic lands and peoples affirms white, masculine, European superiority, *Guns* weaves a tale of adventure replete with such plot devices as the treacherous native, the native informant, and the abducted white female. I foreground Alice Covington, British female protagonist, war correspondent, and Simon's former love interest, as representative of the New Woman who emerged in late-nineteenth-century England. A feminist, anti-imperialist who is adamant on writing the history of the Egyptian-British conflict from an Egyptian perspective, Alice is among the new generation of young women who travel to Egypt in pursuit of a professional career. Although her husband, a colonel in the British army, is part of the campaign on Egypt, she refuses to join him in his tent, preferring instead to stay in the quarters allocated to journalists.

Although this novel is not a bildungsroman in the traditional sense, it presents a developmental structure. I argue that Alice's and Simon's conversion to a pro-occupation stance after what is presented as their experience in the trenches presumably signals their maturity. *Guns* shows a couple who, having been disabused of their romantic notions of freedom for the Other, acknowledge the benevolence of Empire. I argue that in spite of its willingness to imagine anti-imperialist male and female protagonists, not only does the narrative drive the unconventional feminist journalist to condone the British occupation of Egypt, but it also continually undermines her. For instance, the text uses her as a tool that delays and/or jeopardizes the important work of Empire, forcing her to admit her rash behavior, compelling her to capitulate to Empire, and finally re-domesticating her. Although her husband's death releases her from a loveless marriage, by novel's end she is preparing to reenter a second marriage, this time a love union. Thus, due to genre conventions that dictate masculine conquest over the Other and the domestication of women, the use of the imperial romance overpowers the critical, feminist (re)vision of the era.

Chapter 4 on *Wahat al-ghurub*, 2006 (*Sunset Oasis*, 2009), retrieves two female minority voices in the last decades of the nineteenth century and at the dawn of the twentieth century: the young Siwan widow, Maleeka, and the Black Sudanese slave, Niʿma, neither of whom speaks in the narrative. Maleeka's identity as a triply or even quadruply colonized subject makes her important in a work preoccupied with multiple layers of colonialism. She is a woman colonized by a husband in a patriarchal society, a Siwan colonized by Egyptians, a Siwan living in an Egypt colonized by the British, and a woman potentially possessing an unsanctioned sexual orientation. Similarly, Niʿma's image as an extension of Egypt's dominion over Sudan takes precedence over her own identity and history, which remain unknown in the narrative. Although not a bildungsroman per se, *Wahat al-ghurub* follows a middle-aged protagonist whose failure to reach personal and political maturity prompts him to question his past actions. Niʿmas story is central to the male protagonist's stunted growth as his betrayal of the 1881–2 Urabi Revolution parallels his betrayal of Niʿma', and his failure to reach maturity is shown to reflect that of the nation.

The first two sections are dedicated to Maleeka and Niʿma, who, I argue, assert their agency against the text's silencing through art and escape from slavery respectively. First, in piecing together the women's stories and their impact on the male protagonist's journey of self-discovery, I extend to Siwa emergent scholarship on Egypt's vexed position as a colonized colonizer in Sudan, in addition to drawing on scholarship of slavery in the Muslim Mediterranean world. Second, I argue that the novel accords dreams special importance as an indigenous Sufi medium through which Mahmoud, the protagonist, receives guidance from and understands his actions toward both women. Yet, the novel's sensitivity to Egypt's minorities, its exposure of the inequality of the national project, and its effort to recount the point of view of Siwans through use of multiple narrators is undercut by oblivion to the ultimate minority—Siwan women and female slaves whose voices are erased from both the Egyptian historical narrative and the author's fictive (re)vision of the history. Maleeka's murder-suicide and Ni'ma's disappearance channel Mahmoud's move toward suicide, signaling arrested growth and rejection of the classic bildungsroman. Mahmoud sees rebirth in annihilation since the destruction of ancient Egyptian temples and other restrictive structures makes new models possible. Quite ironically, but commensurate with Sufi understanding, Mahmoud's enlightenment coincides with self-annihilation.

1

Egypt the Grotesque: Breaking Leila's Shackle in Lawrence Durrell's *Mountolive*

Lawrence Durrell (1912–1990) is often invoked when mourning an erstwhile Egyptian, more specifically Alexandrian, cosmopolitanism represented by Durrell and the Greek poet Constantine Cavafy (1863–1933). Such nostalgic celebrations, as Hala Halim explains, tend to forget and/or replicate the exclusionary drift of a cosmopolitanism that portrayed Egypt's Arab period as a dark age lying between an enlightening Hellenic period and an equally enlightening nineteenth-century European imperialism. Such studies overlook the fact that whereas many of Alexandria's wealthy foreign residents and elite Egyptians enjoyed a life of privilege, residents of modest means—Egyptian and foreign—lived only on the fringes of this cosmopolitan life, reaping very little of its benefits.[1]

In this chapter, I argue that Durrell's *Mountolive* (1958) confirms the traditional bildungsroman crafting a novel that validates imperialist discourse within which the British presence in Egypt appears as a benign, rational force. The novel marginalizes Leila Hosnani, an elite Coptic Egyptian woman under whose auspices the British official achieves cultural sophistication, diminishing her role from tutor to a symbol of Egypt's decay. Depicting 1934 to 1936 Egypt in nostalgic terms, the novel traces the protagonist's education as he outgrows his love for both Egypt and Leila and recognizes the grotesqueness of both. The text paints Egyptian political life after the 1922 independence as rife with corruption, inaccurately showing this to be the result of limited if not nonexistent British intervention, therefore condemning, rather than celebrating, Egypt's 1919 Revolution. In so doing, it replicates the colonialist master-servant/parent-child relationship by depicting 1919 and the subsequent nominal independence of 1922 as events that sent the child,

Egypt, too early out in the world, and in so doing unleashed an outbreak of corruption and religious zeal that in the end destroyed both Egypt and Britain; the former by separating it too early from Britain's watchful authority and the latter by breaking up an empire.

Mountolive, the third volume of *The Alexandria Quartet* (1957–60), is the only volume in the tetralogy written in an omniscient third-person narrative. It follows the protagonist, David Mountolive, who first visits Egypt in 1918 as a junior officer in the high commission.[2] In order to improve his Arabic, he stays with the prominent Coptic Hosnani family with whom he stays in touch even after he is assigned postings in other parts of the world. In 1934, he returns to Egypt as British ambassador with limited power only to discover that the Hosnanis are involved in a Coptic conspiracy, a fictional anti-British plot to establish a Jewish state in Palestine.

Durrell was born in India to an Anglo-Indian family of Irish descent who had not lived in Britain for two generations.[3] He arrived in Alexandria during the Second World War after escaping a Nazi attack on Corfu, Greece, where, following his father's death, he had moved with his mother and siblings in search of more affordable living.[4] Spending four years in Egypt from 1941 to 1945, he held various positions, writing for the Alexandria-based *Egyptian Gazette*, working as a foreign press service officer for the British Embassy in Cairo, and, in 1944, becoming the press attaché to Alexandria.[5] Although already a published author, it was *Justine* (1957), the first novel of the *Quartet*, which brought Durrell critical acclaim. The *Quartet*, which remains his most prominent work,[6] put him on equal footing with Joyce and Proust, raising calls to award him the Nobel Prize. Indeed, in 1988, Durrell would compete against and lose the prize to the Egyptian writer Naguib Mahfouz.[7]

From praising Durrell for his high artistic style,[8] to applauding his talent in portraying Alexandria's visual, aural, and olfactory aspects,[9] to analyzing his tetralogy in relation to Marquis de Sade,[10] criticism on the *Quartet* abounds.[11] Ignoring the socio-historical and political contexts of the *Quartet*, many studies focus on its modernist and postmodernist aspects exploring its psychological,[12] philosophical,[13] Einsteinian,[14] and Buddhist[15] themes. When his contemporaries addressed the orientalist aspect of the *Quartet*, other scholars rose in defense. For example, in an essay originally published in 1962, sixteen years before the publication of Edward Said's *Orientalism*, Egyptian scholar Mahmoud Manzaloui critiques the Levantinism in the *Quartet*, citing various historical and linguistic inaccuracies and pointing to the erasure of Egyptians from the narrative.[16] In a 1967 response to Manzaloui, American scholar William Leigh Godshalk dismisses the former's argument and, citing Durrell's passages next to their nineteenth-century orientalist sources, determines that Durrell's depictions of Egypt and Egyptians are accurate.[17]

In keeping with most celebrations of cosmopolitanism, critics such as Anna Lillios extend Durrell's orientalization of Egypt by romanticizing Greece then contrasting it to Egypt.[18] Other scholars, such as Rosalind Gwynne, are inclined to forgive Durrell for certain incomplete depictions of Muslims and Islam in the *Quartet* as long as he does not portray the Quran itself negatively.[19] Such scholarly defense of Durrell and his book focuses exclusively on the aesthetics of the *Quartet* as if they were separable from its racial politics and defense of Empire. In so doing, these studies continue to place primary importance on the *Quartet* as a cultural artefact, while Egypt remains an exotic backdrop that aids our understanding of the aesthetics. The novel's erasures, whether of Egyptians, the Quran, Islam, or simply of the way Muslims carry out their lives, mark the author's conceptualization of Islam and Muslims as mysterious beings, which in turn reaffirms orientalist images of Muslim society as mysteriously Other.

In a notable departure from this aesthetic criticism American writer and literary critic, Alfred Kazin, sees Durrell's exotic portrayal of Alexandria as a means of expiating his guilt about Empire, concluding that Durrell is more interested in pleasing his imagination than in using it to make "deeper contact with the world."[20] More recent scholarship has insisted on the importance of the *Quartet's* socio-historical context, employing a postcolonial approach that the current study follows. To cite but a few, Amani Tawfik discusses the portrayal of Egyptians as corrupt and deformed.[21] Similarly, analyzing descriptions of Egypt and Egyptians in terms of ugliness, perversity, and animality, Mohamed Yehia Mohamed Hasan notes Durrell's emphasis on the alterity of Egypt and Egyptians.[22] Michael Diboll relates Durrell's focus on the Hellenistic elements of Alexandria to the *Wafd*'s secularist nationalism with its focus on Mediterranean belonging.[23] Donald Kaczvinsky studies the significance of ornamentalism to colonial and native administration.[24] Joseph Boone reads Durrell among other Victorian writers who traveled to Egypt, such as E. M.

Forster and T. E. Lawrence, seeing in their pictures of Egypt and North Africa sites of pleasure and homoerotic fantasy.[25] Finally, Hala Halim examines the image of Alexandrian cosmopolitanism more closely, pointing to the uncanny image that Durrell produces.[26] The current study follows this trajectory.

The circumstances surrounding the production and publication of the *Quartet* are inseparable from its understanding of Egyptian cultural and political life. Durrell's feelings, his personal life, and his immediate political context overshadowed his Alexandrian experience. Arriving in Alexandria in 1941, Durrell reacted to the city with a mixture of fascination and revulsion, viewing it as a "broken-down version of Naples." He loathed, romanticized, and exoticized it all at the same time, seeing in it "the great hinge where oriental and occidental cultures met—the ancient source of so much western culture."[27] In his introduction to the 1982 edition of E. M. Forster's guidebook to the city, Durrell laments the seventh-century Arab conquest of Egypt, contrasting it to the 1798 French invasion, setting one as a harbinger of darkness and the other as a herald of enlightenment. Recalling his 1977 visit to Alexandria, he disparages the use of Arabic and the emergence of a culture for the native population, attributing the city's decline to the disappearance of foreigners.[28] This tension between what Durrell views as Arab darkness and European rationality informs the *Quartet*. If one adds to Durrell's distaste for Egypt his statement that *Mountolive* was meant to be a "straight naturalistic novel,"[29] or his assertion that he "always want[ed] to get a reality which is either grotesque or sinister—perhaps a bit theatrical,"[30] one begins to see how he formed his picture of Egypt. The image of Egypt that *Mountolive* paints *is* indeed grotesque.

On the personal level, according to American writer and Durrell's official biographer Ian MacNiven, Egypt became synonymous with loss as Durrell missed his prewar life.[31] Displacing his own feelings of loss, separation, and sexual abandon on Egypt, he turned it into a location for sheer animal, sexual, orgiastic existence.[32] Joseph Boone explains how "the dazzling spectacle of Cairene and Alexandrian street life is transformed into an emblem of the psyche's overflowing polymorphous desires. As such, this spectacle becomes a convenient screen on which to project fantasies of illicit, unbridled eroticism."[33] After his separation from his first wife, Durrell sought therapy in sexual promiscuity, and when sex hindered the writing process, he faulted Egypt.[34] Although Egypt provided him with his masterpiece, Durrell was no Egyptophile. He blamed his dry spells on the country announcing that "Egypt is simply lousy with material for good books," leading one to succumb to "apathy and boredom."[35] Boone, however, identifies another reason for Durrell's writer's block where "the fantasized projection of sexual otherness onto Egypt eventually occasions a crisis of writing, of narrative authority, when the writing subject is confronted by (imagined) sensual excess."[36] Needless to say, Egypt—particularly the urban centers of Cairo and Alexandria—was hardly the cultural backwater that Pursewarden, a poet in the novel, makes it out to be.[37] According to Diboll, "At the time of the Armistice Egypt could boast a Europeanised [*sic*] intellectual elite that rivalled that of Europe itself."[38] How ironic is it that it was Durrell's book on Egypt that rendered him the incarnation of Joyce and Proust?

The publication of the tetralogy coincided with another rough period in Durrell's life. He had resigned from the British Foreign Office in December 1952 and was living in Cyprus. Impoverished and in need of money to pay for his divorce and to support his baby daughter, whose mother—his second wife—had left in his charge, he taught at the Greek school in the morning and wrote at night after the baby went to bed.[39] Durrell wrote *Justine* and *Mountolive* (the first and third volumes) each in about twelve weeks, while *Balthazar* (the second volume) took only six weeks, and *Clea* (the last volume) was written in eight weeks, publishing them as separate novels between 1957 and 1960.[40] Remembering the writing process, Durrell himself admitted: "You see, the beauty of it is, that when you are really frantic and worried about money, you find that if it's going to be a question of writing to live, why, you just damn well buckle to and do it."[41]

The *Quartet*'s immediate political context is undeniably important. Having finished *Justine* in 1957 while living in Cyprus, Durrell wrote *Balthazar*, *Mountolive*, and *Clea* in France.[42] Writing in the wake of the 1956 nationalization of the Suez Canal and the subsequent Tripartite aggression by Britain, France, and Israel, he reproduced contemporary anti-Egyptian propaganda that was sure to satisfy his need for money through high sales. Egyptian scholar Sahar Hamouda theorizes that the Coptic conspiracy "must have directed public opinion in Europe against Moslem [*sic*] Arabs, especially as each volume of the *Quartet* met with success as soon as it was published, and that the 1967 war was imminent." Rather than see the tetralogy as an elegy for Empire, she further posits that events such as the Coptic conspiracy and images of Copts alienated from the Egyptian government and threatened by a rising Muslim tide, are attempts to preserve Empire by "giving the West an idea that is more feasible with the new Egyptian regime: that sowing the seeds of religious strife and arousing fanaticism can foment civil war in Egypt."[43]

Leila the Woman

Forming a picture of Leila Hosnani requires wading through high waters of orientalist representation that, by some sleight of hand, transforms her from an exotic Egypt offering herself to be consumed by the British colonizer at the beginning of *Mountolive* to a bestial caricature of an independent Egypt at the end of the volume. Leila is brought into the narrative only inasmuch as she affects the growth of the white, male protagonist, David Mountolive, so that her identity as an Egyptian woman in the early to middle decades of twentieth-century Egypt takes a back seat to his self-involved musings. Although a mentor to the British protagonist, Leila is reduced to a bewitching siren whose spell, when finally broken, exposes a deformed harpy whose monstrosity shocks Mountolive into adulthood as he finally understands Egypt's position within the British imperialist project. But, who is Leila the woman?

Already in her forties when she and her husband host Mountolive in their house in 1918, Leila would have been born in the 1870s, at a time when the Arab *nahda* (cultural awakening) was blooming in Egypt, thanks to a vibrant print culture born in the 1820s that disseminated not only new forms of philosophical and scientific knowledge but also concepts of nationalism and national identity. Around the mid-nineteenth century, books and periodicals printed in Egypt were accessible both nationally and internationally through a network of post offices in Cairo, Alexandria, the Delta, and Upper Egypt.[44] The 1870s and 1880s—the decades that mark Leila's childhood and adolescence—besides witnessing the birth and growth of the women's press as mentioned in the Introduction, saw an increase in printed material no doubt made possible by the spread of private printing presses in Egypt after the 1860s.[45] During those two decades a total of 3,701,500 books were printed, jumping almost twofold from the 1870s to the 1880s (from 1,295,000 books printed between1870 and 1879 to 2,406,500 books printed between 1880 to 1889).[46]

Additionally, reading habits had changed so that by the end of the nineteenth century, reading for women acquired new social meaning as a "mark of prestige."[47] In addition to cultural productions, and particularly taking into consideration Egypt's low literacy rates, the decades leading up to 1919 saw a wealth of printed material circulated through Egypt's mail service.[48] By 1913, five years before Mountolive's first visit to Egypt, the country boasted "427 large post offices and 1,477 smaller postal stations spread throughout Egypt's cities and villages, with roughly 51 million pieces of 'internal' mail delivered every year."[49]

The daughter of a land-owning elite Coptic family from Alexandria, Leila would have attended one of the Western-style schools that Hoda Yousef and Mona Russell tell us were so popular in the late nineteenth century that between 1875 and 1915 demand for these learning institutions far surpassed the number of new schools.[50] We can safely assume that growing up, Leila, an avid reader fluent in four languages besides Arabic, had access to books and periodicals available in her father's library. After finishing her studies "brilliantly" in Cairo,[51] her hopes of studying medicine in Europe are dashed and her marriage to Faltaus Hosnani, a man twenty years her senior from an equally wealthy Coptic family, is arranged in the manner of a business merger.

Leila's dream of going to college predates the first generation of Egyptian women admitted to college as well as the first group of women sent to Europe on study missions by about thirty to forty years.[52] It is worth noting that, in nineteenth-century Britain as well, women's educational opportunities were similarly restricted.[53] Although capable of financing her studies in Europe, Leila's family, it seems, are either not keen on having a doctor for a daughter or want to ensure that she does not abandon Egypt permanently. She is married off to Faltaus at a time when, not much unlike their British sisters, upper-class Egyptian women had little choice in marriage. According to Judith Flanders, marriages in nineteenth-century Britain were business transactions in which financial and social equality outweighed love, with some women even foregoing marriage altogether rather than risking marrying down.[54] In Egypt, as Magda Baraka explains, the main concern was marrying into a "good family," while love "was considered a maverick kind of concept."[55]

However, enabled by wealth, Leila nourishes her love for knowledge through book and periodical subscriptions in four foreign languages to the extent that, as Mountolive attests, her reading material "always overflowed into the house" despite her efforts to confine them to her quarters (21). Indeed, Leila is cultured enough that Mountolive is humbled by her worldliness: "Leila was not only more experienced; to his utter chagrin he found that she was even better read, in his own language, than he was, and better instructed" (31).

Although now living in her husband's country estate in the Egyptian Delta, Leila is no provincial woman. As a young woman, she appears to have been the star of Alexandrian society—the belle of social gatherings earning the sobriquet '"the dark swallow'" (24). Possessing both status and beauty, Leila could savor the cosmopolitan glamor of Alexandria from which native Egyptians of little or no means were barred.[56] Quite the socialite, and unconventional enough to be "among the first Coptic women to abandon the veil,"[57] she has a network of friends among Alexandria's foreign residents. However, a keenness for introspection, sharpened by long stays in the country, has displaced her interest in the trappings of city life.

Leila destabilizes traditional conceptions of the imperial relationship. Besides being Mountolive's lover, which will be addressed further on, Leila becomes his tutor, mentor, and confidant, even assuming a motherly role as he moves from one position to another in different parts of the world. Leila, the Egyptian woman, undertakes the education of the British colonizing subject in her charge, sometimes feigning ignorance so as not to discourage him:

> He was both a lover to her and a sort of *hapless man-child who could be guided by her towards his own growth.* Only (she must have made the reservation quite clearly in her own mind) she must beware of any possible resentment which he might feel at this *tutelage.* So she hid her own experience and became for him almost a companion of his own age, sharing a complicity which somehow seemed so innocent, so beyond reproach, that even his sense of guilt was almost lulled, and he began to drink in through her a new resolution and self-confidence. (30–1, emphasis added)

Leila and Mountolive exchange roles within the framework of the colonial paradigm where she, the colonized subject, takes him under her wing in a paternalistic, or rather maternalistic, supervisory role and he, the colonizer, assumes a filial position as he receives knowledge from an Egyptian woman.

Of note here is that it is the British colonial officer who does not measure up to the native woman in many respects.

Acting as a mentor who "chided his ignorance and provoked his curiosity" (31), Leila molds Mountolive to her own creation. It is the native woman, here, who plays an active role in shaping the British, male protagonist. Being a Levantine—a hybridized Egyptian with a Western education—she shapes him along cosmopolitan lines, merging Egyptian and European cultures, albeit leaning more heavily toward the latter. Once Mountolive leaves Egypt, they keep up a steady correspondence in English and in French. Over nearly two decades, she introduces him to a world of cultural refinement where he "suddenly found the hitherto padlocked worlds of paint, architecture, music and writing opening on every side of him. So she gave him almost a gratuitous education in the world which he would never have been able to compass by himself" (52). Contrary to the narrator's snide remark about rich Egyptians, Europe for Leila is more than just a shopping center. Wherever Mountolive's travels take him in Europe, he receives itinerary suggestions and book requests from Leila, who always seems to know about cultural events taking place at his destinations. Experiencing Europe through him, she asks him to send book packages and visit various venues in which she is interested, such that their long-distance love becomes a "flirtation of minds, in which the roles were now reversed" (52). True to a humanist education, Mountolive's training requires him to report on his experiences to Leila, which pushes him to improve his writing: "Leila became his only mentor and confidant, his only source of encouragement. It was to meet these demands of hers that he taught himself to write well in English and French. Taught himself to appreciate things which normally would have been outside the orbit of his interests—painting and music. He informed himself in order to inform her" (52). However, Mountolive, who in his naïveté believes himself to be Leila's only link to Europe, is unaware that she corresponds with friends in different parts of the world.[58]

Leila is a mentor who polishes him, preparing him for his high position in the diplomatic corps. Ironically, he receives Western culture circulated back through a colonized Levantine. At the end of his apprenticeship, Mountolive emerges as a cultured man, his academic friendship with Leila having in the meantime taken a maternal turn. Besides growing culturally—"so in her skilful [*sic*] fashion she held him year by year until his youthful awkwardness gave place to a maturity which matched her own" (55)—Mountolive grows emotionally, confiding his love affairs to Leila who becomes a mother figure. She has become his anchor so much so that her silence once he is back in Egypt leaves him feeling dejected; "Cut off in this way from Leila, he felt dispossessed, orphaned" (237). She has become a surrogate mother, nurturing him and unleashing emotions long suppressed by an English education. Reflecting on a much-anticipated upcoming reunion with Leila, he expects this meeting to bring him more understanding of himself by determining the contours of his relationship with her: "It was a sort of barrier in himself which had to be crossed, a puberty of the feelings which had to be outgrown" (276).

Leila's agency is striking notwithstanding her marginalization in the narrative. From the very beginning, she calls the shots in the affair, setting boundaries by demanding that Mountolive respect her husband, sometimes mocking Mountolive—as will be discussed further on—altering the terms of their liaison from lovers to pen pals, deciding not to visit him in Europe even after her husband's death, and, last, taking her time to meet him when he is finally posted in Egypt at the end of two decades of their acquaintance. Mountolive's inability to negotiate these parameters—for example, his failure to show up unannounced at the Hosnani country estate—is testament to her power in the relationship.

Leila's determination to plan her life rationally is backed by a strong resolve. Her long silence when Mountolive reappears in Egypt speaks of an agency that is simply not upended by Mountolive's sudden materialization, or by a passionate desire to rekindle an old flame. Having moved Mountolive to a different category, she now has to assess the criteria of a possible reunion—the same thought that she considers earlier as she contemplates visiting Mountolive in Europe after her husband's death: "I found myself entertaining a thought which for years now I have rigorously excluded. The thought of *seeing you again*. Only I could not for the life of me see the terms and conditions of such a meeting" (57, emphasis in original). While Leila's later silence may seem to be the result of female vanity caused by her disfigurement by the smallpox, in reality it is motivated by introspection that always demands a rational meaning for actions. When she does meet him, at the end of the novel, she is unafraid to go with her face unveiled. Despite confiding to a friend elsewhere in the *Quartet* that, in actuality, she is dying of heart sickness now that Mountolive has outgrown her love, or rather her mentorship, Leila will not hide her face "'for I have in reality the heart of a man.'"[59]

Driven less by affection than by an attempt to use him to hide her sons' involvement in the conspiracy against the British, Leila's last meeting with Mountolive reveals another aspect of her agency even as it confirms the stereotype of the duplicitous Other. Although in *Mountolive* she feigns ignorance of her sons' involvement in the conspiracy, in *Balthazar*, Leila who is in on the plot, asks Nessim if they can trust Mountolive.[60] It appears that she briefly considers trusting him with their scheme in order to take advantage of his new role as ambassador of Egypt to both further as well as mask their plans. Once the plan is exposed, she pleads with Mountolive not to act upon this information, appealing to her position as friend and former lover. In a continued reversal of the colonial paradigm, Leila can easily move Mountolive from lover, to friend, to idea, conjuring him up when necessary.

Much in the same way that Mountolive insists on seeing Leila as an image of an exotic Egypt, Leila transforms him into an idea, out of a desire to live the relationship on her own terms. For Leila, Mountolive is a protégé modelled after herself, allowing her to taste European culture vicariously to the point where she questions his reality. In this case, it is the imperial officer who becomes the colonized subject's colonial fantasy, as Leila's words to Mountolive indicate; "You may be now simply a figment instead of a flesh and blood dignitary … I can't find the courage to compare the truth to reality as yet" (145).

The Leila-Mountolive Affair: Re-creating the Myth of the Fantastic Other

Durrell's use of the bildungsroman to record Mountolive's education is inextricably intertwined with the fantastic, which serves two functions. First, it validates the bildungsroman as a traditionalist genre in which the individual cannot locate his or her voice outside the social order but rather has to reconcile with it. In Durrell's text, reconciliation with the colonial paradigm marks Mountolive's attainment of education. Second, in reinforcing the bildungsroman, the fantastic validates orientalist, colonialist discourse forcing Mountolive to accept the colonial binary. In the end he views

Egyptians not only as dangerous, threatening, and *unheimlich* (unfamiliar, uncanny) but also as grotesque. My reading agrees with Halim's while noting that the representation of Egypt and Egyptians leans more heavily toward the grotesque.[61] Mountolive's experience of two important periods of British history in Egypt, 1918 and 1934 to 1936, allows him to live the colonial fantasy and eventually outgrow it, resulting in an embrace of the English social order.

Mountolive at first approaches Egypt through colonial fantasy where Leila first poses as a sultry female whose sensuality unleashes emotions long suppressed by a rational English education and replaced by a reserved masculinity before he finally transforms her into a grotesque Caliban-like figure. Accepting as real the exotic world of orientalist writing, such as Edward William Lane's *The Manners and Customs of Modern Egyptians* (1836), which Mountolive believes to be the "true Gospel on Egypt" (44), he is enthralled by Egypt's magical difference. Expecting to relive the same marvelous experience, he reenacts the colonial fantasy in his sexual relationship with Leila, which itself mirrors his changing relationship with Egypt. Mountolive's initial perception of Egypt invests it with fantastic elements, where he is perplexed by his new feelings toward an exotic, almost supernatural world. He accepts unquestioned the exoticism of Egyptian life believing in its magical difference before identifying it as uncanny, ugly, and grotesque, within which Egypt's difference is rationally explained away in terms of lack. Thus, embracing the English colonialist social order, he accepts its "rational" classification of Egypt as incapable of self-governance. Durrell achieves this by rejecting Egypt's marvelous charms, which lure Mountolive at first, and replacing them with a disenchanted, and thus ostensibly rational, perspective that exposes Egyptians as corrupt, irrational beings ruled by mysterious religious forces that are rightly incomprehensible to a civilized man.

The fishing episode with which the novel opens introduces two Mountolives and two Egypts. This highlights the protagonist's state of innocence as reflected in the image of Egypt that the text creates in this episode. First, the fishing scene establishes the fantastic image of Egypt that the novel contests and confirms at the same time. In this scene, Mountolive imagines himself in a magical world that appears to be "mirrored in a soap-bubble trembling on the edge of disappearance" (11). The passage paints Egypt as a world that plays magical tricks on one's senses leaving one wondering about its reality. It is beautiful but unfamiliar. To Mountolive's eyes, nature projects itself as a "tapestry" that evokes nineteenth-century orientalist paintings. He sees a breathless race in wild nature where natives blend with their environment to become part of the landscape. Wild excited birds dashing to obtain a share in the catch, loud noises, and speedy movement, all paint a communion between natives and birds that subtly links 1918 Egypt to ancient Egypt in uninterrupted continuity. Mountolive's impressions point to the tension between the Egypt that he and Durrell create, on the one hand, and the actual Egypt that they experience, on the other hand. Both figures impose a magical ambience that disappears upon contact with the real world.

Second, as if anticipating Mountolive's final disenchantment and mocking his initial innocence, the fishing scene paints a beautiful world that is tempered with ugliness, thus emphasizing its "otherliness" and foreshadowing Mountolive's discovery of Leila toward the end of the novel as just a fattish Egyptian woman reeking of sesame, mint, and whisky—a "pitiable grotesque" (281). For example, the lake waters are "turbid" (11). Mountolive also perceives Egyptians as primitively sensual and, to evoke Boone, somewhat projects on them homoerotic fantasies as he observes the "Arabs with their long white robes tucked up to the waist. … The light gleamed on their dark thighs. The darkness was full of their barbaric blitheness" (16). Describing the scene at the lake "it was all beautiful, but it stank so: yet to his surprise he found he rather enjoyed the rotting smells of the estuary" (12), the narrator emphasizes Egypt's alterity, to evoke Hasan. This renders Egypt grotesquely beautiful, to be appreciated despite, or because of, its ugliness and marks Mountolive's embrace of the fantastic, denoting his innocence corresponding to his prematurity phase in the bildungsroman.

In a further confirmation of the imperial paradigm, Egypt's sensuality is contrasted to the rationality of Britain. At the end of the very first paragraph of the novel, readers are told that Egypt appeals to the senses rather than to reason. It is a place that unleashes one's passion and contaminates Mountolive for whom "somehow today it was rather more difficult than usual to be reserved, so exciting had the fish-drive become" (11). The narrator juxtaposes two Mountolives; the British and the Egyptianized who, shedding his English reserve, "had in fact quite forgotten about his once-crisp tennis flannels and college blazer and the fact that the wash of bilge rising through the floor-boards had toe-capped his white plimsolls with a black stain. *In Egypt one seemed to forget oneself continually like this*" (11, emphasis added). Mountolive is implied to be heading down a dangerous path under Leila's/Egypt's spell. The British protagonist is, thus, painted as regressing by embracing the Other's insidious exoticism. One might say that *Mountolive* starts with a reverse bildungsroman where the British protagonist unlearns certain aspects of European modernity before attaining experience and embracing a modernity that classifies civilizations hierarchically.

Mountolive's journey on the path of maturity reflects vacillation between two seductive discourses: an anticolonialist ideology that exposes the moral corruption of Empire and an imperialist ideology about exotic, debased Egyptians. This fluctuation is seen in a lecture delivered to Mountolive by Faltaus Hosnani, the head of the family. Following a faux pas in which Mountolive mistakenly refers to the Hosnanis as Muslim, he is presented with a pointed critique of Britain's imperial practice in Egypt. Faltaus' lecture and the subsequent epilogue by Leila and Nessim, appearing at the start of the novel and occupying over six pages, is where Durrell delivers his strongest critique of imperialism. Faltaus juxtaposes European discrimination against Copts during the Crusades to acceptance and inclusion by Muslims and blames Britain for sowing the seeds of hatred between modern-day Christians and Muslims. This brief critique of Empire occurs at a point where Mountolive's infatuation with Egypt is sustained by a blossoming affair with Leila during his 1918 visit at a time when he is innocent enough to accept the rosy, romantic picture of the country. Mountolive is seduced by the language of religious harmony.

In this episode, the Hosnanis interpret the British occupation as a modern-day Crusade where hunger for power and wealth are invested with Christian civilizational overtones in order to sanitize the exploitation. To examples of Copts rising to political power in nineteenth-century Egypt, the Hosnanis contrast the exclusion of the Copts under British rule.[62] In her study of Egyptian sectarian strife between 1882 and 1919, Rabihah Sulayman explains that, historically, the British favored Syrian Christians for a purportedly superior mathematical knowledge that was pronounced lacking in both Coptic and Muslim Egyptians. The British confined Egyptians to low-profile and manual labor, countering Coptic protests by claiming the religious prejudice of the Egyptian government.[63] Vivian Ibrahim, however, finds that reports dating back to the first decade of the twentieth century show Copts to be, in fact, overrepresented in both the state education system and the bureaucracy.[64] Casting what he sees as contemporary British-backed discriminatory practices as another iteration of the injustices that Eastern Christians suffered at the hands of Crusaders, Faltaus reminds Mountolive that, despite the common bond of Christianity, the latter had massacred the former. Once more, he sees in unjust British policies a refiguration of another historical exclusion when the Copts, whom he describes as the "only branch of the Christian Church which was thoroughly integrated into the Orient," were debarred from entering the newly captured Jerusalem after the first Crusade (41).

Leila's and Faltaus' Oxford-educated son, Nessim, concludes the lecture by equating the British occupation with the Crusades and accusing Mountolive, and by implication Britain and Europe, that they "have remained Crusaders at heart" (46). In a premature allusion to the famous 1919 Revolution slogan "Long Live the Crescent with the Cross," (Faltaus delivers this lecture in 1918), Nessim corroborates his father's proclamations, adding that "for us there was no real war between Cross and Crescent [.] That was entirely a Western European creation. So indeed was the idea of the cruel Moslem [*sic*] infidel" (45). In echoing nascent Egyptian nationalism, the Hosnanis paint a picture of Egyptians united by territory and history despite British attempts to divide them.[65] This brief history lesson constitutes the novel's only critique of Empire. Seen in light of ensuing events, such as the bribery scene, or the Coptic plot, it is clear that this episode serves to mock Mountolive's initial naïveté attributing his embrace of the Hosnanis' critique to his infatuation with Leila and, by extension, her family. This reflects ambivalence on Durrell's part as he attempted to negotiate the waning Empire.

According to Jed Esty, the 1930s brought economic depression (which made colonies expensive to maintain), calls for independence in the colonies, and the looming crisis of British imperial contraction. British authors attempted to come to terms with these events until "World War II exposed the cracks and patches in Britain's imperial structure with a kind of historical finality, precipitating (despite the Allied victory) the formal process of decolonization."[66] Durrell is no exception. His choice of the mid-1930s for a setting is highly significant as these years are a shifting point in Britain's imperial relationship with Egypt. Thus, while the 1919 Revolution marks the onset of British imperial decline in Egypt, for Durrell it is not the prime cause of the demise of the British Empire in the country. Instead, it is the period leading up to the 1936 treaty that begins the process by granting Egypt more liberties and constricting those of Britain.

The narrator exposes Mountolive's arrogance in thinking that through his knowledge of Arabic ("the open sesame of language" (22)) he has penetrated Egypt, while foreshadowing his bitter disappointment as he later finds out that indeed he has not. As noted earlier on, Mountolive's education moves in reverse direction under Leila's mentorship. In his innocence, he oscillates between embracing Leila's and Egypt's otherness and exoticizing them. Egyptian culture ceases to be exotic as Mountolive lives its daily realities. Yet, his admission that his imagination has painted this "canvas" of Egypt (22) is belied by his reference to the "open sesame of language," exposing his persistence in perceiving Egypt in fairy-tale terms. Pages later Mountolive admits that "through [Leila's] eyes he began to see Egypt once more—but extended through a new dimension. To have a grasp of the language was nothing, he now realized; for Leila exposed the hollowness of the knowledge when pitted against understanding" (31). Here, Mountolive views his interpretation of Egypt as concomitant to his penetration of Leila. The irony is that Leila herself turns out to be a mirage. This is precisely what Mountolive discovers when, at the end of the novel, he heads to the Arab quarter wearing the garb of a Syrian businessman. Thinking that his knowledge of the culture will allow him to pass as Arab, he attempts to re-create the illusion of the magical Egypt one final time and fails.

Mountolive recasts Egypt's distasteful aspects into fanciful representations of it, succumbing to competing fantasies about Leila and Egypt. This ambivalence strongly surfaces in his relationship with Leila whose exotic and monstrous images are themselves Mountolive's fantasy. The Mountolive-Leila affair is both a confirmation and a reversal of the colonialist narrative. On the one hand, *Mountolive* depicts the Egyptian woman as a passive object available for the white man's pleasure. On the other hand, receiving a sentimental education from Leila, Mountolive becomes the "brown woman's burden," as Diboll rightly notes.[67] During Mountolive's first visit to Egypt and over the course of the following years, Leila teaches him to appreciate poetry, the arts, and love, as noted earlier on. Yet, despite this reversal, because an Egyptian woman is teaching a British male subject how to feel, the novel becomes a subtle confirmation of orientalist discourse that represents the Egyptian woman as emotional and the British colonial officer as more rational.

Ruminating on Leila's impact on him, Mountolive reflects that "he had been formally educated in England, educated not to wish to feel" (18). Contrasting his earlier self with the current one, he discovers that Leila's passion overwhelms him. In a manner that evokes Boone's attribution of Durrell's writer's block to the sexual excess that he has projected on Egypt, Mountolive's sexual initiation is deemed grotesque for shaking his ability for rational thinking: "It was unpleasant to be forced to grow. It was thrilling to grow. He gravitated between fear and *grotesque* elation" (27–8, emphasis added). Mountolive insists on forcing an exotic framework on his relationship with Leila. Drawing a picture of an Egypt that appeals to his wild passion, he senses an initiation that causes his nascent emotional side to overpower his rational side. Noticeable here is Mountolive's identification of his new emotions as non-English feelings that Leila has awakened in him, introducing him to a world of grotesque happiness.

For all their cosmopolitanism, Leila and the Hosnanis are cast as mimics; flawed copies of the West, in Homi Bhabha's words "*almost the same, but not quite*."[68] Mimicry derives from the ambivalence of the colonial power whose contradictory depictions of natives—in this context Egyptians—as similar but different, evokes an inscrutable, grotesque Egyptian that forever inhabits the fantastic. Ambivalence, then, is a state that locates the Other on a continuum between the uncanny mimic (almost the same but not quite) and the menace (utterly different and even threatening). In the world of the novel, however, the picture of Egyptians as menace lurks beneath their fantastic surface, insidiously conveying itself in their mimicry and quite dangerously so because it goes undetected due to their hybridity. This hybridity, their remarkable sameness, and their defiance of classification exclusively under one cultural group renders them difficult to read and, therefore, masks the menace beneath the mimicry.[69]

The Hosnanis' hybridity—their mimicry that renders them fantastic—deceives Mountolive, causing first his enthrallment, then his uncertainty, and, finally, his enlightenment. Mountolive's initial fascination with the reeking Egypt, while conveying his innocence, poignantly captures the ambivalence of colonial discourse, which paints Egyptians as at once beautiful and ugly, the same and different, mimic and menace, and ultimately exaggerates the menace because of the potential danger that lies in the ambiguity of the exotic. Such depictions deny Egyptians agency in the form of resistance via strategic positioning, known à la Bhabha as sly civility, where subjects may show outward compliance while choosing a course of action that best suits them.[70] The Hosnanis identity as Levantine (bourgeois and Western-educated) is what turns them from cosmopolitan to suspect mimics, to rephrase Hala Halim. Halim traces the changes that the term underwent first to refer to bourgeois, Westernized foreign and/or minority communities living in the eastern Mediterranean during colonial times, then to denote mercenary mimics under colonial rule, and finally, at the hands of Durrell, to point to an uncanny menace in postindependence Egypt, such that the term Levantine denotes Bhabha's concept of elusive sameness.[71] Interestingly, these changes correspond to differing phases in Mountolive's educational experience until he is completely disabused of his love for Leila and Egypt.

At the beginning Mountolive romanticizes Nessim with his "flawless head" and "Byzantine face such as one might find among the frescoes of Ravenna—almond-shaped, dark-eyed, clear-featured" (17). Diboll identifies this as Durrell's tracing of the Mediterranean/Byzantine elements of Western culture in Egypt.[72] As Mountolive's education progresses and he learns about the Coptic conspiracy, Nessim and the Hosnanis become a threat, their hybridity masking their danger. Thus, the hybrid Alexandria in the *Quartet*, in Halim's words, is "an 'uncanny' space of 'colonial hybridity,' a space that poses a 'menace' to a (would-be) sovereign, and decidedly male, imperial subject—whether that of the colonial administrator or of the Western writer."[73] To appropriate Mohamed Yehia Mohamed Hasan's words, Alexandria occupies a middle ground between Self and Other.[74]

While the narrative portrays Leila as a mimic who idealizes Britain, the character's occasional over-performance mocks Mountolive's innocence. One such example is when she quotes to Mountolive John Ruskin's 1870 inaugural lecture at Oxford University extolling Britain's imperial duty.[75] While Diboll reads in this proof that Leila is a perfectly colonized subject who idolizes Britain, Hasan comes closer to the point when he argues that Mountolive falls in love with an image of Britain whose reflection he sees in Egypt.[76] I favor Hasan's analysis because, rather than seeing Leila as a blind admirer of Britain, he acknowledges her character as Mountolive's creation. To take Hasan's words a step further, Mountolive uses Leila as a screen on which to project his nostalgia for a once glorious Britain. In other words, wishing to revive the past world of Empire, he creates an exotic image of Egypt, missing its agency vis-à-vis Britain's civilizational discourse. Mountolive falls in love with the discourse of the civilizing mission that Leila represents.

However, this is one of the moments where the text mocks Mountolive's conviction that Egypt can be civilized. Struggling to preserve the romantic ideas he has read in Lane's *Manners*, Mountolive insists on projecting onto Leila the stereotype of an exotic Egypt that is fascinated by the greatness of Britain. Not only does he want to believe that she adores him because he represents an ideal Britain, but he also tries to elicit an affirming statement by asking: "'But why me, Leila?' as if there was all the choice in the wide world before her, and was astonished when she lay back and repeated the words after him with what seemed like a musical *contempt*; the puerility of his question indeed annoyed her" (28, emphasis added). A keyword here is "contempt."

Mountolive mistakes contempt and sly civility for infatuation. When Leila recites part of Ruskin's speech glorifying England's duty to civilize the world, he takes that for adoration. In his mind, Leila sees in him "something like a prototype of a nation which existed now only in her imagination. She was kissing and cherishing a painted image of England" (29). However, Leila's mimicry denotes sarcasm rather than adoration. As the narrative goes, she varies her tone of voice "*to the melody of the prose*" (29, emphasis added). When Mountolive asks her if she can fall in love "with the stone effigy of a dead crusader," she delivers a mocking response: "'You asked me *why*,' (emphasis in original) she said, *still with contempt*. 'Because,' with a sigh, 'you are English, *I suppose*,'" (30, emphasis added). Leila's answer to Mountolive is one that he desires, but her derision coupled with her use of the words "I suppose" indicate awareness of her lover's dream of falling in love with a reflection of Britain. In short, where Mountolive insists on casting Leila in the role of an oriental seductress, in instances such as this one, the text mocks him.

Although Mountolive recognizes what he thinks is Leila's "absurd book-fed dream" (29) he persists in pursuing his own ridiculous book-fed dream. Earlier during the fish drive, he dreams about Egypt, the rotting Egypt that stinks yet that he loves: "'Egypt,' he said to himself as one might repeat the name of a woman. 'Egypt'" (12). After Leila picks a crumb on his lip with her tongue he feels "the small warm tongue of an Egyptian cat upon his underlip for a moment" (28). Leila's assertion that it is her husband who, in his wisdom, has suggested that she take Mountolive for a lover (30) feeds the latter's fantasies and conjures up orientalist images of women made available for the white man's sexual gratification. The novel presents this as part of the irrationality and immorality of Egypt: "What on earth was an Englishman to make of these strange patterns of thought, these confused and contending loyalties?" (30). It is this same kind of irrationality that permeates Durrell's rendition of Egyptian political life.

While Diboll reads the Leila-Mountolive affair through the *Wafd* Party's relationship with Britain,[77] adding that Leila's "enthusiastic endorsement of Ruskin's "Imperial Duty" illustrates the depth of the *Wafd*'s Europeanism,"[78] I wish to extend this reading. Their affair mirrors Durrell's interpretation of Egypt's political life, which mixes brief praise with condemnation of moral corruption, claiming that although Egyptian nationalism might seem sincere and beautiful, in reality it is grotesque. Even though at this moment the text ridicules Mountolive's naïveté in thinking that Leila had a wide range of lovers to choose from, it reaffirms another stereotype of Egypt—that of the secluded woman.

While at first Mountolive views Leila as an aesthetic object, when he meets her again almost twenty years later at the end of the novel he substitutes another art object, a grotesque one this time, for the earlier marvel. Kaczvinsky sees in this second meeting with Leila a "last-ditch effort to recapture his youthful romanticizing of Egypt."[79] Suddenly, seeing her in animalistic terms, he describes Leila's eyes as "the mutinous sad eyes of some clumsy cartoon creature: a cartoon of animals dressed up and acting as human beings" (281). This description of Leila, hovering between grotesqueness and animality, signals a shift in Mountolive's view of the Hosnanis (particularly the refined Leila and Nessim) and calls to mind Amani Tawfik's reading of the *Quartet* where descriptions of Egyptians associate them with disease, animality, deformity, and mutilation.[80] Thus, in place of her image as a sophisticated, Western-educated Levantine, Leila joins Egyptians, collectively depicted as diseased and/or mutilated. Mountolive continues to ponder Leila's appearance, which "had a rakish and impoverished air," her skin, disfigured by smallpox, looking "coarse as the skin of an elephant" (281). The repetition of grotesque descriptions cements the new bestial image of both Leila and Egypt: "Each time the lamps came up he looked again, and each time he saw himself confronting something like an animal cartoon figure—an elephant, say" (281). Occurring after his discovery of the Coptic conspiracy, this meeting wakes him up to the reality of Egypt, resetting him on the path of education by reorienting him toward Britain.

Mountolive's initial ambivalence captures hesitation between two seductive narratives, that of the power of Empire and its officials enacting a so-called civilizing mission and that of the exotic Egypt. The novel's identification of Egyptians as grotesque shifts the hesitation from Mountolive's mind, that is from his inability to see Egyptians for what they are at the beginning to the inscrutability of Egyptians—their amorphousness that renders them sometimes fantastic and sometimes uncanny while in reality they are dangerously uncanny, particularly the Westernized Hosnani family. This inscrutability defies both a rational explanation of Egypt's difference as well as an embrace of a magical culture.

Leila's harsh reality shatters the romantic dreams of the former colonizer. Mountolive's awakening to the "real" Leila, a stand-in for Egypt, frames Egyptian political life in brutish as well as brutal terms. Not only does the meeting follow his discovery of her sons' involvement in the Coptic conspiracy, it also occurs after various descriptions of Egyptian violence; Muslims cutting camels alive, Narouz's (Leila's other son) new pastime killing bats with a whip, as well as Memlik Pasha's reported pleasure at telephoning the prison in order to hear the cries of prisoners while being tortured. Thus, Mountolive's conceptualization of Leila is also a framing of Egyptian political life as deformed and grotesquely violent.

While continuing to focus on the experience of the current-day colonial official, Durrell shifts the reader's attention from the grotesque Leila to the suffering Mountolive indicating his growing pains:

> Leila had suddenly left him face to face with a reality which, he supposed, had always lain lurking behind the dusty tapestry of his romantic notions. In a sense, she had *been* Egypt, his own private Egypt of the mind; and now this old image had been husked, stripped bare. … He had never been … natural, outward-going in his attitude to life. He had always hidden behind measure and compromise; and this defection had somehow lost him the

picture of the Egypt which had nourished him for so long. Was it, then, all a lie? (284–5, emphasis in original)

Mountolive's thoughts point to his mistake: abandonment of English reserve and involvement with Egypt brings one face to face with its ugly reality. He realizes that the fascinating picture of Egypt is a fallacy and that, equally, the civilizing mission is just another fallacy because Egyptians are incapable of change. Restored to his English sensibilities, he decides to "waste no more time upon this Egypt of deceptions and squalor, this betraying landscape which turned emotions and memories to dust, which beggared friendship and destroyed love. He did not even think of Leila now … it was as if she had never existed" (295). The narrator marks Mountolive's maturity as he "reached a new frontier in himself; life was going to be something completely different from now on. He had been in some sort of bondage all this time; now the links had snapped" (295).

Through fantasy Durrell investigates the state of the British official in the ex-colony. The novel evokes pity for a diplomat whose days of glory are long gone and who is helpless in the face of a politically and morally corrupt native government. A dwarfed image of earlier diplomats, he is naïve enough to believe in the ideology of the civilizing mission. Mountolive, with his second-hand uniform (which Kaczvinsky sees as a "symbol of ornamentalist rule—braided and splendid but a bit out of style"),[81] his small, indifferent dog given to him by the Chancery wives to keep him company, his unrealistically romantic ideas of Egypt and Leila, and, finally, his loneliness, incite both laughter and pity at the same time. Durrell shows that, in the end, Mountolive learns his lesson as he realizes that Egypt is deceitful and decides to leave forever.

Historically, Sir Miles Lampson, later Lord Killearn, was the real holder of David Mountolive's job. He arrived in Egypt in summer 1934 as "the last colonial British High Commissioner to Egypt and became Britain's first Ambassador to a supposedly free Egypt in 1936." He continued in this post until 1946. Quite unlike Mountolive, Lampson was an imposing imperialist who was disdainful toward Egyptians, very much in the manner of Lord Cromer, British high commissioner in Egypt from 1883 to 1907.[82] As Kaczvinsky notes, Durrell makes Mountolive ambassador when, arriving in Egypt in 1934, he would still have been high commissioner until the 1936 Anglo-Egyptian treaty.[83]

Anne Ricketson Zahlan believes that creating Mountolive as the polar opposite of the high-handed Lampson conveys the "real impotence of England in a rapidly-changing world, the actual inevitability of the deconstructing of the imperial self."[84] To Zahlan's point, I would add that Durrell's lamentation of Britain's receding power, with the underlying argument that Britain's departure is causing Egyptians to revert to their corrupt, barbaric ways, advocates for the Western power's continued presence in Egypt. Seen in the immediate historical context of the novel—Nasser's nationalization of the Suez Canal and the failed Tripartite Invasion of 1956—Durrell's liberties with Lampson's character further elicit sympathy for the colonial officer who is putatively threatened, if not outmaneuvered, by recently empowered corrupt, backward Egyptians.

Ultimately, this ambivalence is resolved by the embrace of Britain as a superior, rational force. Although Mountolive sometimes resists colonial discourse, as in his complex relationship with Leila, he affirms it by attributing the failure of the imperial mission to widespread and intransigent Egyptian corruption. In this sense, both the civilized Egypt that Britain is allegedly trying to create and the spectacular Egypt that Mountolive is creating in his mind are mirages—soap-bubbles that will explode upon contact. In reconciling with colonial ideology, which condemns incorrigible Egyptians, Mountolive classifies Egypt as Calibanesque. Egyptian society as seen in the novel poses a quandary as it exposes the failure of the British occupation to turn Egyptians into civilized people. Mountolive rejects the dream of the romantic, exotic Egypt in favor of the grotesque Egypt that cannot be rationally explained.

Durrell's inclusion of a prominent Coptic family by no means constitutes a humanization of Egypt's Copts for, far from proving to be redeemable mimics, they reveal themselves to be no better than their Muslim compatriots. Congruent with imperialist discourse, Durrell sees religious feeling as an anachronism signifying irrationality and thus marks it as premodern.[85] His portrayal of political life in mid-1930s Egypt is inextricably entangled with his understanding of the role of Islam in Egypt and its effects on both Muslims and Christians. According to the novel, the proneness of Egyptians to mysterious spiritual feeling makes them impervious to modern democratic ways. Even the Copts who, in Faltaus' lecture to Mountolive at the beginning of the novel, are elevated to the brains of Egypt, are reduced to mere puppets controlled by their ancient Egyptian ancestors who engage them in a plot against the British instead of copying their putatively ideal political system. Their transformation corresponds to Mountolive's progressive enlightenment. Eventually, Egyptians, whether Coptic or Muslim, are deemed to be a threat since not only do they plot against Britain but they also conceal their seditiousness through the very symbols of religion, as seen in the bribery scene discussed further on.

One of Durrell's most direct indictments of all Egyptians occurs in the novel's bribery scene that locates Islam as a contagion that has infected Egypt's Copts. In this telling scene, the Quran becomes the very medium and the symbol of the supposedly corrupting nature of Islam, through which Christians are defiled. The Coptic Nessim visits the home of Memlik Pasha, the Muslim Minister of Interior, as a Quran recitation is about to start.[86] He is there to bribe the latter to get him to overlook Nessim's role in a plot to establish a Jewish state in Palestine, a plot with no basis in history in which Halim sees a reaction to anti-British activism that occurred in Cyprus between 1953 and 1956 and therefore immediately preceded the writing of the *Quartet* and overlapped with the publication of *Justine*.[87] However, situating the work in its commercial background, Kenneth Rexroth explains that, because Durrell had sold *Justine* before the rest of the work was completed, he had to produce a novel a year to meet a deadline. As a result, "plotting, which at the start was careful and wise, became sensational. It not only became sensational, it became frivolous and irresponsible."[88]

Of importance is the fact that the Christian delivers to the expectant Muslim a rare copy of the Quran at a Quran recitation with money hidden in its pages. His participation in this process marks his seduction by Muslim corruption, which is completed when he stays to listen to the reading that warms his heart. That a Copt—a Europeanized, Oxford-educated one at that—enjoys a Quran recital allegedly testifies to the dangerously hypnotic power of Islam over both groups. Because the goal of the bribe is to cover for the Hosnani boys' implication in the Coptic plot, the scene identifies religion as seditious. In this instance, it is the harmonious coexistence between Christian and Muslim Egyptians, this closeness, which causes the presumably infectious spirit of Islam to affect Copts. As a result, both Muslims and Copts are coded as equally dangerous, uncivilized, corrupt, and, in short, irredeemably Other. In addition to further highlighting Mountolive's immature enchantment with Egypt as well as his obliviousness to the menace posed by the Levantine Hosnanis, this incident shows Egyptians to be vulnerable to mysterious religious forces regardless of their source or of the audience's religious beliefs.

The gradually shrinking distance between the author and Mountolive marks the latter's progress from ignorant, unreliable young man to mature protagonist. The text moves from indulging his fantasy of an exotic Egypt, to distancing him for naïvely embracing its rotting, stinking beauty, as in the fishing scene mentioned earlier, to validating the epiphany of a now-educated protagonist whose point of view converges with that of the social order. He concludes that the beauty, rationality—in a word, civilization—that Egypt offers is a dream and that beneath this mimicry lies a real menace. Consequently, Durrell absolves Britain of guilt for occupying Egypt and, in an amusing reversal of the situation, Britain poses as the victim of this colonial project, finally gaining freedom from Egypt's shackles. Durrell casts the British occupation as a burden endured by the white man in return for ingratitude.

Mountolive's Awakening

Durrell's nostalgia is ambiguous. For one thing, *Mountolive* does not acknowledge the success of the civilizing mission, depicting Egypt as in need of Britain's constant vigilance to keep it from lapsing into a state of abjection. Moreover, it departs from the imperialist, colonialist ideology by showing that Britain's civilizing efforts will only bring forth the grotesque in Egyptians, mildly hinting at the discourse of voluntary decolonization mentioned in the Introduction to this study. To be clear, I am not suggesting that Durrell briefly entertains an anti-imperialist stance born out of conviction that Egyptians have a right to self-rule. On the contrary, the novel underscores the incorrigibility of Egyptians.

Nonetheless, and despite his exposure of the imperial mission's futility, Durrell legitimates Empire by attributing the failure to Egypt's intractable primitivism. When evoking pity for the now powerless British official in Egypt, Durrell exhibits nostalgia for the heyday of Empire. In this sense, he arguably longs for the once-enchanted Mountolive in himself. This constitutes nostalgia for an earlier, simpler time when personally Durrell might have thought that Empire could work. On the other hand, one may read his text as quite the opposite of nostalgia—as a rejection, but not a condemnation, of Empire. It is worth noting that his depiction of powerless British officials is counterfactual. In reality, Britain continued to intervene in Egypt's affairs to the point of surrounding the King's palace with tanks in 1942 in order to force him to appoint a pro-British prime minister.[89]

Mountolive's grotesque experience at the child brothel eliminates the text's punctuated ambivalence. By confirming Durrell's depiction of Egypt as grotesque, it constitutes both his and the protagonist's final disillusionment. Mountolive's trip to the native quarter at the end of the novel is his and the author's final, desperate attempt at reviving the illusion of a marvelous Egypt. In this scene, gothic elements combine to foreground the mimicry of Egyptians placing them in a third space between the uncanny and the marvelous. Unlike Bhabha's potentially freeing third space, a hybridity that allows the Other to combine various cultural values and practices, this space identifies Egyptians as grotesque, Caliban-like figures, who, neither conforming to Britain's illusion of a magical East nor following the British model of rational governance, are incapable of copying what is implied to be a rational British system.

Following in the footsteps of Edward William Lane who, according to Egyptian scholar Azza Kararah, went by Mansur Effendi in Egypt, Mountolive goes native and, confident that his dress and command of Arabic will confer authenticity on him, orders a meal and some drinks in the Arab quarter.[90] He is approached by an Egyptian whose "face had all the candour [*sic*] and purity of some desert saint" (289). Mountolive believes this man to be a venerable sheikh about to reveal to him secrets about his future, whereas in fact the Egyptian takes him to a child brothel. In a reversal of the gothic novel formula, where a damsel in distress is rescued by a brave hero, it is the former British colonial officer who is abducted, locked up in an unknown location, and subjected to frightening trials before he is mysteriously released.

The episode delivers a harsh lesson to Mountolive who still believes that by simply going native and demonstrating his fluency in Arabic he can pass, in his words, for "a Moslem [*sic*]," and unlock the mysteries of the country reviving the mirage of a mysterious, magical Egypt. Because he cannot remember or explain certain details of his experience, his fantastic account of the incident is somewhat doubtful. For example, upon entering the child brothel, Mountolive says that he "felt rather than saw the worm-eaten staircases" (290). Sometime during his ordeal he falls unconscious and dreams of his mother reading *Gulliver's Travels* to him as a child. He is riveted by the fantastic image of Gulliver fixed to the ground by Lilliputians who, like the child prostitutes, are crawling over his body. Additionally, in his eagerness to re-create the myth of exotic Egypt, Mountolive has set the stage for his own delirious experience. He goes to the Arab quarter having already had two glasses of whiskey. Once there, he orders *arak* "his first drink of the Levant" (288) then "forgetting also how strong it was, and overcome with nostalgia … [he] ordered himself a second glass" (288). The *arak* transports him to a mythical world: "He was in the seventh heaven of delight now. He was on the way to recovering, to restoring the blurred image of an Egypt which the meeting with Leila had damaged or somehow stolen from him" (288). Mountolive heads to the brothel already intoxicated with nostalgia. Yet, instead of recovering the magical Egypt, he encounters grotesque Egypt.

The resolution of the brothel scene defies classification as either wholly fantastic or wholly uncanny. Mountolive knows that he has been subjected to a harrowing experience from which he managed to escape but does not know how "he found himself (though he had no idea how he had finally escaped) leaning upon the icy stone embankment of the Corniche with the dawn sea beneath him" (293). He realizes that the sheikh played a trick on him—an explanation that, despite its logic, does not explain why the man assumes that Mountolive is looking for a prostitute, whether or not he recognizes him as an Englishman, whether he takes him to the brothel out of sheer malice or out of depravity, and whether he is a sheikh to begin with. Mountolive finally realizes that in its squalor and grotesqueness, the child brothel is Egypt and decides to leave the country.

Mountolive's epiphany—that Egypt is a grotesque dream—validates colonialist discourse by reinforcing the bildungsroman as a genre that equates the protagonist's maturity with recognition of and reconciliation with the established social order. After the child brothel episode, Mountolive, now sullied by his initiation into an ugly, mature world, "seething with self-contempt and disgust" (294) experiences the sadness that comes with maturity. Mountolive, who is not saved through any heroic acts of his own, but instead inexplicably finds himself next to his car with no recollection of the details of his escape, reflects the frailty of Britain and its alleged loss of power and grandeur. Feeling like a "mummy" in "the splendours [*sic*] of [his] second-hand uniform" Durrell, through Mountolive, mourns Britain's loss of limitless power that Cromer and other high commissioners once had in Egypt. Durrell argues that this power was benign because the British used it to control a corrupt people. This is the image that frames Egyptian national life in the novel.

By the end of the novel, a more mature Mountolive refigures Egypt, represented by Islamic symbols, as a violent place, drenched in blood. A telling instance of this reconfiguration occurs on his drive into Alexandria for his final meeting with Leila. Mountolive sees a "blood-stained cloud" (277) deflowered by the phallic minarets, highlighting the alleged bloodiness and violence of Islam that caused Egypt to lose her innocence and predicting his own imminent loss of innocence after the child brothel scene. After his escape from the brothel, Mountolive looks "back once [at Alexandria], with a shudder of disgust, at the pearly mirage of minarets rising from the smoke of the lake, the dawn mist" (295). His disgust marks his initiation into the world of the mature. His exotic image of Egypt is shattered and replaced by an image of an oppressive Eastern religion that destroys even nature.

Mountolive's colonial education is now complete. In the dawn, which tropes his awakened consciousness, he perceives the true face of Islam to be a barbaric religion that is incompatible with the rational social, political life of the European Enlightenment imaginary. He embraces the English social order that argues that the Egyptians are incapable of self-rule because Islam is inimical to progress. This incapacity extends to Coptic Egyptians who are increasingly portrayed as doubly dangerous: first, because they have been seduced into a Muslim lifestyle and, second, because they are particularly susceptible to outbreaks of religious fervor. The novel codes this susceptibility as an intergenerational pathology active in and passed on by ancient Egyptian ancestors, which figure as an evil spirit that possesses Narouz as he delivers a seditious speech in a trance. These prove to be evil as Narouz becomes so violent in the end that his fellow Copts cast him off.[91]

Mountolive confirms Pursewarden's (a poet in the novel) view that Egypt is a "rabble-ridden grotesque which we now apparently regard as a sovereign state" (105). The novel refuses to see Egyptians—Muslims or Christians—on other than religious terms. The text creates an imperialist image of an imaginary Egypt whose religion, with its putative brutality, lethargy, and irrationality, controls it rendering Egyptians at odds with modernity. This lack is what marks them as menace. The novel suggests that religion, or religious sentiment, is the stage that once Egyptians outgrow will allow them to join advanced Western nations who have presumably moved beyond religion. *Mountolive* gracefully glosses over continued British support of corruption and disruption of a healthy constitutional life as long as this furthered British interests.[92]

Although Diboll sees Durrell as a pro-Copt whose interest in ancient Egyptian religion extended to the Coptic Church, images of plotting or of possessed Copts challenge this.[93] Gordon Bowker notes that Durrell found the dominance of Islamic culture in Egypt oppressive: "If he already hated 'cannibalistic' Christianity, he found Islam suffocating and beastly."[94] The novel equates both Muslims and Christians once in the bribery scene and again when, fearful of the Egyptian government's response to their meetings, a Coptic character asks Nessim if he has intended to invoke a "jehad" against the government (218).

In his portrayal of Egyptians, Durrell creates a racialized, religion-based Egyptian national identity that transforms religious difference into different national belongings absolving Empire of guilt while dissociating Alexandria from Egypt, as Halim justifiably argues. As a justification of British presence in Egypt, nineteenth-century imperialists such as Cromer denied the existence of such a thing as an Egyptian race claiming Egyptians to be racial hybrids.[95] Durrell destabilizes the category "Egyptian" sometimes using "Egyptians" and "Moslems [*sic*]" interchangeably to refer to Muslim Egyptians while other times referring to them as the "Arabs," but almost never referring to Copts as "Egyptians." Even more, the novel refers to other European nationals residing in Alexandria as "Alexandrians." In Halim's words the term "Alexandrian" in the *Quartet*, "not only precludes those of European descent who did not see themselves as strangers and exiles, such as Cavafy, but more startlingly Egyptians, and specifically Muslims … In construing the Alexandrians as European(ized) strangers and exiles, the text has recourse to a species of 'imaginative geography used by other writers too to dispossess the city from the country and ascribes it to Europe.' "[96] In the end, echoing Cromer's argument, *Mountolive* contends that Egyptian nationalism, if the concept even exists, cannot succeed because the Egyptian people cannot easily be defined under a clear national category. By the same token, the novel illustrates that only experienced British administration guarantees the success of such a diverse nation.

Conclusion

Mountolive follows the protagonist's education on the cultural and imperial levels, in both of which Leila's role is instrumental. Through Mountolive's relationship with Leila and her family, the novel first reverses the imperial narrative before confirming it. First, by making Leila bear the burden of Mountolive's education, the novel offers a new civilizing mission where the Levantine woman shapes the imperial officer. His intellectual superior, Leila's mentorship during the early stages of his career and over the years help him attain a cultural sophistication that matches that of the colonized Levantine woman herself. This marks his first maturation, later to be marked as regression. Second, by shocking Mountolive with the ugly face of Leila, making her (and by extension the Hosnanis) an incarnation of the scheming Levantine, *Mountolive* turns them into a grotesque menace, occasioning the protagonist's second and final maturity at the end of the novel. Ultimately, despite Durrell's ambivalence, the novel confirms imperialist discourse with its claims about evil Egyptians. Mountolive's imperial maturation occurs at the moment that his views converge with those of the English social order. Outgrowing his enchantment with both Leila and Egypt he recognizes that even its Western-educated Coptic people are not to be trusted particularly because of their elusive sameness that turns into a menace.

2

Lessons in Modernity: Naguib Mahfouz's *Sugar Street* and the Female National Intellectual

Not many readers may remember the feminist journalist Sawsan Hammad in Naguib Mahfouz's *Cairo Trilogy* (1956–7).[1] Indeed, there is no reason to remember her, for she is a minor character who appears very briefly at the end of *al-Sukkariyya*, 1957 (*Sugar Street*, 1992), the last volume of the *Trilogy*. Rather than highlighted, her story is buried deep in the novel, making her very easy to gloss over. Yet, Sawsan is an interesting character. Not only is she the educated new Egyptian woman but also her lessons in an indigenous modernity are instrumental to the male protagonist's education and final maturity. For this reason, I center her in my reading and argue that she emerges as a female national intellectual. Through Sawsan, *Sugar Street*, inadvertently or not, presents a brief female bildungsroman, a story portraying a journey of education. This bildungsroman differs from traditional female narratives where domesticity is at the center. Sawsan's story needs to be pieced together, but it is a female narrative of education where woman as agent is struggling to come out of the text as a franchised subject.

Even though it is Ahmad who emerges as the male protagonist of Mahfouz's Egyptian bildungsroman at the end of *Sugar Street*, as I argue, his journey is modeled on Sawsan's route. Through Ahmad, *Sugar Street* rejects the classic bildungsroman as a fit vehicle for the other's self-realization while at the same time repudiating traditional native forms, presenting both as models that produce flawed protagonists. Offering an alternate bildungsroman, Mahfouz revises the genre to allow the Egyptian intellectual to fashion a model that fits the native sociohistorical context. Sawsan's training of the male protagonist as journalist and, more importantly, as critical thinker, reflects the process that she has gone through as a female national intellectual.

Together, Sawsan and Ahmad embody various segments of Egyptian society: the petit bourgeoisie represented in Ahmad as a merchant's grandson and in Sawsan who could not attend college but is a well-read journalist; the new educated Egyptian *effendiya* class seen again in Ahmad; and the proletariat, which, as a laborer, Sawsan's father stands for. She is also the new woman: the antithesis of the aristocratic, colonized Aïda whom Kamal loves hopelessly; the females in Ahmad's family who represent the traditional urban middle class; and Zubayda the entertainer, who represents the exploited women of Cairo's working class. Sawsan takes on an active role guiding Ahmad's development as a thinker.

The *Trilogy* covers the years from 1917 to 1944. Over the period of twenty-eight years, Mahfouz interweaves Egypt's 1919 Revolution, life under two world wars, and constant struggle with the British over governance with changes in Al-Sayyid Ahmad Abd al-Jawad's family—the patriarch who reigns strictly at home but spends his nights in drunken revelry, cavorting with Cairo's female entertainers.[2] *Sugar Street* follows the Abd al-Jawad family from 1935 to 1944. Two-thirds into the novel, Al-Sayyid Ahmad, the patriarch whose waning power reflects that of Britain, dies shortly after a German air raid during the Second World War. Kamal, his youngest son, publishes articles in periodicals as he continues to search for the meaning of life, while Al-Sayyid Ahmad's grandchildren and Kamal's nephews, Ahmad and Abd al-Muni'm, engage in Egyptian political life each in his own way, one taking a leftist track and the other joining the Muslim Brotherhood.

Although in the *Trilogy* Saad Zaghloul, the revolution, and Egyptian political life remain on the margins, coming to the forefront only as they intersect with the Abd al-Jawad family life, their impact on the family, whether direct or indirect, makes their presence pervasive. Without question, the fullest treatment of the revolution occurs near the end of the first volume, *Palace Walk*, the most prominent effect of which is the death of Fahmy, second son of Ahmad Abd al-Jawad, during a peaceful demonstration. Its presence fades thereafter. However, Zaghloul, his companions and successors, and the rich intellectual, political life that emerged before and continued to flourish under the revolution remain a source of inspiration for Kamal and his fellow intellectuals, so much so that at the end of the second volume Kamal reacts more strongly to Zaghloul's death than to the multiple deaths in his own family. Throughout the *Trilogy*, and particularly in *Sugar Street*, the 1919 Revolution poses as a golden age against which the current political scene is constantly evaluated. This is most apparent in Riyad Qaldas' nostalgic praise for the *Wafd*'s success at including all Egyptians in a democratic parliamentary life by erasing religious divisions. Kamal and his nephews' choices are a direct commentary on, or rather an elegy of, 1919. But, where Kamal represents the intellectual's failure to live up to the revolutionary spirit of 1919, Ahmad provides hope.

Critics usually see Kamal as the protagonist of Mahfouz's *Trilogy*, but I argue that *Sugar Street* endorses Ahmad as a representative of a new male Egyptian modernism—someone who revises the *nahda* (cultural awakening) of the late-nineteenth and early-twentieth centuries to forge a specifically Egyptian structure.[3] Ahmad Ibrahim Shawkat is one of two grandsons of the notorious al-Sayyid Ahmad Abd al-Jawad. Kamal his son, and Ahmad's uncle, spends most of the second and third volumes looking for the truth but never reaches an epiphany.[4] Rather it is Ahmad who, after some searching, reaches his epiphany, marking himself as the new Egyptian national intellectual in a post-1919 Revolution Egyptian bildungsroman. But, if we examine the text closely, we find that Ahmad's apprenticeship reflects that of Sawsan, a journalist and mentor four years his senior, who later becomes his wife, and that it is actually *her* apprenticeship that we follow as we watch Ahmad progress.

Naguib Mahfouz (1911–2006) is Egypt's most celebrated writer and, in Samia Mehrez's words, the "godfather of the Arabic novel" and "one of the major underground historians."[5] Mahfouz, who won the Nobel Prize for Literature in 1988 after a close competition with the British writer Lawrence Durrell,[6] is, as Roger Allen argues, a foundational figure in the development of the Arabic novel—one who helped the genre advocate and reflect social change as it continues to change itself.[7] Mahfouz's life spanned multiple significant moments in Egyptian history, the most powerful of which was the 1919 Revolution, which he describes as "the one thing which most shook the security of my childhood." Whether from a roof-top room in his family home in Cairo or from his elementary school opposite the famous al-Husayn Mosque, the seven-year-old author witnessed the fallout from the national struggle. From home, he saw "women take part in the demonstrations on donkey-drawn carts … [and] often saw English soldiers firing at the demonstrators," while his school afforded him views of "the bodies of the dead and the wounded laid on the ground." Rasheed Enany identifies this as the reason why Mahfouz constantly recreates the revolution in his works and remains a "spiritual follower of the liberal, democratic principles of the *Wafd* Party which inherited the revolution."[8]

After graduating from Cairo University with a degree in philosophy in 1934 and starting, but never finishing, a master's thesis on aesthetics in Islam, the future author left the university in 1938 and became a civil servant until his retirement in 1971. Following his retirement, he started writing for *al-Ahram*, Egypt's official daily newspaper, but even during his tenure with the civil service Mahfouz held several different other jobs all while publishing his work.[9] For example, from the 1940s until the early 1980s, he became a freelance film script writer, producing twenty-five scripts for films that are today considered the classics of Egyptian cinema. During the Nasser era (1954–70), Mahfouz occupied several important posts, among them secretary to the Minister of National Guidance, member of the Directory of the Film Censorship Office, director-general of the Film Support Organization, adviser to the General Organization for Film Industry, Broadcasting and Television, chairman of the board of directors of the same organization, and adviser to the Minister of Culture.[10]

When the 1952 Revolution occurred, Mahfouz had already written the *Trilogy* and had about eight novels to his name. Originally penning it as a 1,500-page piece entitled "Palace Walk," he had spent the previous seven years working on it. The first part of the *Trilogy* was then serialized in the literary magazine *al-Risala al-Jadida* from April 1954 to April 1956. Following its success, the publisher, who had earlier rejected it on account of its length, decided to divide the book into three parts with three different titles.[11] Mahfouz's initial enthusiasm for the revolution, leading him to stop writing for years, soon waned as disillusionment and anger at the Nasser regime's totalitarianism set in.[12] Although at the time he explained that his break from writing was caused by conviction that the new regime had redressed all the social ills he addressed in his works, he later confessed that he never knew the reason behind this break, adding that he had similar experiences after the 1967 and the 1973 wars.[13] After a five-year hiatus—from 1952 to 1957—he returned with a series of bitter novels in the 1960s.

So harsh was his criticism of the revolution that, but for the personal intervention of the Minister of Culture (Tharwat 'Ukashah), Mahfouz would have joined fellow writers in prison.[14] While Enany suggests that the state's patience with Mahfouz may have been a tactic to create a fiction of tolerance to dissent, he adds that it was commonly known that some of the author's novels of the period were published through the intervention of Muhammad Hasanayn Haykal, Nasser's confidant and editor of *al-Ahram*.[15] In the 1970s under Sadat's crackdown on intellectuals, Mahfouz, along with other intellectuals, was banned from writing.[16]

Because of the profound effect of the 1919 demonstrations on him and his disappointment with the results of the 1952 Revolution, Mahfouz remained haunted by 1919 and continued to revisit its events in his fiction. For example, in *al-Samman wa al-kharif*, 1962 (*Autumn Quail* 1985), he reflects on the corruption of the *Wafd* Party. Further, eight out of the seventy-eight tales in *Hikayat haritna*, 1975 (*The Fountain and the Tomb* 1988), address the 1919 Revolution while *al-Maraya*, 1972 (*Mirrors* 1977), briefly hints at it.[17] Surprisingly, the writer whose first article in 1930 prefers "gradual evolutionary progress" to revolution,[18] in the 1980s and 1990s would call for the use of 1919 as a reference for democracy, religious unity, and national struggle.[19] His belief that revolution will let down its society by failing to fulfill its promise gave way to admiration and regular commemoration of figures of the revolution in his writing.[20]

Although Mahfouz was familiar with Joyce, Kafka, and Proust, when he penned the *Trilogy*, he chose to write it in a social realist mode.[21] In addition to his view that content dictated form,[22] Mahfouz, who found the modernist novel "boring," believed that presenting a chaotic narration was tantamount to dissociating the brain from external life, since the human brain imposed order on the chaos of life. Although after the 1967 war he would go on to write in the style of the Absurd, at the time Mahfouz doubted the suitability of the stream of consciousness technique and the Absurd for Arabic literature.[23] Comparing the Arabic novel tradition at the time to its English counterpart, he declared that Arabic literature had yet to go through a realist phase before moving to introspection and the stream of consciousness, otherwise he would have been a mere imitator. Working alone, Mahfouz had to lay the foundation himself, particularly since eminent figures who wrote Arabic novels, such as Taha Hussein or Abbas Mahmoud al-Aqqad, viewed the genre with disdain and even then their works were closer to biographies than novels.[24] Interestingly, some scholars such as Louis Awad prefer to see the *Trilogy* as a naturalistic work, a school with which Mahfouz did not ally himself despite having read Emile Zola and H. G. Wells.[25]

Refuting claims that the *Trilogy* was a historical novel, Mahfouz asserted that his works always depicted the present. He added that, concerned as he was with the daily life of the Abd al-Jawad family, he had to omit many of the details of the revolution.[26] In actuality, Mahfouz records his and his fellow intellectuals' education—their crisis as they struggled between mimicry and intellectual independence and as Egypt grappled with its national, intellectual, and political identities. Ultimately, Mahfouz revises the genre to allow the Egyptian intellectual to fashion a model that fits the native sociohistorical context.

Sawsan as Mentor

Sawsan hails from a poor, working-class family who occupies a basement room in what seems to be the Jewish quarter in Gamaliya, the neighborhood where Mahfouz grew up and which he immortalized in several of his works. Her father is chief pressman at *al Insan al Jadid* (*The New Man*), the leftist journal where she works and which Ahmad later joins. Financially insecure, Sawsan was unable to join the earliest ranks of women admitted to Fu'ad University (later Cairo University) since 1929.[27] Instead, she has acquired her knowledge through extensive reading facilitated by her job. In contrast to Ahmad's comfortable lifestyle, she has known hunger and poverty. Sawsan appears in six out of fifty-four chapters and, except for the two chapters in which she coaches Ahmad, her appearance is quite marginal, justifying Hoda El Sadda's description of her as a flat character. For, unlike Kamal, Ahmad Abd al-Jawad, the patriarch, and even Amina his wife, El Sadda elaborates, Sawsan does not communicate any of her private thoughts.[28] Yet, Sawsan's importance lies in her role as Ahmad's teacher to whom he owes a great debt, as he himself acknowledges, "My respect for you is beyond words, and I admit that I've been your pupil in the noblest achievements of my life."[29] He regards her as an intellectual superior whose diligence and hard work motivate him. She is a role model and, for that matter, one that he as male protagonist wishes to emulate. Throughout, Ahmad remains in Sawsan's thrall and, even though it is his theory of revolution that we learn about in the last pages of the book, it bears Sawsan's stamp.

Although Ahmad's education as national intellectual takes place in the backdrop of a love story where Sawsan on rare occasion plays the bashful woman, I choose to highlight the intellectual conversations and downplay the courtship in an attempt to bring a new perspective on Sawsan. This hidden female bildungsroman, with Sawsan as national intellectual at its center, is built upon a remarkable reversal of gender roles, where Sawsan, the woman, becomes mentor, critic, work superior, and unrelenting intellectual, while Ahmad is the recipient of her knowledge. When we first meet Ahmad, at the age of fourteen or fifteen, he is already an unconventional character who entertains socialist ideas. His continued education in a gender-blind, socialist nationalism happens gradually. Instrumental to it is the image of Sawsan, who structures his education along three guiding principles: first, active participation in history; second, the functionality of art; and, finally, the urgency to design an egalitarian, gender-blind social code to replace the current bourgeois blueprint.[30]

First, encouraging Ahmad to pick a genre through which to express his views without antagonizing authorities, Sawsan alerts him to the importance of agency in the formation of the national intellectual. Like his uncle Kamal, Ahmad has been translating European pieces in journals without taking a stance. Sawsan rescues him from becoming another Kamal, a detached intellectual who shops around all philosophies. She accomplishes this task by assessing Kamal's methods and contributions in pragmatic terms. She notes that instead of utilizing the knowledge he has amassed in order to form his own theory, he regurgitates old information. Contribution, in her view, is predicated upon intellectual autonomy and putting philosophy to utilitarian use befitting the Egyptian context. Clearly what is missing in Kamal's contribution is his own voice that locates him in Frantz Fanon's adept phase. Theorizing the evolution of national culture in a colonial context, Fanon outlines the intellectual's formation along three steps: first, blind adoption of colonial forms; second, selective adaptation of colonial forms to native scenes; and finally, adept creation of unique native models.[31] Now an independent thinker, the intellectual is actively involved socially and politically, calling upon the people to join the struggle using "combat literature,"[32] a stage which Sawsan already occupies, and which Ahmad is about to enter at the end of the *Trilogy* as he becomes active in distributing subversive political pamphlets.

In contrast to Kamal, Sawsan is an independent thinker who not only holds pronounced opinions about Kamal's contribution, or lack thereof, but also has a clear conception of Egypt's needs at this historical juncture. She knows which thinkers she supports, what should constitute Egypt's contributions to world history, and why Egypt should adopt a secular rather than a religious path, for example. Sawsan ably defends her stance and directs Ahmad toward Marx's "scientific understanding of society" (192) as a starting point from which to devise a social praxis rooted in the exigencies of Egyptian society.

Second, in expounding her theory on the function of art, Sawsan highlights the importance of committed literature. Emerging in Arabic literary criticism in the 1950s and influenced by Jean-Paul Sartre's *engagement*, *al-iltizam* (commitment), according to Egyptian scholar Mohammed Mustafa Badawi, indicated a stance where works conveyed messages born out of the Arab world's sociopolitical realities.[33] Sawsan critiques two types of intellectual: the passive, ivory-tower philosopher and the uninvolved fiction writer. Not a proponent of art for art's sake, Sawsan believes that art should have a practical goal and that the artist or "writer ... must be at the head of the freedom fighters" (192). Anticipating Fanon's remarks on the artist's role in turbulent political times, Sawsan captures the disconnect of Kamal and his friend Riyad Qaldas, the fiction writer, from sociopolitical reality. Kamal and Riyad are not involved writers. On the one hand, Kamal translates Western philosophy without committing to a school of thought. Riyad, on the other hand, writes short stories that, despite centering the proletariat, do not in Sawsan's opinion go beyond the descriptive to offer a remedy for social ills. Incidentally, this is a critique that the Arab literary Left leveled at Mahfouz himself.[34] Sawsan calls for a national program where art is functional and the artist involved.

It is worth noting that Sawsan's views predict the fierce debate and subsequent rift between younger intellectuals post the 1952 Revolution, on the one hand, and, on the other hand, Taha Hussein, the famous *nahda* figure and Dean of Arabic Letters as he was known. Passionate about Egypt's newly gained independence, the former saw art as a medium through which to promote the nationalist cause, blaming the older generation, represented by Hussein, for easy submission to European Enlightenment thought. Hussein, or the last *Nahdawi*, as Hussam Ahmed nicknames him, however, firmly believed that art should not serve propagandist thought. To be clear, Hussein's writing shows profound concern for national causes but, as Ahmed argues, it was his view that artist should be free to choose the content and form of his or her work.[35] Clearly, Sawsan would have joined the opposing camp. Whether or not we agree with her, her philosophy shows her as an analytical thinker capable of forming and defending a stance.

Sawsan emerges as an adept national intellectual in *Sugar Street*. When Ahmad meets her, and when she enters the narrative for the reader, she has already gone through her apprenticeship. Now an independent thinker, she synthesizes the knowledge she has gained, skillfully creating a model that fits the Egyptian context. Sawsan frames Egyptian modernity as an active struggle, constantly evolving to fit the needs of the moment. As an active Marxist, feminist intellectual, she is at the forefront of the national struggle, merging the theoretical, through work at the journal, with the practical through grassroots political organization by giving talks to workers and distributing subversive pamphlets. Sawsan's work at the *New Man*, a dissenting journal that has been previously shut by the government, is by no means a "safe" bourgeois job. Both Sawsan and Ahmad are aware of the threat of arrest, and Sawsan asserts that she owes the government many years in prison (243).

That Ahmad's teacher is a woman is not insignificant because one of her tasks, and Sawsan's third guiding principle, is alerting him to the need for a non-gendered cultural model. Directly as well as indirectly, by virtue of her identity as an educated, intelligent, working woman, she reshapes his bourgeois mentality by prodding him to further question bourgeois ideals with their class and gender biases, tutoring him in Marxism and socialism. As an archetype, she inspires contradictory feelings in Ahmad such that he is caught between treating her as a subject, admiring her independence and intelligence, on the one hand, and, on the other hand, viewing her in traditional bourgeois terms as a sexualized, female object. Beth Baron explains that although women in

Egypt entered legal, medical, and other professions in the 1920s and 1930s, by 1947 they constituted only between 4 and 6 percent of the formal waged labor force.[36] Thus, for Ahmad, whose first meeting with Sawsan likely takes place between 1935 and 1936, the idea of a female employee is a novelty.

Sawsan is, in contrast, professional, decidedly confident, and passionate about her cause, showing her debt to an evolving feminist discourse that owes its birth to journalism, which served as a medium for male and female intellectuals to discuss women's issues. Girls' education in new, Western-style schools had gained ground in the late nineteenth century, so much so that between 1875 and 1915 the government could not meet the population's high demand for such schools.[37] Whereas late-nineteenth- and early-twentieth-century Egyptian feminist writing inscribed women's contribution to the nation on their bodies, extolling their roles as mothers of citizens, in the 1930s and 1940s Egyptian women started demanding more social, political, and economic rights based on national service, rather than motherhood. Laura Bier finds that this period also witnessed the emergence of new feminist voices from other classes, to compete with those of elite women, as well as a rise in female professionalization in such fields as journalism, teaching, and health care.[38] Latifa al-Zayyat, path-breaking Egyptian feminist author and critic, describes Sawsan as the first woman in Mahfouz's work who goes beyond the private to the public and who dedicates her life to the nation and the working classes, proving that women could participate in the social context.[39]

At their first meeting, Sawsan handles Ahmad's sixteen-year-old arrogance and social immaturity with poise. Her image as a female journalist triggers a range of responses to the idea of a female professional in a field that was historically hospitable to the first generations of women who gained a higher education in the 1930s and 1940s.[40] Ahmad who is sixteen years old and about to enter university, visits the offices of *The New Man* to ask for an update on a piece that he has sent and is referred to another room. As he enters the office, Ahmad notices

> three desks in the room. Two were empty, and a girl was sitting at the third. He had not been expecting this and stopped in his tracks. He looked at her inquisitively and apprehensively. She was around twenty, with a dark brown complexion, black eyes, and black hair. There was a resolute look about her delicate nose, pointed chin, and thin lips, but that did not detract from her beauty. (82)

Ahmad's first reaction to a "girl" employee is shock followed by ambivalent emotions. He is perplexed—curious, yet anxious for a host of reasons. First, this is an unfamiliar situation where he comes face to face with a working woman who is not in a lowly position. Second, the near absence of a primer governing conduct with educated women occupying white-collar jobs makes him anxious. Third, he recognizes the need to improvise—to configure a code on his first encounter ever with a professional woman. Finally, Ahmad has no experience interacting with the other sex as a subject—for example he has to "[overcome] nervousness" before asking her about his article (82). As if on cue, the bourgeois man in him promptly appraises her beauty, affirming that work in the public sphere has not defeminized her. These thoughts, which derail his efforts to see the employee in female form, continue to plague Ahmad when he meets Sawsan five years later during his apprenticeship at the journal.

As an educated, working woman, Sawsan shocks Ahmad out of his male bourgeois complacency. His thoughts during this first meeting with Sawsan are colored by discomfort and awkwardness generated in his mind by her gender. These thoughts oscillate between admiration and condescension. For instance, when he learns that she is to summarize his article before publication, he is dismayed. Becoming confrontational, he asks if she is an employee at the journal. Paradoxically, inherited bourgeois patriarchal ideals inspire as well as check his superciliousness. Ahmad's male privilege is tempered by lack of experience in addition to a need to adhere to a code dictating reserve and gentle behavior toward women; "he was tempted to ask what her qualifications for the position were, but his courage failed him at the last moment. So he inquired, 'What is your name, please, so I can ask for you by telephone, if I need to' " (82). Before leaving the room Ahmad, revisited by arrogance, instructs Sawsan: "Please summarize it carefully." (83). Unperturbed, "without looking up she replied, 'I know my job.' " (83). Sawsan's response encapsulates the self-assurance that she exhibits throughout. It is her determination and insistence on being seen as an intellectual that help Ahmad reach emotional maturity as he battles his social class's view of women.

Sawsan and Ahmad's professional-turned-love story serves as a course in a gender-equal modernity. Ahmad struggles to rid himself of bourgeois patriarchal norms that mostly situate women in the realm of the romantic and the sexual. Like their professional relationship, their love relationship is built upon a reversal of gender roles where it is Ahmad who is eventually rewarded with domesticity. He grows from a starry-eyed lover into a more mature man who begins to view male-female relationships in terms of partnership. Ahmad's rebirth as a new man is dependent upon his love relationship with Sawsan who is unlike any woman he has met previously and is certainly nothing like the housebound women in his family. Much like his previous love stories—for example, his adoration of his classmate discussed further on—Ahmad's admiration for Sawsan starts with romantic infatuation with a beautiful object. It is, therefore, apropos that Ahmad receives his professional training from a woman at a journal bearing the title *al Insan al Jadid* (*The New Man*). Not surprisingly, the gender-neutral word *al-insan*, which signifies both male and female in Arabic, much like the rendered English translation "man," (also historically used to refer to both genders) reflects both the language's normalization of male gender as well as early-twentieth-century perceptions of consciousness. Maria Paniconi reports that the Self was seen as primarily male to the extent that women's writing of the period, rather than exploring the coming-of-age narrative as a biological and psychological process, focused on intergenerational interaction.[41] Thus, Sawsan's character pushes the narrative margins in an attempt to break the conventions of the time, paving the way for Layla the protagonist of the first female bildungsroman in Latifa al-Zayyat's *al-Bab al-maftuh*, 1960 (*The Open Door*, 2000).

At the beginning, women for Ahmad are "a beautiful sight" (147), creatures to feast his eyes upon as he does when he "[fills] his eyes with [his classmate's] figure, upper back, delicate neck, and the braided hair that adorned the rear of her head" (147). Unable to interact with women on terms other than the romantic, he expects mere academic collaboration with said female classmate to express his romantic interest. Once employed at the journal he cautions himself against mistaking admiration of Sawsan's intellect for love. Ahmad's conflicting emotions regarding her professionalism and gender, and the conundrum that is her sex, are nowhere more compellingly captured than in his interior perceptions during his very first lesson. Mixed in with his reflection on her philosophy are thoughts about her beautiful eyes and her attractive and fascinating "lively breasts" (193). Ahmad's insistence on placing Sawsan in the romantic and the sexual is symptomatic of the text's unwillingness to acknowledge her as an intellectual superior to, or even on equal footing with, any male intellectual. This is particularly seen in the text's inevitable domestication of Sawsan through marriage to her protégé.

Ahmad's education occurs sometimes through self-reflection, as when he thinks: "our class is perverse … We're unable to see women from more than one perspective" (193). But, mostly, the professional behavior that Sawsan models and her unflagging intellectualism thwart Ahmad's romantic pursuits. This is seen, for example, in her insistence on bringing a book and discussing intellectual matters on what he plans as a date. A year into his training, Ahmad's gradual emotional maturity can be detected in thoughts where frustration is followed by acknowledgement of progress:

> I still occasionally look at women with a traditional bourgeois eye. During hours of lethargic backsliding, I fancy that socialism in the progressive woman is simply another captivating characteristic comparable to playing the piano or to presenting a fine appearance. But it must also be admitted that the year I have worked with Sawsan has changed me a great deal, *cleansing* me to a commendable degree of the bourgeois attitudes implanted in me. (242, emphasis added)

Although at times Ahmad views a woman of intellect as a curiosity, his progress is apparent in his use of words such as "partners" and "comrades" (240) to describe his relationship with Sawsan. Departing from the modernist paradigm of companionate marriage, where men and women's roles are complementary but not equal,[42] Ahmad introduces the concept of partnership along with socialist rhetoric of comradeship, thereby demonstrating openness to an egalitarian framework. Yet, his self-admittedly incomplete education can be seen in behavior that readers today would recognize as sexual harassment. He kisses Sawsan in the office and, managing to kiss her despite resistance on another occasion, assumes it was consensual since she could have taken other precautions to avert the kiss (242). Ahmad is evidently not yet fully "cleansed" of bourgeois attitudes toward women.

By rejecting his dreamy sentimentality, insisting on her identity as a professional by focusing on intellectual topics, and calling him out on his bourgeois gender notions, Sawsan helps Ahmad begin his transition to a new kind of postbourgeois love where husband and wife are equal partners in the national struggle. Sawsan's level-headedness, leading her to critique Ahmad's bourgeois expectations of her as lover, is at times tempered by responsiveness to his love. For instance, her response to his desire to hear words of love from her—"this is the traditional, bourgeois view of women, isn't it?"—is counterbalanced by deliberate failure to note Ahmad's reference to her as "darling" despite initial protestations. Although Sawsan disapproves of his talk about love (240), glares at him and "reprimands" him when he admires her beauty, we are told that "discreetly and cautiously, she had begun using cosmetics" (240). While it is highly possible that Sawsan's actions arise from reciprocity and coyness, she holds power in both relationships, the professional and the romantic. Although we never hear her unfiltered voice, neither Ahmad's interior monologues nor the omniscient narrative voice reports playfulness, giggling, or simpering on her part. If anything, Ahmad criticizes her for never tiring of intellectual discussions. Sawsan's love does not blind her to the need for "a new dictionary for old terms like 'love,' 'marriage,' 'jealousy,' 'faithfulness,' and 'the past' " (245).

Despite the text's willingness to portray a female intellectual, even if briefly, the narrative insists on domesticating Sawsan. *Sugar Street* cannot imagine a relationship between man and woman that is not governed by love and sexual desire. Sawsan despises the bourgeois gender dynamic yet enacts her role within this framework as beloved and wife, thus prompting El Sadda's remark that Sawsan "embodies the enigmatic construct that occupied the *nahda* imaginary."[43] Ahmad himself is a reflection of what El Sadda identifies as the *nahda* hero in Arabic literature in the first half of the twentieth century—a hero holding equivocal views on women, "aspiring to a more egalitarian relationship with women that does not … compromise male dominance and control."[44] El Sadda sees that the relative paleness of female characters in the *Trilogy*, particularly the modern types in *Sugar Street*, is congruent with the *nahda* ambivalence about what is meant by the "new woman."[45] Ahmad's struggle to rid himself of the bourgeois norm of seeing woman as a sexed being is one that the text itself undergoes, as evidenced by its insistence on domesticating Sawsan. *Sugar Street* silences Sawsan such that, in El Sadda's words, "we get to know about her political views, but not about her inner self, the way we do about Kamal and 'Abd al-Jawwad and even Amina to some extent."[46] The text eventually contains her within a bourgeois patriarchal norm, fixing the focus of the bildungsroman on the "new man." It is little wonder then that Mahmoud Amin El Alem and Abdel-Rahman Abu Ouf fault Mahfouz for not capturing the crisis of the female intellectual activist. Glossing over Sawsan, Abu Ouf goes on to say that due to the absence of a female activist as a counterpart to Fahmy, the eldest son of Ahmad Abd al-Jawad and Amina who dies at the end of *Palace Walk*, women in Mahfouz's fiction figure as a symbol for a victimized Egypt.[47]

To conclude, on the margins of Ahmad's bildungsroman, through what is said about him and not mentioned about Sawsan who mentors him, we can trace a female education narrative. These erasures show Ahmad's apprenticeship to mirror Sawsan's so that, for this part of the narrative, it is Sawsan whose story readers follow without much notice. Her female voice fights the text's silencing, struggling to break out of the repressive confines of this male-authored text, but the only way it speaks is through Ahmad. In this vicarious female bildungsroman, the intellectual female voice demands a genderless modernity, where men and women are equal partners in the national struggle. One may argue that Ahmad's marriage to Sawsan denotes both hope and failure—hope that he will traverse to a postbourgeois gender politics as well as failure to step outside bourgeois norms that relate to women mainly through love.

Which Path?: The New Man

Sugar Street includes one female national intellectual and three aspiring male national intellectuals: Sawsan, whose role as Ahmad's mentor helps him reach an enlightenment that reconciles him with modern-day Egypt; Kamal, whose journey of self-discovery remains incomplete until the end of the series; and his nephews, the brothers Ahmad and Abd al-Muni'm, who, in Rasheed Enany's view, represent his "spiritual schism" that leave him wavering between past and present, East and West.[48] The novel's juxtaposition of Ahmad and Abd al-Muni'm as national intellectuals best illustrates the fissures in Egyptian political life. The first, a communist, and the second, a Muslim Brother, they are counterparts to each other and more pointedly to Kamal. Their stories represent two alternative formation narratives. On the one hand, Abd al-Muni'm embraces the religion that his uncle repudiates. On the other hand, after a short-lived love story with an aristocratic woman, Ahmad rejects the classical Arabic poetic tradition of *al-hubb al-ʿudhri* (romantic unrequited love), which entraps his uncle, and plunges more deeply into Marxism. His flexible approach toward governance and national culture marks him as the protagonist of a new indigenous Egyptian bildungsroman that marries European Enlightenment principles to the cultural specificities of early-twentieth-century Egypt.

Through Kamal, *Sugar Street* explores the plight of the national intellectual whose enslavement to an imposed, foreign system isolates him from his people—whether educated or uneducated. To evoke Abdul JanMohamed, Mahfouz uses Kamal to condemn the national intellectual's surrender to the Manicheanism of colonialist ideology that pathologizes indigenous culture and valorizes colonialist culture. As a result, the Other cannot escape the double-bind of catalepsy and petrification, where merging indigenous culture with Western tradition signifies mimicry while clinging to tradition denotes recalcitrance.[49] Kamal, who thinks of himself as a national intellectual, never blossoms into an independent thinker. If we overlook Fanon's tendency to ignore the negotiation process that the colonized often went through, at least in the case of Egypt, we find that Kamal remains a passive recipient of European knowledge—one who is alienated from the society that he claims to educate.

The symbiotic relationship between national intellectual and people, much like Mahfouz's conceptualization of that between writer and reader, hinges on the work's utility to the nation. In the same way that the success of combat literature is dependent, first, on its relevance to the national struggle and, second, on a mutual recognition between the intellectual and the people, Mahfouz defines a writer as someone whose readership extends beyond the critics—a politically involved citizen who speaks against social ills.[50] Sawsan, later to become Ahmad's wife, demonstrates both the irrelevance of Kamal's work as well as the discrepancy between his view of himself and society's view of him. Describing him as "a writer who rambles through the wilderness of metaphysics" (191), she notes that instead of utilizing the knowledge he has amassed in order to form his own theory he regurgitates old information.

Not only do Kamal's articles target an insular group of like-minded individuals, but they are also deemed to be obscure and/or irrelevant by the educated elite, such as Fuad al-Hamzawi, his childhood friend who is now a public prosecutor. Neither representative of nor accessible to the mass population, the culture that Kamal manufactures is elitist excluding even educated Egyptians who hold prestigious positions. His attempts to acculturate fellow Egyptians in the Western values of doubt and rejection of religious truth for scientific method are undermined by his dry content, not to mention his conscious decision to publish in periodicals that his father, the average Egyptian, does not read.

The novel's critical portrait of Kamal evokes such Western-oriented intellectuals as Mahfouz's mentor Salama Musa (1887–1958). Musa, whom Mahfouz describes as an independent thinker far ahead of his time, was plagued by self-contradictions, leading him to call for publishing in colloquial Egyptian while writing in Standard Arabic himself. More notably, his extreme leaning toward Europe led him to argue for writing Arabic using Latin script. Yet, Musa was instrumental in founding a company that sold only Egyptian goods and encouraged Egyptians to buy only Egyptian-made products. Mahfouz ascribes this contradiction to the time itself and, while Kamal shares Musa's strong inclination toward the West, he does not share his ability to act independently within national interests.[51]

Kamal wavers between admitting and refusing to accept his failed responsibility as an intellectual. Half aware of his failure he chooses inaction, continuing a life of mimicry. This endless waiting recalls Western assignments of non-European countries to the waiting room of history. As Riyad Qaldas, his Coptic friend, tells him, "You read and understand. You're a historian with no history. I hope you observe the day you emerge from this condition as your true birthday" (138). Riyad's poignant observation points to Kamal's copying phase as an eternal gestation period that places him outside a multi-vocal historical project. Riyad urges Kamal to become an active intellectual. While Kamal, at times, seems to be aware of his predicament, as, for example, in his first meeting with Riyad when Kamal describes himself as "a tourist in a museum where nothing belongs to me. I'm merely a historian. I don't know where I stand" (94), he strips himself of agency and, with it, participation in history. By submitting to the delusion of the objectivity and universality of Enlightenment thinking, he remains a scribe who faithfully, yet selectively, records the history that Europeans make.

Kamal's struggle for intellectual independence is one that Mahfouz himself underwent. In a 1978 interview Mahfouz outlines his development from the adopt into the adept phase, admitting that he only achieved intellectual independence in the last fifteen years. He adds that he has recently started creating his own model. Prior to that, he explains, he and other writers assumed that the proper way to write a novel was to produce a European novel. Therefore, he elaborates, for third-world writers, literary success meant negating oneself, as a result of which there was a proper novel and an incorrect one. Alternatively, Mahfouz views any mimicking, even of old traditional indigenous forms, as a form of imprisonment—precisely the state in which Kamal exists.[52] Unlike him, however, his nephews struggle to make their voices heard.

Enany explains that Ahmad and Abd al-Muni'm represent two directions that existed in Egyptian society at the time: Islamism and Marxism.[53] On the one hand, the Society of the Muslim Brothers was founded in 1928 as an indigenous reformative force calling for coupling the use of science and technology with a return to the true teachings of Islam as a gateway toward a native modernity that reconciled the country's historical Islamic character with the twentieth century. The Muslim Brothers encouraged Egyptians to ask for their rights in the workplace, contest the British occupation, and resist the "de-Islamisation [*sic*]" of Egypt.[54] On the other hand, stood leftist communism, which critiqued capitalism for its tendency to generate social injustice. Until 1928 the movement was dominated by foreigners, who enjoyed a degree of tolerance by the British and were allowed to form organizations. The British, however, suppressed Egyptian communism, which mainly concerned itself with labor issues.[55]

While Mahfouz acknowledges the importance of a deep understanding of Islam and its ethics, his mistrust of a nationalism that mobilizes religious discourse stems from an awareness of the difference between the religious teachings of a given faith and individual interpretations of that faith—a view that he delivers through Riyad Qaldas who remarks "'the problem is that we interact with Muslims, not with Islam'" (139). Mahfouz's advocacy for democracy and multiple political parties as guarantors of a healthy political life derives from his conviction that Islam is compatible with democracy.[56] He asserts that by embracing values and principles found in all religions a particular government follows religion even as it claims the opposite.[57]

Mahfouz's rejection of religious nationalism is specifically demonstrated in his portrayal of Abd al-Muni'm whom the novel distances through humor as, for example, when the narrator describes him as coming into a room preceded by his beard; or in his own mother's classist declaration that the beard makes him look like the couscous street vendor; or when his colleagues ask if they stone their dissenters. On various other occasions Abd al-Muni'm and his friends are referred to as fanatics, sometimes by the former's parents or by other family members. Although Abd al-Muni'm is supposed to serve as testament to the danger of using religious discourse as a foundation for nationalism, Mahfouz's presentation of him is puzzling since the latter's actions do not reflect fanaticism. Apart from the path he chooses, his actions do not differ much from those of his brother. When we first meet him in *Sugar Street*, he is enjoying clandestine meetings with the neighbors' daughter. Later, he regrets his deviousness deciding to get married while still a university student and leaving the choice of bride to his mother. He graduates from college, secures a government job and, at the end of the novel, both he and his brother hold meetings with their respective supporters in their apartments.

Sugar Street does not convey a clear picture of Abd al-Muni'm's understanding and application of religion and in so doing almost presents religion and modernity as antagonistic. Sawsan too, despite her critical acumen, treats them as mutually exclusive concepts. Since women's issues became a hot topic in late-nineteenth-century Egypt and in the Arab world, "feminism" has been a suspect term. Its association with the West and its deployment as an ideology that justifies colonialism and exploitation under the guise of introducing modern civilization not only alienated many Arabs and Muslims but also inspired persons whose work might well be described as feminist to dissociate themselves from the term. As a result, it remains a topic that eludes definition. Whether secular or religious in conviction each camp excludes alternative iterations of feminism, either deeming it an exclusively secular idea or attempting to locate women's empowerment solely in Islam. Antifeminists, too, share the view that religion is antithetical to modernity. In the same way that many enthusiastic secularists claim that one cannot use religion, particularly Islam, to articulate women's rights in a modern society, diehard supporters of patriarchy maintain that feminism is against Islam, seeing it as a Western conspiracy, either refusing to admit the existence of gender inequality or justifying it in religious terms, and even dismissing the concept of feminism altogether. Meanwhile, some contemporary feminists locate what is seen as the patriarchy of Islam in patriarchal interpretations of the Quran. Pointing to the need for female exegesis, they produce fresh perspectives that look at women as individuals.[58] Sawsan fails to see that feminism and/or modernity can exist on a religio-secular continuum.

In her conversations with Ahmad, Sawsan reveals a pattern and a problem well-identified by scholars of gender working within different feminist traditions. For example, Mervat Hatem, like many Arab women feminists, critiques secular Arab feminists for making religion the other of modernity.[59] In a similar vein, Joan Scott points to a structural fault in the discourses of Western modernity and feminism, both of which rely on a binary opposition between modernity and religion, therefore precluding the possibility of existence of the modern and the religious, or of modern, religious feminists.[60] Feminism, in this sense, replicates the universalism of the Enlightenment by othering difference and relegating it to the premodern realm. This manifests in the novel's comical portrayal of Abd al-Muni'm's religiosity, which reduces him and his fellow Muslim Brothers to stereotypes. It is also visible in Sawsan's modernist project (which is also Ahmed's modernist project) that involves jettisoning religion to speed up the modernizing project. For example, reassuring his uncle that he married Sawsan according to Muslim tradition, Ahmad declares, " 'We marry and bury according to the percepts of our former religion, but we live according to the Marxist faith' " (251). While Sawsan is justified in her call for a new social taxonomy where women are equals, a model that discredits religiously inclined women suppresses female/feminist voices that see themselves as both religious and feminist.

Commenting on Abd al-Muni'm's support of the Muslim Brothers, she pronounces religion a utopian socialism, relegating it to the realm of mythology and suggesting that no modernist project can include a religious component. As readers, we are expected to assume that, because of his connection with the Muslim Brotherhood, Abd al-Muni'm is dangerous. Sasson Somekh seems to agree, even identifying both Abd al-Muni'm and Ahmad as caricatures of the Muslim Brotherhood and communism due to their lack of depth.[61] Such generalized portrayal may result from Mahfouz's prejudice against the Muslim Brothers, whose message he never understood, and what critics see as his idealistic understanding of communism. Mahfouz mainly viewed the Muslim Brothers as a political power that used religion to compete with the *Wafd*

Party. Because of his staunch loyalty to the *Wafd*, Mahfouz once wrote that any war against them before achieving nationalist goals weakened the cause.[62] Of course, the Muslim Brothers' militancy did not endear them to the nation. One might say, however, that in marginalizing Abd al-Muni'm the novel condemns any group that purports to institute the rule of any given religion. Presenting the democratic practice of Kamal's editor, an Islam scholar who publishes alternative viewpoints including Kamal's atheist voice, *Sugar Street* demonstrates that religion and modernity can harmoniously coexist.

Riyad's and the author's endorsement of the *Wafd* as the nationalist party par excellence for transcendence of religious identification to meet Egyptians on a human ground foreshadows Ahmad's epiphany toward the end of the novel.[63] Rather than perceiving religion as an obstacle to political evolution, Riyad, and consequently Mahfouz, blame Egyptians for their own disempowerment by painting a picture of a complex struggle between a King whose dictatorial tendencies are supported by corrupt Egyptian officials such as Sidqi Pasha who promoted British interests; politicians, such as al-Nuqrashi, who deserted the nationalist side to cooperate with the King and/or the British; patriotic politicians of integrity, such as the Copt Makram ʿUbayd; and the Egyptian masses.[64] *Sugar Street* emphasizes inclusive ideologies as the first step toward the success of the nationalist struggle. This is the truth that Ahmad stumbles upon while in prison: "'Without regard to the differences of taste between us, our common human condition has united us in this dark and humid place: the Muslim Brother, the Communist, and drunkard, and the thief. Despite dissimilarities in our luck and success at looking after ourselves, we are all human beings'" (301).

Missing from Sawsan's and Ahmad's view of the nation are Egypt's Jews, some of whom showed patriotism by supporting the 1919 Revolution. At its peak in the 1940s, Egypt's Jewish population ranged between 75,000 and 80,000. Deborah Starr informs us that this was a polyglot, cosmopolitan community that included non-Arabic-speaking foreign nationals.[65] According to Gudrun Krämer Sephardic Jews in Egypt generally preferred to keep a low profile. Whether to protect economic interests or, later, to avoid instigating anti-Semitic sentiments that might threaten the communal life they enjoyed with Muslims during the liberal period from 1919 to 1936, Jews avoided taking a stance on political matters.[66] However, many Jews supported the 1919

Revolution with some joining the *Wafd*.[67] Krämer goes on to say that "at least until the early 1930s, even the local Zionist movement supported the Arab and Egyptian national aspirations and … it was by no means rare to find Egyptian Jews sympathizing at the same time with both the Zionist and the Egyptian national movements."[68]

However, the Jewish community was not only culturally, linguistically, and economically diverse, but also politically heterogeneous, counting among its ranks royalists, communists, Zionists, and Egyptian patriots.[69] As a result, "limited to a handful of lawyers, writers, and journalists who joined the Wafd and who, even in the 1930s and 1940s, retained their sympathies for the Egyptian national cause," Egyptian patriotism did not strike roots deep enough to Arabize and Egyptianize the Jewish community. After the 1948 war and around the time Mahfouz was composing the *Trilogy*, the Jewish community came under attack by many groups including leftists, Islamists, and the government. This made it harder for them to pursue political activity.[70]

Ahmad's turn to Marxism is significant since, as Ahmad Muhammad 'Atiyya points out, the 1919 Revolution, by limiting itself to political independence, failed to address the socioeconomic grievances of the peasants.[71] This is due to the *Wafd* Party's bourgeois leanings, which excluded peasants and laborers.[72] For this reason, in the later days of the *Wafd*, Mahfouz became a leftist *Wafdist* insisting on social justice and democracy. The author's admiration of communism's belief in social justice, although it brought him rapprochement with the Left, did not represent a move toward Marxism.[73] Rather, he preferred British socialism for its democracy and recognition of religion.[74]

An Egyptian Bildungsroman

Ahmad, who represents the novel's vision of the national intellectual post-1919 and who is primarily guided by his wife, Sawsan, recasts the European paradigm that entraps his uncle to actively create his individual bildungsroman. His route at first resembles Kamal's, seen, for example, in his infatuation with his aristocratic classmate who rejects him. However, harboring none of his uncle's delusions about finding pleasure in the pain of unreciprocated love (*al-hubb al-'udhri*), he decides to forget a woman whose ideal husband is one who can only provide material comforts.[75] Through his work at the newspaper, he meets Sawsan who, four years his senior, becomes instrumental in his evolution as an independent thinker and who facilitates his ultimate transition from Fanon's adopt into the adapt phase. Her marriage to Ahmad presents the working class as infusing the petit bourgeoisie with new blood, new life, new ways of thinking and being. To appropriate Ahmad Muhammad 'Atiyya, it regenerates him, liberating him of his bourgeois beliefs.[76]

Sawsan demarcates the parameters of what Ahmad later terms "perpetual revolution" by highlighting the importance of political commitment. Her perceptive evaluation of Kamal's personality encapsulates his elitism, indecision, passivity as a national intellectual, as well as his fascination by all theories and failure to endorse one. Equally critiquing Riyad Qaldas she pronounces his stories more descriptive than pragmatic (192). Sawsan calls for commitment—for a national program where art is functional and the artist involved: " 'Our society is in deep pain. So first and foremost we must stop this pain. After that we can play around and philosophize. Imagine a man musing happily about abstruse points of philosophy while his life's blood drains away. What would you say of a man like that?' " (192).

Sawsan's meditations on the value of philosophy and literature to a society in pain echoes Mahfouz's own dilemma and his ultimate journey from the first to the second and from writing historical fiction on ancient Egypt to penning narratives that directly addressed Egypt's contemporary realities during the turbulent 1940s.[77] Nicknamed the writer of the petit bourgeoisie, a title which he resented at first,[78] Mahfouz was earlier criticized for not portraying various social classes and regions.[79] Earlier Marxist criticism focuses on his preoccupation with the petit bourgeoisie to the exclusion of the proletariat,[80] faulting Mahfouz for depicting the petit bourgeoisie seeking escape, focusing on personal problems instead of pondering the bigger, national problem. In consequence, novels' endings provide individual, rather than national, resolutions, ending tragically either through suicide, murder, tragic death, or scandal.[81] This failure is attributed to the absence of the concept of a revolutionary protagonist in Egyptian fiction for which reason Mahfouz, like many bourgeois writers of the age, fails to see that the laborer is this future hero.[82]

Unlike a rebel who stops at rejection without moving toward an ideological vision of a utopia (one is reminded of Kamal), a revolutionary hero, as defined by Ghali Shukri, is a progressive character who believes in radical change for society and who possesses unflagging belief in hard work. She or he is one whose faith is progressive rather than reactionary. In other words, this hero does not wish to return to the past, regardless of its merits—one thinks of Abd al-Muni'm—rather she or he looks ahead to the future, believes in science instead of metaphysics, in society rather than heaven, and in socialism rather than human competition. A revolutionary hero is a catalyst for change. She or he works for the revolution, not for the government, effecting one revolution after the other. Shukri calls this radical protagonist *al-muntami*; the believer—or, for lack of a better term, the one who belongs—an individual who is dedicated to the issues of society espousing a certain set of scientific, socialist principles. This interest starts with theoretical interest and develops into joining a party or a group devoted to these issues,[83] the figure that Sawsan represents in *Sugar Street*.

Thanks to Sawsan's training, Ahmad transforms into this radical protagonist who, in Shukri's words, exemplifies mature leftist belonging. He transcends his bourgeois identity, concerning himself with the rights of the masses, refusing to settle for a secure government post, as his brother does, and preferring to work for no pay.[84] Ahmad's commitment makes him a different kind of protagonist from the fifteen-year-old Muhsin in Tawfiq al-Hakim's *'Awdat al-ruh*, 1933 (*Return of the Spirit*, 1984), whose maturation, Maria Paniconi indicates, occurs along elitist, aesthetic terms. Muhsin's apprenticeship prepares him to be the spokesperson of the nation as he assumes pedagogical leadership over his people.[85] In contrast to Mushin's hierarchical position, Ahmad's involvement and his willingness to go to prison for his ideas, bring him closer to the masses. Through Marxism Ahmad fashions a vision that suits Egyptian society. At the end, he is about to transition from his adapt into his adept phase. He reaches a crossroads when facing common Egyptians in prison, including his brother the Muslim Brother,

> Clad in his overcoat, he had often written about "the people" in his beautiful study. Here they were—cursing or snoring in their sleep. For a few seconds by the light of the torch he had seen their wretched sullen faces, including that of the man who was scratching his head and armpits. At this very moment his lice might be advancing resolutely toward Ahmad and his brother.

> "You are devoting your life to people like this," he told himself. "Why should the thought of contact with them worry you? The person on whom mankind's hopes for salvation are pinned should stop snoring and wake to his historic role. Let him rear up and rescue the entire world." (301)

Faced with the choice of remaining a detached intellectual, like his uncle, or becoming an engaged intellectual, Ahmad chooses engagement. He overcomes class biases that pathologize the working class as a source of contagion yet envisions the fight in masculine terms, seeing the savior as a man, neutrally rendered as "person" in the English translation quoted earlier on. Despite the vestige of romanticism seen in his perception of Egypt's future as contingent upon one person's awakening from a deep slumber to fulfill a historic role and, unlike his irresolute uncle, Ahmad melds European philosophy, that is the Marxist dialectic of class struggle, and Egyptian nationalism, embracing solidarity with his brothers and, by implication, openness to their experiential knowledge as necessary supplements to Western history making.

This is the point where the Egyptian protagonist achieves epiphany in a native bildungsroman, emerging from the adapt to the adept phase. Ahmad is arguably discarding one European model—that of Enlightenment skepticism and capitalism—for another European model by adopting Marxism. Yet, what distinguishes this modernity from the Western modern is its malleability. His program of action, as quoted by Kamal, names perpetual revolution, *not* Marxism or another ideology as the solution: " 'The duty common to all human beings is perpetual revolution, and that is nothing other than an unceasing effort to further the will of life represented by its progress toward the ideal' " (306). Ahmad defines perpetual revolution as an obligation to " 'revolt against ideals I believe to be false, since recoiling from this rebellion would be a form of treason' " (306). Ahmad's manifesto identifies constant change as the paradigm and, by implication, the philosophy as the variable. Therefore, Marxism, for Ahmad, is a point of departure in critical practices that aim to understand and remake the exploitative world in which we live. He steps into adulthood, modernity, and being not by adopting European Enlightenment values but by using appropriate values from that paradigm to create an individual Egyptian modernity. He creates where Kamal adopts. It is important to note here that both Ahmad and Abd al-Muni'm agree on this theory although they differ on the application.

Ahmad exemplifies Fanon's involved national intellectual who calls his people to action. Unlike his uncle, he succeeds in demystifying Europe as the source of Enlightenment and modernity. He matures when he realizes that Marxism, though useful in thinking about class politics, emerged out of a historically specific context and that it must be revised to fit the contemporary Egyptian context.

Some scholars, such as Atiyya and Abdel-Rahman Abu Ouf, point to Ahmad's belonging to the middle bourgeoisie, his work for free, and his reliance on his father's money for survival as a reflection of Mahfouz's idealistic view of communism as an ideology of social justice.[86] In their view, in a colonized country like Egypt where colonialism is the first obstacle toward social justice, the nationalist cause cannot be separated from the social struggle. Additionally, Mahfouz's vision of communism entails only a view of social justice, not a nationalist stance regarding the 1936 treaty and the oppressive 1930 Constitution.[87] Yet, criticism of Mahfouz's "shallow understanding" of Marxism holds the author to a fixed understanding of the ideology reinforcing an inflexible European paradigm without allowing for a culturally specific vision. It is important to remember Mahfouz's declaration that the social justice of Marxism appealed to him, that he preferred socialism, and that he set out to write the *Trilogy* to explore socialism as a solution.[88] Shukri rightly observes that at the end of *Sugar Street* Mahfouz sees hope in the positive Left which cares about the social aspect as well.[89]

Conclusion

Sugar Street offers a female bildungsroman where the new Egyptian woman shapes the new Egyptian man, guiding him through his quest for a modern Egyptian national identity. Sawsan's training of Ahmad prepares him for his role as a nonelitist, committed national intellectual who will act as the conscience of his people. It is through her mentorship that the male protagonist achieves intellectual education in an Egyptian bildungsroman. Although women are still missing from the masculinist vision articulated in Ahmad's prison cell, his continued interaction with Sawsan will help him outgrow the bourgeois paradigm where women are companions but not equal partners. Noticeable in both protagonists' visions is a hesitance to include religion, still positioning religion as Other of modernity, thus seeing modernity as progressing along a single-track, secularist paradigm. Yet, hope for an inclusionary framework presents itself in the example of Kamal's journal editor, a scholar of Islam who does not silence Kamal's atheist voice.

3

Alice in Wonderland: Egypt and the Benevolent Empire in *The Guns of El Kebir*

Self-admittedly nostalgic for Empire, John Wilcox (1933–2018) recalled his pride as a child at seeing the pink spots signifying British dominions on a world map. His sense of British uniqueness extended to include the country's postimperial history seen in its debatably voluntary relinquishment of colonies and support of South Africa's struggle against apartheid.[1] At the same time, in his autobiography, he enthusiastically recorded his father's break with the Conservative party shortly before the Second World War, upon which the elder Wilcox adopted left-wing views and read communist newspapers, which the nine-year-old author devoured.[2] In short, this son of a working-class family viewed Empire as an exploitative project yet described imperial domination as a system that was characteristic of the nineteenth century and one that *did* do a measure of good in certain parts of the world. Wilcox's ambivalence toward Britain's imperial past colored his views of Egypt's 1881–2 Urabi Revolution leading him to argue that, Britain's egotistic goals notwithstanding, nineteenth-century Egyptians were poor and uneducated and Colonel Urabi had to be reprimanded for endangering the Suez Canal.[3]

This chapter stretches the definition of bildungsroman by reading *The Guns of El Kebir* (2007), an adventure novel, as a formation narrative. Both protagonists, already in their mid- to late-twenties, move from innocence to experience while their attempts at thinking critically against the discourse of Empire are proven to be naïve. I focus on Alice Covington, a professional woman, feminist, and anti-imperialist, who insists on traveling to Egypt to report on the Urabi events from an Egyptian point of view. In centering Alice, whom the narrative insists on marginalizing, I argue that her journey through Egypt becomes an educational one, affecting hers and Simon Fonthill's (the male protagonist's) maturation and their ultimate reconciliation with Empire. The novel ultimately justifies British dominance, with the masculine genre of the imperial romance domesticating Alice.

In *The Guns of El Kebir* (*Guns*), Sir Garnet Wolseley, adjutant general of the British army, recruits the twenty-seven-year-old Simon Fonthill and his Welsh petty officer, Jenkins, to conduct undercover scouting missions in Egypt in preparation for the British invasion. Along with Ahmed, an Egyptian sidekick who represents the British imperial view, Simon and Jenkins battle Bedouins and angry Egyptians in various locations. Always appearing at the right moment, they rescue the British consul during the Alexandria massacre, help protect a European community taking refuge at the Anglo-Egyptian Bank during the bombardment of Alexandria by British invading forces, and facilitate the British invasion. In the meantime, Alice Covington, the marginalized feminist, anti-imperialist journalist and Simon's former love interest, makes history by becoming the first woman to report on events from the front lines.

Falling in Love with the Victorians

Born in Birmingham, England, in 1933, John Wilcox started his career as a subs' boy for the *Birmingham Despatch* before working as a reporter for the daily newspaper *The Birmingham Gazette* and eventually winning the "Young Journalist of the Year" award.[4] He later became head of public relations at the Rootes Group, one of England's largest automakers, which he joined in the mid-1950s, and in 1963 took a position as a public relations manager with the International Wool Secretariat. In his late forties, Wilcox left the company to start his own business as a marketing consultant in textiles. Then he partnered with the Lonsdale Advertising Group. During this time, he also served as nonexecutive chairman of Wilcox, Brown and Madden, a textile-based marketing consultancy started by his former colleagues in the International Wool Secretariat. In the mid-nineties he sold the company, moved to South-West Wiltshire, and started writing fiction.[5] Between 2004 and 2018 he published seventeen books including sixteen novels, sometimes almost moving at the rate of a novel each year (and occasionally two a year), an autobiography, and a short story in addition to two nonfiction books.

Wilcox's family background is the main inspiration behind his novels. His father came from a late-Victorian working-class family, whose seven sons—Wilcox's father and all his six brothers—fought in the First World War. All seven brothers survived the war and three of Wilcox's uncles earned medals. One uncle received the Victoria Cross, another the Military Medal, and a third uncle won the Distinguished Service Medal. His uncles' honorable performance in the First World War prompted him to question the nature of courage and his ability to be "as venerable as … [his] Victorian uncles."[6]

Wilcox's uncles, however, were not the sole source of his fascination with the Victorians. Nor was his reading limited to nineteenth-century imperialist writers. While his reading spectrum included contemporary writers of postcolonial fiction, such as A. S. Byatt and Salman Rushdie, whom he compared to great Victorian writers, he confessed to being "tainted a bit by Empire." Having avidly read and been influenced by imperialist writers such as G. A. Henty and H. Rider Haggard, it is no surprise that Wilcox's work has been compared to imperialist works.[7] For example, *The Sunday Express* has compared his novels to the Victorian boys' magazine *Boys Own* while *The Northern Echo* has described Simon Fonthill, the protagonist who appears in several of Wilcox's novels, as "a hero to match Sharpe or Hornblower," fictional characters exemplifying British bravado.[8] The *Good Book Guide* describes one of Wilcox's novels as "a swashbuckling tale, slashed through with adventure, bravery, and the utmost danger" and finally *The Historical Novels Review* describes another of his novels as "a thrilling tale of courage and fortitude."[9] Identifying his love of history as the reason behind writing historical novels, Wilcox explains that the nineteenth century's wealth of material for adventure narrative makes it an appropriate time setting since during the period from 1850 to 1914 the British army was "always in action in some far-flung area." In his view, the imperial content of his novels is dictated by the era.[10]

Speaking in 2010, Wilcox regretted the absence of serious reviews of his work, attributing this to his choice of the genre of the popular adventure narrative. While pleased with the comparison to C. S. Forester's *Horatio Hornblower*, which he read as a child, he "winc[ed]" at the comparison with *Boys Own* because, to his mind, his stories are "deeper than that." In the same year, he counted forty rejections by publishers for various reasons, among which is the unpopularity of the kind of novel that he wrote. Acknowledging himself as a writer of formulaic stories, he explained that he could not write a modern philosophical novel. In a theory evincing somewhat generalized views of readership, particularly female readers, their expectations, reading habits, and preferences, Wilcox declared that he was at a disadvantage. Constituting the majority of readers in the United Kingdom and dominating publishing houses, women, he surmised, were not enamored with "blood and thunder" books. For this reason, he tried to insert romance into his novels. Still, Wilcox was proud of his following. In addition to fan letters and appreciative comments on his online blog, he was gratified by the existence of "a market in first-edition hardbacks" of his novels.[11]

Guns is also the product of a trend emerging around the middle of the twentieth century and marked by a surge of interest in all things Victorian, including art, fashion, architecture, and literature. In her study of the Victorian period in British cultural memory, Kate Mitchell points to a shift in perception toward the era, contrasting feelings of repulsion experienced by authors in the earlier half of the century with those of nostalgia harbored by their counterparts in the second half of the century. Thus, whereas the former distanced themselves from the era and its values, which to them denoted repression and injustice, the latter resolved their feelings toward life after two world wars by recasting the era in more favorable terms. According to Mitchell, in the span of a century, the Victorian era changed roles from "Other" to precursor of the then contemporary moment.[12]

Dana Shiller explains that nostalgic literary and historical studies were particularly inspired by Margaret Thatcher's call in the 1980s for a return to Victorian morals. The former prime minister's extolment of Victorian values and of her Victorian grandparents helped popularize the period, which in turn spawned neo-Victorian genres. These spanned magazines, biographies, and fiction, among other things. According to Shiller, this neo-Victorian genre features novels that are "set at least partly in the nineteenth century. This capacious umbrella includes texts that revise specific Victorian precursors, texts that imagine new adventures for familiar Victorian characters, and 'new' Victorian fictions that imitate nineteenth-century literary conventions."[13] *Guns* belongs to the last category. While scholars such as Shiller, Louisa Hadley, and Cora Kaplan point out that, in its reflection upon historiography and the ability of history-writing to access the past, neo-Victorian fiction adopts postmodern views of history, *Guns*, in contrast, follows a more conservative path.[14]

In his re-creation of events in late-nineteenth-century Egypt, Wilcox employs adventure narrative that, Martin Green asserts, "became the literary counterpart to Empire," for English writers in the seventeenth century and beyond.[15] In infusing it with the imperial romance (a subgenre of the Victorian novel), with its postimperial permutation, the romance of the archive, the author delivers a work that upholds Empire. In his study of the imperial romance, John McClure defines the genre as an adventure narrative that follows a male European hero as he explores exotic lands and battles disorder, and conquers uncivilized foes/natives, bringing stability to an "otherly world."[16] Prominent writers of the genre include H. Rider Haggard and Rudyard Kipling.

Guns is charged with elements of the imperial romance such as the chivalric hero who travels to primitive lands and battles an uncivilized people (Simon), the white woman to whom the hero is devoted and whom he rescues from evil natives (Alice), the native sidekick whose job it is to affirm the righteousness of the hero and of Empire (Ahmed), and, finally, the villain who is punished in the end (George, a British Thomas Cook employee and smuggler of artefacts).[17] Alongside the hero are so-called vicious Egyptians, whom the narrative constantly describes as the "mob," when contrasting their savagery to the magnanimity of the British, who allegedly take pains to preserve Egyptian civilian life while invading the country. *Guns*' romantic emplotment advances the story of an anarchic Egypt that is rescued by a superior, rational British force.

The romance of the archive, the second genre that *Guns* straddles, is an extension of the adventure narrative. In her study of the genre in contemporary British fiction, Suzanne Keen notes that, following post-1956 decolonization, British imperial romances mutated into romances of the archives, often producing fictions that defended Britain's imperial past. Many later fictions, however, adopt a critical approach toward history-writing. Keen defines the genre as a narrative that chases historical archives (such as important documents) or which takes place in locations significant to that history (such as libraries). She explains that the definition of "archive" has extended to include museum collections, mappings, and "fictional representations of memory."[18] A representative of the genre in *Guns*, is Alice, who, in search of the truth, travels to Egypt, and interviews Colonel Urabi, the leader of the revolution, and Admiral Seymour, mastermind of the bombardment of Alexandria, in an attempt to provide an assessment of the Egyptian desire for autonomy. The imperial romance and the romance of the archive, thus, intersect through Simon and Alice. The use of the determinedly masculine imperial romance establishes the imperialist narrative of the Urabi Revolution in *Guns* while working seamlessly to obscure female voices.

In traditional bildungsroman narratives youth is central to the idea of bildung. Education follows a climactic event, which serves as a watershed moment after which the protagonist reaches enlightenment. In reality, transformative events are hardly limited to a certain age or frequency, nor is formation linear. One might encounter sudden detours, follow a circular pattern, or exist in stasis that causes a state of eternal youth, as Jed Esty illustrates in his analysis of the modernist bildungsroman.[19] Formation is also one of life's events, existing on the margins of other multiple experiences. Each transformative moment serves a purpose, causing progression or regression, each time counting as a life lesson. In this case, youth is incidental to learning, and the flexibility of life entails a looser approach to the bildungsroman. Therefore, formation, or lack thereof, is a lifelong experience that exists in every story including *The Guns of El Kebir*.

By merging the imperial romance with the romance of the archive *Guns* produces a bildungsroman. The plot structure and genre mixing work in such a way as to portray the British occupation as inevitable. By depicting the 1881–2 Urabi Revolution as an anarchic movement, the novel contrasts Egypt's political immaturity with Simon's and Alice's personal and political maturity at the end of the novel. Although the novel occasionally acknowledges Urabi and his supporters as nationalists, most of the time it portrays them as imposters motivated by personal gain. In this respect, *Guns* presents the British occupation as introducing stability to a country torn by irrational-rebels-turned-dictators and portrays the British occupation as justifiable. Very briefly, *Guns* is an apology for Empire. Rather than focus solely on Simon, the male protagonist, I bring focus to two other characters: first, Fatima, Ahmed's cousin and the owner of the hotel in Alexandria where the trio (Simon, Jenkins, and Ahmed) shelter during the occupation and, second, Alice, who is trapped in a loveless marriage to an officer in the occupying forces and whose role as an independent female professional and protagonist of the romance of the archive the novel consistently undermines. Her testimony, serving to justify British encroachment on Egyptian sovereignty, is key to hers and Simon's education.

Fatima: An Egyptian Businesswoman in Nineteenth-Century Egypt

Like her cousin Ahmed, Fatima appears in the narrative only to render services to the British protagonists. Her marginalization in the novel is replicated in her geographical liminality in Alexandria in a "little hotel, a few streets back from the harbour [*sic*], not quite in the native quarter but certainly not smart enough for most Europeans."[20] Despite being silenced and deprived even of the comic utterances granted to Ahmed, Fatima is an interesting character. For one thing, by virtue of owning and managing a hotel in Alexandria, she is an independent businesswoman in nineteenth-century Egypt. At no time does the novel mention a husband or a guardian figure such as a father or a brother. She is presented as discreet, trustworthy, and shrewd. Not only does she receive Simon and his party at her hotel, but she also provides them with native clothes to help their disguise. Later when they return to the hotel from a street fight, she is unperturbed by their messy appearance, nor does she show curiosity. Through her resourcefulness she provides baths for all three of them despite the strain it puts on the hotel. Clearly not an impressionable, sheltered woman, Fatima is not squeamish about killing in self-defense. For example, after the bombardment of Alexandria, Simon, who thinks that "Fatima may need protection" (143), instructs Ahmed to stay behind while he and Jenkins look for Europeans in need of help. Ahmed refuses, "No, no. I come [*sic*] with you … Fatima has old [*sic*] shotgun she can use if people come" (143).

Fatima is implied to be running a tolerably, if not highly, functional business, supervising employees and feeding her guests scrumptious food in the middle of a foreign invasion. Though subservient to the British characters, she is portrayed as extremely efficient, highly resourceful, and well connected. Her "informants" (189), as the novel refers to her network of friends, prove useful when Simon wants to locate George, a dubious Thomas Cooke employee. Her skills also include nursing, as when she ministers to Alice after George kidnaps and nearly strangles her. In fact, her nursing skills are so commendable that the Greek doctor who examines Alice praises Fatima and asks her to continue the treatment (209). Ironically, these traits that make her powerful are the same ones that make her an indispensable agent to Egypt's imperial subjugation. Needless to say, Simon rewards her with a huge sum of money before leaving.

What makes Fatima's character intriguing is the slim chance that such a character would have existed in real life at the time. Egypt historian Afaf Lutfi Sayyid-Marsot tells us that under Mamluk rule in the eighteenth century, women in Egypt managed and accumulated great wealth that was either handed over by fathers or spouses or transferred through inheritance. Women from all classes invested by buying, renting, and selling property and, in a relationship of mutual support, relied on religious scholars to guard their rights. However, with Muhammad Ali's modernizing efforts in the nineteenth century came a dwindling of women's power. His desire to build a centralized government led him to dismantle older economic systems replacing them with modern institutions that further entrenched patriarchy. As Marsot explains, while under the older system women may have relied on men to act on their behalf, women's legal status was not contested whereas modern institutions (such as banks) only recognized men.

As patriarchy became more normative in the nineteenth century—with men becoming breadwinners and women further alienated from economic life—women continued to lose power in society and in the family as well. For example, although Muslim women were granted property and inheritance rights with the advent of Islam in the seventh century CE, the reinforcement of a normative patriarchy meant that human practice was at odds with religious legal code, and it was not unusual for wealthy women to be deprived of their inheritance.[21] Additionally, at the time of the novel, Western-style education (including girls' education) had gained ground so much so that the government could not meet public demand.[22] Gendered school education aimed to provide girls with the skills needed for their respective social class. Regarded as a necessity for working-class women, work outside the home for elite and middle-class women was seen as an inversion of what many believed to be the natural, sexual order.[23] This makes it unlikely for Fatima to own and manage a hotel.

Fatima's presence in the narrative justifies Empire. Together, Fatima and Ahmed act as counterparts to Simon and Alice who entertain anti-imperialist views. By including an improbable narrative, *Guns* offers what looks like native testimony by an Egyptian career woman. Her business acumen corresponds to Alice's while exposing the latter's naivety on the matter of Empire. Fatima, a "modern" woman who runs her own business, becomes an agent in her own subjugation. By aiding Empire, she embraces British modernity, legitimating it as "the" proper model. In the world of the imperial romance crafted by *Guns*, Fatima and Ahmed are good natives who know their place and whose actions illustrate the journey of education that Simon and Alice have to undertake.

Romancing the Archive: A Feminist, Anti-Imperialist Damsel in Distress

Third-person omniscient narration enables *Guns*' account of the Urabi Revolution and the ensuing occupation to pose as a detached ethnographic account. In actuality, this reportage is focalized through biased Western subjectivities: Simon, Alice, and Ahmed, who is simply a third Western consciousness posing as an Egyptian voice. In "The Point of Narratology," Mieke Bal intervenes in criticism of non-Western populations and their cultures, attributing the othering that many scholars have cited to the discipline's reliance on third-person narrative. In Bal's words, "the subjective focalization no speaker can avoid adopting shape[s] the fabula or content of narrative decisively."[24] Alice's approval of the invasion despite her anti-imperialist stance shows Britain to be acting out of altruistic motives. Simon's military training, perspicacity in previous battles, and reservations about the army provide a supposedly detached opinion about military intervention. Together, their assessment masks their subjective judgment where British interests rank first, as it points to their newly gained knowledge and reconciliation with the British social order. This section focuses on Alice while the next one focuses on Simon.

Alice Covington is a trailblazer on two fronts. First, she represents a novel social phenomenon that, having taken nineteenth-century Britain by storm, warranted the coinage of the term "New Woman" in 1894. According to John Tosh, this New Woman was an educated, independent, young middle-class woman who challenged patriarchal norms that assigned women to domesticity and male protection. She worked mostly in teaching or journalism, lived by herself or with other young women in the city, smoked, and cycled. She disrupted gender norms by going unchaperoned in private as well as in public and competing with men in the workspace.[25]

Second, Alice represents a new type of woman traveler to the Orient, who could be said to be attempting their version of the imperial romance. In the eighteenth century, pilgrimage to biblical lands allowed women to venture to the East with society's blessing. Since the trip was viewed as an experience that completed their education, many women travelers wrote their journeys as bildungsroman narratives. Additionally, women traveled to the region either as companions to husbands holding diplomatic postings in the region or as individuals (usually unmarried women—"spinsters," in the parlance of the day) engaged in missionary work. In her study of female British travel writing Billie Melman notes the emergence of a new category of woman traveler in the 1870s and 1880s. These were new, self-taught orientalists, existing "on the periphery of the metropolitan sites of knowledge about the Middle East, apprenticed outside the universities in the last two decades of the nineteenth century and grudgingly accepted as members of the community of knowledge in the beginning of the twentieth." However, according to Melman, the most important shift in the last decade of the nineteenth century is "from work to a career and from pilgrimage, or literary travel to specialist travel," as women increasingly began to engage in areas such as field archeology, Egyptology, and Ethnography.[26]

Alice embodies the contradictions of the era. Despite her feminism and her love for Simon, she marries Ralph Covington to honor her father's word. This recalls Judith Flanders' statement that since love held little value in nineteenth-century Britain, marital alliances were more like business transactions. Financial and social equality were assigned such high importance that some women preferred staying single to marrying down.[27] Alice's career, and her marriage—a mix of feminine bowing down to tradition and a resolve not only to work after marriage but also to work as a war correspondent—put her on the cusp of nascent change in late nineteenth-century Britain.

From the beginning Alice is established as a feminist and anti-imperialist, therefore promising a revisionist account of events. As a feminist Alice exhibits fortitude in her confrontations with men who either dismiss her, raise doubts about her ability to work, or try to confine her to the domestic sphere. Her conversation with her husband shows her to be a skilled negotiator who can be firm and assertive when needed. Alice coaxes Ralph but when he forbids her to go back to work, she asserts her autonomy and equality by distinguishing between prohibition and persuasion. She exhibits the same pluck and resoluteness during her meeting with her editor, reminding him that she is a mature woman who is financially and sociologically independent.

In pursuit of her professional goals, Alice is intrepid, this being an important characteristic of male heroes of the imperial romance, according to Linda Dryden.[28] Once in Egypt, she is the only one who takes initiative by evading the officer keeping an eye on the journalists stationed by the Suez Canal in Ismailia and looking for news on her own. When she learns from her husband that she might be sent back, her negotiation moves skillfully from a plea to a veiled threat, promising to raise a "hell of a fuss back in England" such that Wolseley "will be accused of muzzling the press"(320). Despite his disapproval, her husband cannot argue with her.

As a journalist in pursuit of facts, Alice Covington is the hero of the romance of the archive par excellence. Pointing to the importance of research to the plot, Keen explains that such romances are usually set in places that include archives, such as libraries or country houses and include characters that also feature as researchers. These characters are "endowed with the corporeality and 'round' psychology of the realistic novel."[29] They meet obstacles and are rewarded at the end with sex and physical pleasure—seen in the convenient combat death of Alice's disagreeable husband and her upcoming marriage to Simon.[30] In the context of the novel, the archive can be the location(s) to which Alice travels, the sights that she sees, the people with whom she interacts, the specific persons whom she interviews, as well as her reports for *The Morning Post*. Her archive, therefore, is Egypt itself and, in more specific terms, Urabi and Seymour. While, as Keen explains, many authors use the genre to subvert imperial discourse, in *Guns* the romance of the archive serves as a lesson to Alice by having her discover firsthand that she was misguided in her anti-imperialism.

Thus, Alice's interviews with Urabi, the leader of the revolution, and Seymour, the mastermind of the bombardment of Alexandria, function as two reconstructed archives. Both interviews are crucial to her rehabilitative experience, revealing to Alice her error in believing in the right of the Other to create alternative modernities. Occurring after the most poignant use of prolepsis (flashforward),[31] their respective positions impact her assessment of events. According to the plot, Alice meets Urabi in Cairo as Simon enters

Alexandria for the second time after having accepted Ahmed (a native sidekick) as a third member of the team. Chronologically speaking, neither the Alexandria massacre nor the bombardment had occurred yet. Alice interviews Urabi *before* these two turbulent incidents. The narrator, however, structures the plot so that this interview anachronistically appears after the massacre and is cut short by news of the bombardment. The text's manipulation of narrative speed colors Alice's impression of Urabi, causing her to foreground his inscrutability as Other, his unchecked militance, his possible duplicity, and his peasant looks, in the end deeming him a "potentially dangerous" man (160). As neo-Victorian fiction, *Guns* does not belong to romances of the archive to which Hadley, Kaplan, and Keen attribute a desire to revise the imperial past.

Such restructuring of historical events distances Alice by indicating her innocence, seen in her inability to recognize the wisdom of the British Empire whose goals in attacking Egypt are the restoration of order and the protection of European Christian residents. Alice's interview with Seymour further justifies the attack. The bombardment of Alexandria, sandwiched between both interviews, emphasizes the chaos that governs Egypt, more so because the interval between them is collapsed into a matter of days although, in reality, at least a whole month would have elapsed between Alice's meeting with Urabi and her interview with Seymour.

As a result, Urabi's declaration about economic grievances as one reason for the revolution poses as deceitful. Instead, reflecting the author's sensibilities, Alice anachronistically reads one Suez Crisis through another more recent Suez Crisis when 1956, as Stuart Ward reminds us, "mark[ed] the point when the very idea of the 'end of empire' began to emerge more fully into the public arena."[32] Impressing Britain's waning power on British national consciousness (and no doubt on the then twenty-three-year-old author), the Suez Crisis, in John MacKenzie's words, caused "a sort of implosion of confidence, a moment of truth when the British realised [*sic*] that they could no longer discipline the 'awkward squad' at the periphery in the way that they had in the nineteenth century."[33] The novel's more recent historical context, such as British support of American involvement in Afghanistan and Iraq, following the September 11 attacks, is another rude reminder of Britain's demotion. The text manifests nostalgia for a glorious Victorian era (which the author's venerable Victorian uncles witnessed) before Britain started playing second fiddle to the United States.[34]

Because her anti-imperialism is what distinguishes her professionally, Alice figures as an analyst who acknowledges the right to independence of Egyptians as long as this does not interfere with Britain's interests—a stance which the novel validates. For instance, in her meeting with the editor of her newspaper, she worries about two things: embroiling Britain in another expensive war and losing the Suez Canal, both of which do not consider the ramifications for Egyptians. More important in her critique of Britain's "hypocritical" and "unwise" stance is her orientalist view that classifies the world according to an imperialist scale where Turks pose as the "most backward and barbaric of all the imperial powers" (113) and the British, by implication, as a superior imperial power. In this sense, Egyptians are justified in their demands because they aim to free themselves from (an)"other" empire.

Although Alice's focalization of Seymour shows him in ridiculous light—for instance his sometimes inconsistent answers and his constant swearing, or his reluctance to admit that he acted without permission when he decided to attack Egypt—she makes subtle distinctions between him and Urabi.[35] Whereas the latter is portrayed as an uncouth peasant who keeps her waiting for one and a half hours, Seymour grants her immediate attendance and offers her tea and "some excellent muffins," which constitute her breakfast (174–5). As if to further confirm the difference between the two men, the narrator mentions that Alice sends prior notification to Seymour implying that she has followed the same procedure with Urabi, who despite that keeps her waiting and ends the meeting brusquely. Despite Alice's ridicule of Seymour, the novel makes sure to show a human side to the leader of an attack on a sovereign country.

While his actual interview answers occupy five short statements, ranging between two to three lines and a sixth longer paragraph justifying the attack on Alexandria, the rest of his utterances are small talk that humanizes him. The novel's mild criticism of Seymour is consistent with Alice's portrayal as critic of Empire with a predilection for antagonistic engagement with British officials. This trait manifests in her suggestion that perhaps the Egyptians fortified their defenses because "they felt that your squadron, with all these magnificent ironclads anchored out here off the port with their huge guns, was threatening *them*" (175, emphasis in original). Yet, she shows sympathy to Seymour. After his statement about attacking Egypt to restore order, she ponders his answer: "It was clear that Sir Frederick was uneasy on these issues, so Alice led the conversation back to the bombardment, the attack on the European quarter by the mob and the subsequent looting" (176). Her tact with Seymour, an Admiral, versus her straightforward attitude with Urabi, a war minister, indicates unequal treatment leaving her without giving the Egyptian side a fair hearing.

To evoke Hayden White, Alice's manipulation of her material in order to advance her career points to the corrupt archive that she produces—her reportage. Falling within the bounds of career satisfaction that Keen cites among the characteristics of the protagonist of the romance of the archive, Alice's obsession with the newness of her information is expected of a female war correspondent wishing to prove her professional excellence in a male-dominated career. However, the contradiction between her wish to give a "balanced view" and "adding just a touch of colour [*sic*]" to Urabi's words reflects a divided self. Despite her earlier promise to Urabi to "*articulate [his] views as fairly as [she] possibly can*" (157, emphasis in original), she is willing to abuse her authoritative voice by twisting his words in order to further her career prospects by achieving a scoop. Her use of the term "tale" to refer to Urabi's statement betrays her search for sensational news and points to her conceptualization of the whole story as an oriental, romantic tale in the fashion of the *Arabian Nights*. To evoke White again, Alice's archives deliver elusive, literary accounts by selectively emplotting events in a coherent, yet sensationalized, historical narrative.[36]

Alice's sensational emplotment is reflected in her evaluation of her story to the *Morning Post*. Describing it as a "good piece" and a "colour [*sic*] piece" that mixes evidence with drama, she uses terms such as "terror unleashed;" and "mob" to refer to Egyptians. Her account of the effects of the British attack on Alexandria shows Egyptians as aggressors and Europeans as the real victims. Alice neither attempts to assess the losses in the native quarter, nor does she, or anyone else, speak about Egyptians displaced by the attack. When she finds the European quarter she declares that it has suffered the most, humanizing it with allusions to skeletons of houses, remains of doors, and stains left by dead bodies.[37] Whatever concern Alice has harbored for Egyptians is outweighed by her professional aspirations. The exclusion of Egyptian victims of the same event points to a shift in Alice's stance on Empire. Alice's archives create a genre conflict where the romance of the archive with its revisionist strain battles the imperial romance, each attempting to force its conventions on the narrative.

In *Guns* the imperial romance woos and, indeed, subjugates Alice, first, by undermining her feminism and, second, by assimilating her into an imperialist narrative that normalizes a European paradigm. Alice tries to enact a female imperial romance, but the formula undermines her because of her gender. Whereas Simon, as a male, slips smoothly into the genre, she is portrayed as a threat to British military operations in Egypt since he has to continually leave important matters in order to rescue her. When Simon is in danger, the narrative formula provides him with an opportunity to show his British mettle through courage and resourcefulness, but when Alice is in danger this raises fears of abduction and miscegenation that would threaten British racial purity.

Alice's multiple abductions confine her within the role of the damsel in distress whose lack of shrewdness leads her in one instance to travel across the desert with none other than George, the corrupt Thomas Cooke employee. On several occasions Alice is made to admit her folly. For example, after her first kidnapping by George, she tells Simon, "'How I wished I had never started that stupid game'" (210). Then adds, "'Simon, I am so ashamed of myself for getting you into this terrible situation and so grateful to you for saving me'" (211). Addressing her husband, Simon, and Jenkins after her second kidnapping, she says, "'I felt I had been selfish and unthinking'" (391). The formula pushes her within the role of damsel in distress by further emphasizing her frailty even when she has just killed her captor; Simon "had longed to rush across and take her in his arms and comfort her; tell her how much he loved her frailty and admired her pluck" (395). Noticeable here is how frailty, deserving love, precedes pluck.

By the end of the novel, even though Alice succeeds professionally, the narrative reinscribes her in a domestic structure, this time promising her a marriage of love. Nevertheless, such an ending offers a compromise on the traditional resolution for female bildungsroman narratives, where women are subsumed into the domestic sphere. In this sense, Alice as a New Woman who, the novel implies, will continue with her professional career after her marriage to the less traditional Simon, partially succeeds in inserting her voice in a patriarchal narrative that assigns her narrow parameters. Yet, how much room does the imperial romance allow for a feminist/female imperial romance or a feminist/female history of the occupation? Deeply masculinist and Eurocentric, the imperial romance imposes its formula on revisionist strains. To reappropriate David Medalie, the competing genres in *Guns* tip the balance toward the imperial romance. Because the genre requires certain components, such as the intrepid male hero, the vulnerable female in need of protection, and the exotic yet evil natives in dire need of civilization, it triumphs over the anti-imperialist mode or, one might add, the feminist mode.[38]

Embracing Empire

Simon, the brave hero of this imperial romance, illustrates the danger lurking in Egypt through examples of bravado where he rescues the British consul during the events of the Alexandria massacre, protects a group of Europeans taking refuge in a bank, and rescues Alice from multiple abductions (although ironically the abductor is the British George who is assisted by evil Egyptians). Simon's experience, in which Alice plays an important part, leads him up an arc of education to conclude the necessity of the occupation.

Guns' narrative structure and its strategic employment of prolepsis (flash-forward) lend more cogency to Simon and Alice's evaluation of the events, which, in turn, furthers an imperialist delivery of events, thus validating the genre of the bildungsroman with its standardization of the European paradigm. The narrator uses prolepsis so that the first time we meet Simon and Jenkins in Egypt after leaving them in England, they are in the middle of the desert about to be attacked by Bedouins. The novel then pauses to go back to the pair's arrival in Alexandria reporting hostility toward Europeans before returning to the desert scene. Such departures from the storyline, "anachronies" as Gérard Genette calls them, cultivate an image of Egyptian violence, which *Guns* shows to be the result of the Urabi Revolution. *Guns'* manipulation of narrative speed and its reliance on repetitious structures, which retard the narrative, supports its depiction of Urabi as creating an anarchic state. Writing on narrative speed, Kathryn Hume lists "repetitious structures[,] the framing of tales within tales," and characters among techniques that writers use to delay narrative.[39] In *Guns*, for instance, highly dramatized episodes describing how Simon and his group are constantly attacked by "Arabs," or "Bedawis [*sic*]," slow down the pace to teach Simon a lesson by demonstrating that anarchy rules rampant in Egypt. The two abductions of Alice are also illustrative, all incidents becoming instrumental in Simon's education.

Significant to Simon's understanding of the revolution is Ahmed, Simon's native informant who represents native Egyptian opinion, and whose credibility stems from his sensible recognition that Egyptians are not ready for self-rule. In reality, he is another British voice disguised as an Egyptian whose native support solidifies Britain's invasion of Egypt as an action that Egypt itself desires. Bal's critique of Western ethnography's attempts to speak for the Other through the Western Self captures his character: " 'We' speak, and focalize, the focalization of 'them,' but 'they' do not speak, and 'their' focalization only comes to us filtered by 'ours.' "[40] Ahmed's "insider" knowledge of Egypt is a conglomerate of British assumptions among which are the political immaturity of his country, Urabi's intention to seize the Canal, and his dictatorial tendencies. All of his tips about the current state of affairs cater to Britain's imperial aspirations, legitimating the occupation, which he depicts as delivering Egypt from chaos: "I think it has to be done, this big fight. Otherwise this silly man Arabi [*sic*] will continue to muck up country [*sic*]. Egypt needs stability, quietness [*sic*]" (402).

Simon's identity as the unconventional son of a military man promises a hero who is loyal to Empire yet one who could sympathize with the Egyptian desire to create their own modernity. He functions as a "reflector," whom Manfred Jahn describes as "a foregrounded character, a 'central consciousness,' whose perceptions 'reflect' the fictional world." Jahn refers to the reflector's thoughts, perceptions, and feelings as "consciousness-data" and points to the use of psychonarration in presenting this data: "In reflectorial mode, a reflector's inside views are shown 'from within,' the text foregrounds the reflector's consciousness-data, the narrative tempo is scenic, and the reader is cast into the role of a witness."[41] Simon's judgment of events is instrumental to the picture that *Guns* paints and to his maturation as he embraces the imperialist narrative. The journey of education that he undergoes in this imperial romance cum bildungsroman, and the use of psychonarration, create an illusion of transparency that validates the archive that he produces as he embraces the British view. He receives his education firsthand and, if his human sources are subjective, Egypt becomes an archive that is mediated through what the text establishes as his unique consciousness.

As reflector, his credibility is of prime importance, promising a different kind of hero of the imperial romance. The narrator establishes it by referring to Simon's past through several sources, therefore maximizing the effects of the traditional bildungsroman resolution. For example, we meet his mother who hates "Mr Gladstone and ... all things radical. She disliked the unconventional—and her son *was* unconventional" (3, emphasis in original). Despite his dislike for the hierarchical structure of the army, he is no coward. The novel presents Simon as the new blood whose creative thinking regenerates the army and, therefore, Empire. Coming from a non-titled, middle-class family, he believes in hard work and rejects the army with its rigid system of respect for seniority and rank superseding shrewd tactical planning. The novel presents his knack for good military tactics, despite his young age, as a gift that the army is now beginning to use to its advantage. Wolseley solicits Simon's assistance because as a former military man he will not shy away from armed intervention while his level-headedness will guarantee sound judgment.

In further genre merging, *Guns* flirts with the spy thriller, which Michael Denning identifies as the successor of the imperial romance.[42] Because Simon gathers information through clandestine means, the text persistently asserts his credibility. His is an irregular military role. He is an indispensable member of the team, yet he is expendable if the whole affair were to come to light. For these reasons the narrator painstakingly establishes Simon's shrewdness, his reliability, and devotion to the Queen. His non-conformity and espionage, instead of endangering Empire, become an asset because the job that he undertakes is an unconventional one—one that needs a creative mind that is unfettered by the kind of traditional thinking that Simon despises. Wolseley's reiteration of Simon's rejection of a commission in the army and a promotion, information provided earlier by his mother, ward off any remaining doubts about his loyalty, taking the tarnish off espionage.[43]

Readers follow Simon's education as he moves from mild sympathy with Egyptians to support of British imperialism. His education is structured along three main lines: an interpretation of events in classist terms, an evaluation of the revolution's effects on British interests, and a dismissal of serious grievances among Egyptians.

First, acknowledging ethnic and racial tensions while overlooking them at the same time, Simon recodes materialist grievances as dissatisfaction on the part of Egyptian peasant underdogs with the privileges of their Turkish overlords. Historically, as noted in the Introduction to this study, the upper ranks of the military were populated with Turco-Circassians, while Egyptians—mostly drawn from the peasant classes—were kept in the lower ranks. However, Simon's conclusion is anachronistic when, in his first meeting with Wolseley, he frames the revolution as an attempt to overthrow Ottoman rule in Egypt. Not only was Urabi an Ottomanist, but nationalist ideas promoting Egyptian independence from the Ottoman Empire did not emerge until the beginning of the twentieth century.[44] Simon internalizes racialized Ottoman views of Egyptians as "*fellahin* [*sic*]" (peasants), a loaded term that aligns with colonialist representations. As Turks used it, it denoted naïveté, incompetence, stubbornness, and sometimes subhuman qualities. By referring to Egyptians siding with the revolution as *fellahin* [*sic*] and describing Urabi as "a formerly obscure colonel … a *fellaheen* [*sic*] or member of the peasant classes" (41), Simon frames the revolution as an ignorant class warfare. After his arrival in Egypt, he observes the "*low-bred* Egyptian officers grown arrogant because of their newly acquired power" (80 emphasis added). For all his non-conformity, Simon's reference to Egyptian troops as mostly composed of "low-born *fellaheen*, like Arabi [*sic*] himself" (80), betrays his own classism. As he reiterates Simon's views, Stone Pasha's expert analysis by an outsider with no stakes in the British-Egyptian affair validates Simon and Empire.

Second, Simon's assessment of the Urabi Revolution, like Alice's, remains tethered to British interests. He sees it as a menacing military coup that aims to oust Turkish leaders who support European interests in Egypt. This justifies intervention in the name of civilization while masking Britain's desire to safeguard its route to India by snatching Egypt before France and other rivals such as Russia and Germany.[45] Scattered references to Urabi's control of the army and to the Khedive as a prisoner in his own palace construct Urabi's rule as Minister of War as a reign of terror. Stone Pasha, historically the American chief staff of the Egyptian army, confirms this interpretation when, in his meeting with Simon, he paints the image of a Khedive being chased by Urabi from Cairo to Alexandria—a portrayal showing the purpose of the Urabists to be seizure of power.

Third, despite the somewhat sympathetic portrayal in places—for example, "Simon felt a pang of sympathy for the rank and file of the Egyptian army, paid a pittance, treated badly by their Turkish officers and living in what was virtually an occupied country" (47)—Urabi is presented as a pretender, who uses political demands to achieve personal gain, and his cause is always qualified. Although, or because, Stone Pasha tells Simon that Urabi's promotion was held back for sixteen years under Khedive Ismail, his account of Urabi's investment in the revolution casts it as a personal vendetta. Stone states, "I guess he wants the Turks out, a lessening of foreign influence and a new constitution" (87). Earlier, Simon tells Wolseley that "the Egyptian army is adopting nationalistic postures," adding that at the Abdin demonstration Urabi demanded "some sort of a new constitution" (41, 42). Qualifying terms such as "I guess," "nationalistic" instead of "nationalist," and "some sort of" together with "postures" depict Urabi and his supporters as insincere while overriding Egyptian concerns. Much like nineteenth-century imperialist accounts of the revolution, the narrative dismisses the existence of nationalist feeling in Egypt, or such tangible fears as dissatisfaction with European influence tolerated by the Ottoman Empire, fear of a French invasion after the French annexation of Tunis, or demands for a new constitution that allows Egyptians to share in the government, and finally for equal rights for Egyptians and Turco-Circassians in the military.

Throughout, Simon is reluctant to name the revolution as such, sometimes referring to it as a "movement" (42), a "nationalistic movement" (42), or "this Egyptian nationalism" (43). This reluctance to name the events indicates his gradual rapprochement with imperial discourse, exonerating Britain and denying its responsibility for Egypt's political and economic problems while validating the occupation. Referring to the revolution as "insurrection" and "revolt" (432) in his Author's Note, Wilcox delegitimizes Urabi's movement. In an interview with the author of this study, he added that that time lacked "democratic ways" of voicing dissatisfaction, gracefully overlooking the lack of democratic governance.[46]

Wilcox is also unaware of Egyptian nationalist accounts and sympathetic British views of the revolution, such as Wilfred Scawen Blunt's *Secret History of the English Occupation of Egypt*.[47] A nineteenth-century English poet, anti-imperialist and personal friend of Urabi, Blunt became the "unofficial adviser" to *al-Hizb al-Watani*, the National Party that Urabi had formed, negotiating with the British government on Egypt's behalf. He supported the causes of

Algeria, Egypt, Ireland, and India, even leading to his imprisonment in Ireland for two months between 1875–6. Blunt was such a powerful player in the events that, Peter Mansfield reports, he was discussed in the House of Commons and, after the British occupation of Egypt, barred from entering the country for three years.[48]

It is not clear either whether Wilcox was aware of the *nahda* debates brewing in the Egyptian press roughly since mid-century. Lisa Pollard writes that, quite a while before the British occupation, male and female Egyptian intellectuals had started discussing the means to modernity. Egyptian intellectuals had accepted the imperialist rhetoric maintaining that Egyptian political life was unsound because family life was unsound. Deciding that a democratically governed family led to a democratically governed nation, they had named family reform as the panacea for all social and political ills. More specifically, the road to modernity lay in monogamy and the education of women. The British, however, ignored these debates as well as various attempts at reform going on in Egypt.[49] The novel's skipping over such details paints a picture of a culturally stagnant Egypt, stifling alternative visions of modernity, and making inevitable the success of both the traditional imperial romance and the traditional bildungsroman narrative, to which Simon contributes.

Despite the narrator's efforts to present Simon as a reliable reflector, the latter's dependence on rumor and conjecture for his account of the Alexandria massacre points to his lack of reliability, which the novel's narrative techniques mask. The episode, which the novel chooses to refer to as riots, lasts close to ten pages. Because Simon does not catch the event from the beginning, the story of the riot is truncated and the reason behind it appears to be meaningless anger at the British consul. Simon first becomes aware of it when he hears a commotion on the street. When he enquires about it, Ahmed reports that Fatima, his cousin, says it is about "something to do with British consul. Big riot" (129). There is no mention of the stabbing of the Egyptian boy by the Maltese national.[50] Thus, manipulation of narrative dictates the imperialist account of the events. Simon focalizes the riot as if it truly *were* about the British consul. He is content with hearsay and spins his yarn accordingly, reporting what he expects to see rather than what he witnesses. Approaching the consul's carriage, he reports that the "the noise grew louder until they turned a corner to find a crowd of Arabs, including, *Simon felt sure*, some black-shrouded Bedawis, jostling around an open carriage so that it was completely surrounded" (129, emphasis added). According to Egyptian historian Mahmoud al-Khafif, acting upon the Khedive's directions, the governor of Alexandria enlisted the help of Bedouins to tarnish the revolution with chaotic lawlessness that included looting and acts of violence against Europeans.[51]

The narrator uses prolepsis again so that Seymour's ultimatum, instead of occurring almost a month after the Alexandria massacre, not only precedes it but becomes the reason behind what is presented as gratuitous violence against Europeans. Historically, Seymour issued the ultimatum on July 10, 1882, almost a whole month after the Alexandria riots and twenty-four hours before the bombardment of Alexandria. Commenting on the use of narrative speed, David Herman explains that "longer or shorter duration can cue readers to focus on some narrative details as more salient than others. When a storyteller passes over events quickly or fails to mention them altogether, story-recipients regularly infer those events to be of relatively little importance vis-à-vis the narrative as a whole."[52] The narrator spends close to ten pages dramatizing the attack on Cookson and his rescue by the trio but skips over the events preceding the British invasion. Slowing down the narrative pace slows down the narrative speed, cueing readers to the importance of events illustrating lawlessness and animosity against Europeans.

Rearranging incidents heightens the drama of adventure as well as the sense of impending doom. Such manipulation of narrative transforms Egyptians from exploited victims shot at by Europeans to an angry "mob," a term that the narrator frequently uses to refer to them. More dangerously, it shows Egyptians as the initiators of the Alexandria massacre and therefore as provocateurs of the invasion, thus denying Britain's active role in the aggression. Most importantly, his portrayal of events brings Simon closer to the traditional protagonist of the European bildungsroman, facilitating his reconciliation with the discourse of Empire, which, in turn, signals the true maturation of the twenty-seven-year-old after his life-changing experience in Egypt. As Keen notes, closure and the existence of truth characterize romances of the archive, which "create temporarily risky worlds in which the character—and by extension the reader—can seek and find that truth."[53] Both Alice and Simon find their truths in the end.

Conclusion

Although not a bildungsroman per se, *Guns* blends the romance of the archive with the imperial romance to form a bildungsroman that justifies Empire. It is a swashbuckling tale in a chaotic landscape that needs the kind, civilizing hand of Britain. Egyptians are reduced to lawless mobs siding with a low-born, dictatorial officer. Simon and Alice, having gone through their respective journeys, emerge with a newfound conviction of the benevolence of Empire. Alice, the anti-imperialist researcher, finds her truth when she recognizes the danger of Egyptians once in power. Siding with Britain, she deems the revolution anarchic, accepting the necessity of British intervention. Although the imperial romance imposes on her the role of the vulnerable female, she insists on writing her own story. In Alice, readers see a determined feminist reporter working from the front lines. Despite some detours, her trip to wonderland ends happily for her. She is promised a marriage of love after her husband conveniently dies in Egypt. Simon, too, his liberalism notwithstanding, is a catalyst for the British annexation of Egypt. As he looks upon the bodies of the dead at the battle of Tel el Kebir, he ponders "so many lives lost, to preserve … what? The ownership of a few miles of waterway carved out of sand dunes [the Suez Canal]? The restoration of stability to a country unsettled by foreign domination? Well, at least Ahmed seemed to think it had all been worthwhile" (419). Simon's doubt, though at first seeming to interrogate the validity of imperial war, serves not so much a question but as a confirmation of the "truth" that *Guns* has offered through the imperial romance and the romance of the archive.

4

The Women of Mahmoud's Dreams: Bahaa Taher's *Sunset Oasis* and the National Mosaic

Bahaa Taher's *Wahat al-ghurub*, 2006 (*Sunset Oasis*, 2009), is one of many twenty-first-century "new-consciousness" novels that reflect a rising sensitivity to the Arab world's gender, racial, ethnic, sexual, and geographic minorities. According to Mary Youssef, by centering marginalized voices, authors manifest a new consciousness—a heightened awareness of their pluralistic societies—and call for a redrawing of the national imaginary to represent the full mosaic of their respective nations.[1] In this chapter I argue that *Sunset Oasis* includes two minority female bildungsromane eclipsed by Mahmoud's angst but contributing to his own growth. The novel eventually rejects the idea of bildung, or formation, as a forward-moving journey that ends in social harmony. In his exploration of the bildungsroman, Taher employs the Sufi concepts of journey and dreams as a familiar, local, religious epistemology through which to explore the stunted personal and political growth of Mahmoud, the protagonist.[2] Ironically, Mahmoud's enlightenment coincides with his death, consequently dismissing knowledge as the precursor of harmonious existence.

With a focus on the character Mahmoud Abd el Zahir and his struggle to come to terms with his betrayal of the Urabi Revolution, *Sunset Oasis* begins in 1902, twenty years into the British occupation. The novel's events take place in Egypt between the late nineteenth century and the early years of the twentieth century, and travel between Cairo, Alexandria, and Siwa, an oasis in Egypt's western desert close to the Libyan border where Mahmoud is posted as the new chief of police. Mahmoud has taken part in the 1881–2 Urabi Revolution, later crushed in 1882 by British occupying forces who reinstated Khedive Tawfiq as the ruler of Egypt. To escape retribution by the government,

Mahmoud has had to denounce both the revolution and its leader, Colonel Ahmed Urabi, a betrayal that torments him throughout the novel.

Despite his rapprochement with the regime, he does not get ahead professionally, and his promotion as new chief of police in Siwa is a form of exile. The farthest point on Egyptian land, the oasis used to be part of Egypt in ancient times before its recapture in the early nineteenth century. Siwa was also Alexander the Great's stop at the Oracle of Amun in the fourth century BCE, where he reportedly communicated with the god Amun and was made a god himself. Mahmoud's assignment is to dispatch exorbitant taxes collected from Siwans to a British-controlled government in Cairo. His duties include balancing tense relationships among Siwan tribes; managing a love-, but mostly, hate relationship between these tribes and the Egyptian government; convincing his Irish wife, Catherine, to stop intruding upon Siwan sites in her quest for Alexander the Great's tomb; all while trying to avoid the fate of his predecessor who was killed by the Siwans.

In place of omniscient narration focalizing a central consciousness, and a linear narrative progressing teleologically toward knowledge, the novel utilizes a postmodern multiple narrative technique. The presence of multiple narrators with sometimes jarring points of view, themselves reflecting the dissonance involved in a forced restructuring of consciousness, destabilizes the bildungsroman's unitary vision of harmony with the social order. As narrators take turns, several formation narratives appear on the margins of the text.

The novel's location in Siwa, as a geographic, social, economic, and ethnic periphery, allows for an interrogation of the bildungsroman's tendency to endorse dominant narratives, making it possible to recover minor female narratives. A liminal place lying on the seams between Egypt and Libya, Siwa was ruled for centuries by a Libyan family before falling under ancient Egypt's authority.[3] According to Ahmed Fakhry, during Ottoman times and until the violent Egyptian conquest of 1820, the oasis enjoyed relative autonomy, traded with various regions and—although Siwans had to acknowledge the Sultan of Turkey as Caliph—paid no yearly taxes.[4]

Revolution and the national imaginary were ever present in Taher's mind, as major political events in Egypt coincided with milestones in his life. For example, Taher (1935–2022) recalls that the first big demonstration calling for the fall of King Farouk (r. 1936–1952) and his repatriation to Turkey came out of his secondary school. Soon after, Taher's own college experience was bookended by the 1952 Military Coup and the 1956 Tripartite Aggression on Egypt. For the young, excited author, the 1952 Coup evoked the Urabi Revolution. In 2004, he was one of the founding members of the political group *Kefaya* (enough) that protested Hosni Mubarak's long rule (r. 1981–2011) and the possible ascendance of his son, Gamal, to Egypt's presidency. Although barred by ailing health from regular participation in the 2011 Tahrir Square demonstrations, the author was among the first ardent supporters of Egypt's revolution.[5]

Not surprisingly, Taher, who held a bachelor's degree in history and a graduate diploma in modern history, continued to explore revolution, gender, as well as ethnic and religious relations in his works. For instance, *Khalti Safiyya wa al-dayr*, 1991 (*Aunt Safiyya and the Monastery*, 1996), investigates Muslim-Coptic relations in an Upper Egyptian village, while *al-Hubb fi al-manfa*, 1995 (*Love in Exile*, 2001), reevaluates the Nasser era with its autocratic policies, the subsequent rise of Islamism, and the changing attitudes toward feminist voices. In *Sunset Oasis*, which won Taher the 2008 inaugural prize for *al-Ja'iza al-'alamiyya li al-riwaya al-'arabiyya*, the International Prize for Arabic Fiction (the Arabic Booker, presented by Abu Dhabi Department of Culture and Tourism), the Siwa Oasis, with its isolated desert setting, serves as a backdrop upon which Mahmoud, the protagonist, projects his past, while helping him reflect on his actions as he goes through his midlife crisis. His contradictory position as at once nationalist and collaborator, colonized and colonizer, hero and coward, victim and oppressor, allows both him and the author to reflect on the position of Egypt's ethnic populations within the nationalist project.

Most studies of the novel justifiably focus on the depiction of Siwa and the Siwans in the novel. For Mary Youssef, the novel's focus on Siwa as the geographic periphery highlights the Siwans' fight against colonial oppression in its British and Egyptian forms. She reads Siwa as a "spatial emblem of self-quest," where characters attempt to find themselves, and concludes that the marginalized female voices belonging to different racial, cultural, and linguistic communities in the novel reflect women's peripheral social realities.[6] Discussing speech as freedom versus being spoken for as delegation of freedom, Hatem Hafez questions whether the *zajjala* (the peasant farmers) in the novel do not speak because they simply do not wish to or because they have delegated that right to Sheikh Sabir and Sheikh Yahya, esteemed members of the Eastern and Western tribes respectively.[7] Mustafa al-Dab', reads Sheikh Sabir and Sheikh Yahya, both members of the council of *al-ajwad* (heads of families) as representative of the spatial authority, which regards intruders in the oasis as enemies that should be dealt with or eliminated. In this case, Mahmoud stands for intrusive state authority.[8]

Rather than bring Mahmoud into focus immediately, this chapter centers two female characters whose lives are strongly affected by Mahmoud's stunted growth. These minority voices engage in a conversation that comments on the bildungsroman and the national struggle. These women are Maleeka, a rebellious young Siwan woman whose interactions with Mahmoud's family against her tribe's customs indirectly cause her death, and Ni'ma, Mahmoud's Sudanese slave and the love of his life who leaves him. Justified in her view that Maleeka, Fiona (Catherine's sister), and Ni'ma "represent women and their marginalized status irrespective of their racial, cultural, and linguistic difference in male-dominated societies," Youssef argues that Taher "reflects their social reality aesthetically by denying them individual voices and providing them with existence only in the consciousness of the other characters."[9] However, Maleeka and Ni'ma resist by speaking through art and storytelling alternatively.

Siwan Women between Writing and Self-Writing

Maleeka's story is a submerged female narrative struggling to come out through other voices. Readers only learn about her from other characters whose views of her are colored by their own frustrations, desires, and ideological perceptions. Maleeka's bildungsroman must, therefore, be constructed out of these fragments. I argue that through fragmented narrative Maleeka, at least fifteen years old, emerges as a protagonist who insists on writing her own story, resisting epistemic violence wrought on her by characters who recount or redefine her story, as well as physical violence inflicted by her mother and other women. Maleeka creates an alternative mode of self-writing through art. Her identity as a triply colonized subject—quadruply so if we include her homoerotic encounter with Catherine—makes her important in a work preoccupied with multiple layers of colonialism.

Related to western Amazigh (Berber) tribes that populated North Africa and speaking a language that is very close to theirs, Siwans are ethnically Amazigh, and their language incomprehensible to Egyptians. Today, Siwans are linguistically assimilated into Egyptian culture, Arabic being the language of instruction in schools, although they may continue to speak Siwan at home.[10] As a Siwan living on Egyptian territory, Maleeka is colonized by the British. As a Siwan, she is colonized by Egypt whose people the Siwans regard as foreign intruders. As a woman she is colonized, metaphorically, by her elderly, impotent husband and a male worldview whose boundaries are safeguarded by the women of the tribe, who, having internalized these views, have become agents of self-subjugation. Additionally, Maleeka's potential homoerotic sexuality does not conform to either British or emergent Egyptian modern sexuality.[11]

Despite the novel's attempt at granting historically suppressed voices a chance to speak, with the exception of Catherine (Mahmoud's Irish wife), these voices, as Youssef observes, belong to educated males who express their thoughts through lengthy introspection. This narrative mode, in Youssef's words, "enables Tahir, the intellectual, to discuss complex views and practices of critical issues like race, religion, and imperialism without the interruption of much direct speech."[12] In contrast, Mahmoud, the colonized colonizer, to use Eve Troutt Powell's term,[13] and protagonist of this bildungsroman, narrates eight out of eighteen chapters. Catherine, who approaches Siwa as an imperialist adventurer, narrates six chapters, while Sheikh Yahya and Sheikh Sabir, patriarchs of the Western and Eastern tribes respectively, narrate one chapter each. Mahmoud, Catherine, and Yahya also share a chapter. Even the long dead Alexander the Great fares better than Maleeka, having a chapter all to himself. Youssef rightly notes that "the reader's inability to have direct access to these women's thoughts and emotions parallels their isolation from public life."[14] We never hear the voice of Maleeka (or Niʿma) whose story is told through her sympathetic uncle, Yahya, her mother and brothers whose voices are also filtered through the educated Yahya, and through Mahmoud and his wife, Catherine, who orientalizes Siwa and its people.

Maleeka endures epistemic violence as her voice is continually hijacked by characters who shape her according to their own perceptions. Only her loving uncle sees in her intelligence and independence, which he respects. To her superstitious mother and the women of her tribe, she is a demon-child, possessed by the evil spirits to which she exposes herself in the temples of the infidels (the ancient Egyptians). The village elders only see her as an intransigent wife who abandons her husband and whose revolt poses a threat to the history and very existence of their community. Mahmoud views her as a native who is defiling his white wife, while Catherine, romanticizing her to the point of ethereality, projects on Maeeka homoerotic fantasies in a manner reminiscent of nineteenth-century travelers analyzed by Joseph Boone.[15] Always enduring physical violence, Maleeka is brutally beaten with sticks by her mother and tribeswomen to rid her of spirits that may have possessed her during one of her trips to the ruins. Her husband batters her for no reason. Mahmoud kicks her and almost shoots her when he thinks she is attacking Catherine, and Catherine herself beats her with a palm rib.

Maleeka's refusal to comply with societal norms, as child or adult, coupled with her character that eludes clear definition, leads others to impose their narratives on her. As an independent and precocious woman, her rejection of the confines of the roles expected of her as a female is caused by a desire for agency in charting her own path. As a child her transgressions include violating gender segregation norms by dressing up as a boy and leaving the house. Her forays into public space are rendered even more criminal because she visits much-feared ancient Egyptian temples built by pagans. Undeterred, Maleeka persistently rejects her role as guardian of patriarchal gender boundaries. She continues to roam the village in her disguise and when Catherine intrudes on their living area during a visit to a historical site, Maleeka is the only one to open the door in an attempt to establish contact. Determined to seek friendship outside her community, Maleeka later risks severe punishment to visit Catherine, ultimately bringing about her own death. Such incidents of sartorial and spatial infractions cause Siwans to write her in terms of insubordination, particularly when she leaves her husband and asks for a divorce.

Eager to forge her narrative against the confines of another masculine genre popular in the nineteenth century—the imperial romance—Catherine is guilty of epistemic violence against Siwans in general and Maleeka in particular. Like the protagonist of an imperial romance, Catherine sees herself in masculine terms as an adventurous hero who will penetrate Siwa and tame the inferior Siwans.[16] She has read everything about them, undoubtedly including material that notes homosexual practices among Siwans.[17] Having recently experienced a sexual awakening with Mahmoud, whom she also sexualizes as a virile male Other, she arrives in Siwa predisposed to view the location through a sexualized lens, which sets the stage for her encounter with Maleeka. While Maleeka's sexual identity cannot be ascertained, it is important to account for Catherine's own role in narrating Maleeka through her own desires.

When Catherine meets Maleeka, she is ready for an adventure. From the minute she lays eyes on Maleeka, she is smitten by her beauty. Later, Maleeka comes to Catherine in a sexual dream in which her braids are replaced by snakes, "which started to slither towards me and wrap themselves around my body."[18] Thus, when Maleeka tries to cross language barriers and establish friendship with Catherine, the latter first mistakes this friendly move for a homoerotic advance before she questions her judgment of the episode, wondering who has attempted to seduce whom and whether in fact there has been any seduction to begin with.

Catherine's second meeting with Maleeka ends disastrously. In a defiant spirit, the widowed Maleeka, seeking new friends, dresses up as a man and visits Catherine. As Catherine recalls the details of the visit, she recollects that, at the sight of Maleeka, her mind "seemed suddenly to have stopped working" and adds that she "stood there, [her] eyes fastened on [Maleeka's] scarlet lips and her bewitching grey eyes" (188). When Maleeka faces Catherine, the latter recalls that "her heavy breathing was hot on my neck" (188). When Maleeka embraces Catherine, Catherine first embraces her, then she thinks of Sappho and pushes Maleeka away and shouts "No! No! I'm not Sappho!" (188). Catherine adds, "In agitation, I kept muttering to myself the same sentence, 'I am not Sappho! I am not Sappho!' while at the same time resisting the temptation to stretch out my hand once more and raise her from the ground and clasp her face to my bosom'" (189). Catherine experiences a rush of contradictory urges that render her incapable of judging the episode.

On two occasions, Catherine tries to understand the incident and admits that "there's nothing but fog" in her mind (224). At first, she casts the episode as a seduction but later ponders whether *she* has been the one to press Maleeka's face to her breasts. Her perplexity remains unresolved as she questions whether she shuddered with disgust or with pleasure when Maleeka kissed her. Finally, she settles the matter by pronouncing it a "moment of weakness, a moment of confusion brought about by the killing loneliness of this oasis" (224). Ibrahim 'Awad, who strongly rejects the episode as highly improbable, overlooks Catherine's attraction to Maleeka, her awakening sexuality, and her orientalist approach to Egypt that leads her to exoticize the place and the people. Despite questioning Maleeka's seduction of Catherine, 'Awad, interestingly, does not interrogate Catherine's reliability as narrator and seems to accept her story even when she herself is not completely clear on the details.[19]

Much later, Catherine's thoughts indicate that Maleeka has not seduced her: "I still live the shudder that swept over me when she kissed me and I pressed her head to my breast" (267). Very much like an orientalist, Catherine blames what she views as illicit sexual feeling on Siwa and further invests the geographic location with sexual qualities. Catherine's self-questioning, although it shifts the focus from Maleeka's story to her own, emphasizes the problem of forced narratives hinting that Maleeka's true voice may never be fully recovered. Indeed, we only hear of Maleeka "making a noise like an injured cat" (165). We do not know Maleeka's true age. Catherine's reference to her as a "child" (171), if not accurate, points to Catherine's imperialist tendencies and her paternalistic attitude toward Siwans. Mahmoud, who is incriminated in Egypt's colonization of Siwans, also refers to her as a "girl" (165).

Through art, Maleeka finds an alternative mode of speaking. On her ill-fated visit to Catherine, Maleeka takes two statues, which she has fashioned out of clay and made to look like herself and Catherine. She moves them to signal to Catherine her wish to become friends. Yet, her alternative narrative mode is constantly misread, whether as demonic expressions by the uneducated tribespeople or as "primitive" by Catherine. Her uncle is the only one who recognizes her art, deeming her clay statues to be identical to those she used to bring back from the temples. Later, her identity as a widow and her violation of widow practices trigger the events leading to her death, an incident in which epistemic and physical violence meet.

The fight over upholding patriarchy, divergent local nationalisms, and Egyptian and British colonialism is staged on Maleeka's body, which in addition to that becomes the battleground for the fight over autonomy to write her own story. These two forms of violence coalesce in the circumstances surrounding Maleeka's image as a widow and her subsequent death, by far the most ferocious act of violence enacted on her body. From beginning to end, whether as child or wife, Maleeka exists as a symbol—a cultural signifier who is denied writing her own story. For the Siwans, Maleeka's marriage—that is, her life—is an experiment. Belonging to the Westerners, she is married off to an Easterner in an attempt to bridge the nationalist schism between the two tribes. She is part of an exchange in the manner which Gayle Rubin describes; she is a gift that creates social harmony between two different clans who become related by blood. Needless to say, it is the men who are the beneficiaries of such an exchange as it is they who form new social alliances.[20] When her husband dies, Maleeka breaks the widow code dictating that she remain confined for a period of four months and ten days—not to see or be seen by anyone. Otherwise, she will bring disaster to everyone who lays eyes on her. During her confinement the widow is known as the ghoul-woman. When Maleeka is discovered after visiting Catherine, disaster ensues that is immediately attributed to Maleeka's delinquency.

Maleeka contests her definition as a ghoul-woman and even as a widow, insisting on telling her own story, which readers receive through Yahya as told by Maleeka's mother and brothers. Taking issue with her classification as a widow, Maleeka stresses the fictionality of the story, the presence of evidence notwithstanding: "Why did they consider her a widow when Mi'bid wasn't a man? She was still a virgin and the blood that Mi'bid had brought them after his first night with her was faked. She'd never been a wife or a widow, so how could she be a ghoul-woman?" (197). Readers, who are more than three times removed from Maleeka's voice in this episode, learn of Maleeka's suicide of which Yahya is highly suspicious.

As stated in the Introduction, a traditional bildungsroman frames death or suicide as the protagonist's failure to mature. Scholars of the female bildungsroman, however, justifiably read this as a refusal on the part of the protagonist to give up education that she has gained. Maleeka's story, dispersed throughout the narrative, indicts nationalist agendas that stifle women's voices. In this case, tribal belonging acts as a form of local nationalism. Maleeka dies fighting for her right to self-definition. She refuses to submit to genre conventions whatever the genre may be. Whether we believe her death to be murder or suicide, she stays true to her desire to be taken seriously as an independent female subject. In the end, the fight between colonialism and patriarchal local nationalisms takes place over women's bodies. Maleeka emerges as victim of Siwan, Egyptian, and British colonialism, yet one who exercises agency.

Maleeka's death exposes a masculinist national struggle that has no room for women desiring to step into personhood. Maleeka as a subaltern is oppressed by her tribe, who are equally silenced as subalterns and forced to fit in a dominant narrative that orientalizes them. They are embroiled in their own struggle against the British and the Egyptian governments. Thus, Maleeka's attempt to establish contact with Catherine marks her as a traitor of Siwa since women in this struggle figure only as cultural signifiers. Siwans, whether her Western people or the Easterners, invest Maleeka with their mythic lore. Although the oasis historian remarks that the ghoul-woman incident is without precedent in the oasis, he justifies the ancestors' restrictions on widows because they "knew how dangerous it was" (181). In this situation, female behavior not in accordance with an imagined tradition brings about the demise of the whole community, and women defying patriarchal societal norms are construed as diabolic. Thus, Maleeka's identity as a woman and an individual is lost. To Catherine, she is a sexualized other, while to Mahmoud she is an intruder whom he wants to shoot, completely oblivious to the fact that she was seeking refuge in the colonizer's house. Just as he has failed Ni'ma before her, Mahmoud fails Maleeka.

Revisiting the Discourse of the Unity of the Nile Valley

This section focuses on Ni'ma, a Sudanese or Nubian slave who escapes from Mahmoud, her master. Although on the margin, Ni'ma's presence is strongly felt throughout the narrative. Her story is central to Mahmoud's stunted growth as his betrayal of the revolution parallels his betrayal of Ni'ma, and his failure to reach maturity, as a protagonist of a bildungsroman reflects that of the nation. I argue that Ni'ma's agency—seen in her decision to leave Mahmoud's house—indicts a homogenizing late-nineteenth-century Egyptian nationalist project whose legacy is seen today in continued marginalization of Nubian, Siwan, and female voices.[21]

Very little discussion has been devoted to Ni'ma due to her marginality. Ni'ma, the most marginalized character, because dark, woman, slave, and possibly foreign, deserves some attention. Condensed in less than five pages, Ni'ma's life story is filtered through the Egyptian "white," male point of view of her master, Mahmoud, who realizes a little too late that he loves her. Yet, this minor character occupies a major position in a novel that narrates the events of the 1881–2 Urabi Revolution and the subsequent British occupation of 1882. Mahmoud's various recollections of Ni'ma prod him to evaluate the Egyptian nationalist project, exposing its male-, white-centric orientation and questioning his own incrimination in its gender and racial politics. Thus, Ni'ma's presence, or rather her absence, indicts a nationalist identity that is built on the exclusion of gender and ethnic minorities.

Her real name unknown even to herself, Ni'ma is made to represent an essence of Egypt and is therefore denied her history and memory except as an exotic, jasmine-scented Scheherazade whose folktales captivate Mahmoud and whose sexuality satiates him. Despite her minimal appearances and the near-total absence of her voice—she is given only three utterances in the novel—Ni'ma acts agentially, resisting epistemic violence by a text that forces on her an identity other than her own due to her status as an enslaved person.

Despite efforts by Muhammad Ali and his descendants to curtail slavery in nineteenth-century Egypt the practice thrived as slave ownership was a sign of social status. According to John Hunwick enslaved males and females in Egypt, as in much of the Mediterranean Muslim world, were mainly used as domestic servants, with females additionally serving as concubines, wet-nurses, and nannies.[22] Muhammad Ali's 1821 conquest of Sudan had transformed the slave trade into a highly lucrative business. By mid-century, Egypt received thousands of enslaved people directly from south Sudan. As a result, slave ownership, heretofore a privilege of the Ottoman elite, became accessible to Egyptian notables so that, in the 1880s, "almost every household could own at least one."[23] Much in opposition to Islamic law, which identifies religious war as the only avenue for acquiring slaves, enslaved persons were often procured through violent raids.[24] It is estimated in Terence Walz's sources that "as many as 800,000 Africans were forcibly settled in … [Egypt] during the eighteenth and nineteenth centuries."[25] The 1848 Cairo census suggests that there were around 15,000 trans-Saharan Africans, freed and enslaved, living in Cairo only.[26]

Mahmoud's reminiscences, if taken literally, identify him as a twenty-year-old at the time of the British occupation of 1882, marking 1862 as his year of birth. Ni'ma seems to have joined the household at a time when Mahmoud is old enough not only to retain memories but to possess an awareness of his status vis-à-vis slaves. His childhood memories include her arrival at their house, her position as a slave purchased to help his mother with household chores, as well as the fact that neither she nor anyone else knew her parents' names. This puts Mahmoud between the ages of seven and nine. If, to Mahmoud's child's eyes, Ni'ma looks like a "*tifla saghira*" (small child),[27] we can assume that she enters the household at the age of three or four, putting her year of birth at 1866–7 and making her at least sixteen years old at the time of the Urabi Revolution.

The first mention of Ni'ma discloses quite a bit about her history. Mahmoud remembers her as "*Ni'ma al-samra*" (31), (Ni'ma the tan-skinned woman),[28] a descriptor that, Walz observes, had by the nineteenth century in Egypt become one of three standard colors used to refer to enslaved individuals. Identified by complexion rather than by ethnicity, Black slaves were classified as "black (*aswad*) [feminine, *sawda'*], brown (*asmar*) [feminine, *samra'*] and *habashi* [feminine, *habashiyya*]" denoting Ethiopian, who were especially prized for their presumed intelligence and exceptional good looks.[29] Kenneth Cuno explains that the term *'aswad* or *sudani* was reserved for darker Africans living in the sub-Saharan region of *bilad al-Sudan*, literally, the lands of the Blacks.[30] In the Egyptian and Turco-Egyptian writing on the region that Powell examines, and in the Egyptian nineteenth-century nationalist imaginary as well, the further south one traveled the darker people became, signaling further descent into savagery.[31] Nubian women, Hunwick points out, were also popular as concubines in Egypt.[32]

Historically Christian and independent Nubia had held hegemony over the Nile Valley from about the fifteenth century until the Turco-Egyptian invasion of 1821. After the seventh-century Muslim conquest of Egypt, Nubia became a major slave supplier for Egypt.[33] However, as Jay Spaulding states, Egypt's repeated invasions in the fourteenth and fifteenth centuries led to the conversion to Islam of many northern people and to an influx of Nubian slaves in the Islamic world, for which the Turco-Egyptian administration was particularly hungry.[34] Given Egyptian proclivity to Nubian concubines and taking into account Ni'ma's description as *samra'*, rather than *sawda'*, or *habashiyya*, it is safe to assume that she is either Nubian or northern Sudanese—in all probability a non-Arabic speaker and a non-Muslim, but still allowing for the possibility that she is Muslim.

Mahmoud's description imbues Ni'ma with a Nile Valley narrative that subsumes her in the Egyptian-centric nationalist rhetoric of the inseparability of the Nile Valley, particularly Egypt and Sudan. She is made to represent the Nile itself, the lifeblood of Egypt, and becomes in Mahmoud's memory interchangeable with an authentic Egypt as when he says, "When she drew close to me I'd smell the penetrating scent of Egyptian jasmine that seemed to spring from the very pores of her skin" (86). He sees in her a reflection of Egypt's sovereignty over Sudan. She is the Nile that unites both countries; "Dusky Ni'ma got her name from the colour [*sic*] of her smooth, clear, golden-brown skin, which was like the colour [*sic*] of the Nile in flood. They couldn't think of a truer description for that unique colour [*sic*]" (84). Evoking the color of the Nile at flood time, Ni'ma is no longer an individual in her own right.

Ni'ma turns into a symbol representing the true earth of Egypt. She is the silt whose deposits give the Nile its reddish hue during the flood. Colonized sexually as well as culturally, Ni'ma's body is the map upon which Egyptian nationalism is written. She is the land over which Egypt holds mastery. This stance, what Powell calls the "colonized colonizer," was born in Egypt at the end of Muhammad Ali's reign and emerged as a full-fledged nationalist ideology in the 1870s. This dualistic nationalism, again Powell's words, where Egyptian nationalists called for Egypt's independence yet saw Sudan as rightfully belonging to Egypt, continued to be polished especially during the British reconquest of Sudan from 1898 to 1899 so that "by 1919 there was a well-established slogan that called for 'the unity of the Nile Valley.'"[35]

Egypt's image of Sudan was more hierarchical than fraternal, and Powell finds that the image that Egyptian nationalists projected of Sudan did not differ much from British orientalist depictions of Egypt. Many Egyptian nationalists, including Mustafa Kamil (1874–1908), believed that Egypt's mastery over Sudan was nonnegotiable seeing meddling in the Sudan issue as an encroachment upon Egypt's right over Sudan. They used the language of the civilizing mission claiming that enslaved women were educated into Islam and domesticity. Images of Black individuals (free and enslaved) as protégés of benevolent Egyptians fed the discourse of the Egyptian civilizing mission conferring on Egyptians a hypothetical whiteness that inferred civilization.[36] Mustafa Kamil's speeches about Sudan, for example, created an image of Black savagery and barbarity in addition to fanaticism that only white, Muslim Egyptians knew how to tame.[37] Concurrent with the 1882 British occupation, Ni'ma's disappearance foreshadows Egypt's imminent loss of Sudan. At the time, support for the Mahdi's forces grew, culminating in the 1884 rebellion against Egyptian rule, after which Mahdi took control of Sudan.[38]

Ni'ma's life before slavery can only be imagined. However, we can assume that she was separated from her family either at initial kidnapping or along the way. If Ni'ma's village is in the Nuba Mountains in South Kordofan, Sudan, then like other Sudanese slaves from the Nuba Mountains, Ni'ma has walked some or most of the way from Sudan to Cairo on foot.[39] Or, if they had mercy on the small child, like they sometimes did, the *jallaba* (slave traders), may have let Ni'ma ride. So exhausting and treacherous was the journey up the Nile Valley or across the desert that, in many ways, it resembled the Middle Passage.[40]

Ni'ma is totally transplanted and severed not only from familial, ethnic, geographic, and linguistic roots, but from memory as well. Seized at the age of three or four, she is denied the chance to transfer basic early childhood memories into adulthood—such as her name and the names of her parents. As Mahmoud recounts, "and I doubt whether anyone, herself [Ni'ma] perhaps included, knew the names of her father or mother" (84–5). Although Mahmoud once notes that Ni'ma has lost her mother as a young child, it is doubtful that either he, or his father, know anything about her family history. By the time Ni'ma makes it to their house, she has probably passed through several slave traders who would not have cared to keep straight the facts about a little Black slave girl's family origins even if that were possible, considering the number of slaves they trafficked in. By killing the mother, Mahmoud's family relieves itself of any lingering guilt associated with Ni'ma's induction into the household as a human commodity. If anything, according to Ehud Toledano, "the suffering and high mortality that accompanied the slave trade from the sources of supply to the [Ottoman] Empire—if at all known to the majority of slave-holders—were vague and removed notions; they happened in distant and unfamiliar countries and did not seem very real in Istanbul and the other Ottoman cities."[41] Thoughts of Niʿma's trauma when forcefully torn away from mother and siblings can be replaced with complacency about raising/civilizing a poor, dark, orphaned girl. If Niʿma is her given name, she may have descended from a Muslim/monotheistic family and, like other enslaved individuals, been unlawfully captured into slavery.[42] Or, Niʿma may be the name given her by slave traders, who often, as Hunwick writes, bestowed on their charge names indicating happiness, good fortune, and, in Niʿma's case, grace.[43]

Niʿma's arrival at Mahmoud's house as a small child is a moment of birth for her. She has no history, no memory, no language that they can understand, and no name. She enters the household as a worker, but also as a signifier of upward mobility. Mahmoud's father, the wealthy merchant, "[buys] her from the Slavers' Market as a young girl to help [Mahmoud's] mother with the housework," (84–5) and to cement his status as an affluent merchant and owner of a "large house full of slave girls and servants" (11). As children, Niʿma and Mahmoud are inseparable to the point where Mahmoud considers her closer to him than his own brother. Niʿma enthralls him with fantastic tales about enchanted kings and ruthless villains. When she reaches puberty, as was the custom, she is gifted to Mahmoud as a concubine.[44]

Niʿma asserts her agency three times in the novel, first, through storytelling, second through her resolve to stay with Mahmoud even after the family's bankruptcy, and, finally, through her escape from Mahmoud's house. In so doing, she insists on having her voice heard over the narrative's persistent marginalization. Additionally, she resists the discourse of the unity of the Nile Valley where unity leads to an invisibility that highlights only Egypt's dominance.

Niʿma invents herself as a skilled Scheherazade who inserts her own voice in narratives by rewriting the same fantastic story with each retelling. When she recounts stories of enchanted kings and captive princesses, she holds power. She speaks and Mahmoud listens, completely enraptured by her captivating performances; "her voice would tremble as she told of how the villain cast a spell on the good king and seized his throne after turning him into an ape … Niʿma's eyes would overflow with tears as they took the captive princess to marry the evil king, and then her face would shine with joy when the handsome prince arrived" (85). He wonders whether she has heard these stories from her deceased mother or from other slave girls. However, having been captured at a very young age, Ni'ma has no recollection of bedtime stories or folktales her mother may have told her. She *is* the author of her own tales. The stories that she tells are her attempt to insert her voice, to have some autonomy by casting herself as active author and creator rather than passive slave.

Ni'ma's second act of agency, seen in her determination to stay after the family's loss of fortune, is more obvious in the original Arabic edition than in the English translation. Whereas in Arabic Mahmoud recounts that Ni'ma' stayed in the house "*hatta ba'd iflas 'abi*" (*even after* my father went bankrupt),[45] the English edition has Mahmoud saying, "Ni'ma remained in the house *until* my father went bankrupt" (85, emphasis added). Mahmoud then adds that his father "*set free* most of the servants and slave girls, while *the rest fled* and none remained after his death except her [Ni'ma] and the old female servant who had been in my mother's service her whole life."[46] While the English translation uses "*found homes* for most of the servants" (85, emphasis added) instead of "set free," the Arabic "*sarraha*" carries the possibility of either being set up in a new home or being released from slavery—a detail relevant to my next point about Ni'ma's alternatives.

It is not unreasonable, then, to assume that Ni'ma has options. Mahmoud's recollections reveal a master who is intent upon either setting up his slaves in good homes or emancipating them, the latter seen as a pious act in Islamic law whether done posthumously or during one's lifetime.[47] If Mahmoud's father fails to ask Ni'ma which path she prefers, she, on the other hand, does not avail herself of the third alternative of fleeing the house. The fact that this is the only life she has ever known should not diminish Ni'ma's choice not to run away. However, Ni'ma's most authoritative assertion of her agency figures in her final escape from Mahmoud's house.

Ni'ma's flight from the house is an act of self-ownership, and a very brave one at that, considering the dangers faced by runaway slaves in nineteenth-century Egypt. She reaches that resolution upon realizing that despite her love for Mahmoud and his for her, he sees her primarily as a (sexual) commodity. As such, her relationship with Mahmoud mimics Sudan's relationship with Egypt as one of mastery despite the discourse of fraternity. The three utterances that the novel grants her reveal the dichotomous ways she and Mahmoud view each other. For Niʿma, he is master, friend and life partner, and the only man she has ever loved. For the promiscuous Mahmoud, she is one—albeit the only one he has ever loved—among countless other free and slave women with whom he has had sexual relations. Niʿma is wise enough to recognize her weak position as an enslaved person. Rather than confront Mahmoud, she chooses the path of sly civility (outwardly complying with him while resisting inwardly by acting upon her thoughts):[48] "She asked me, as she lay next to me on the bed, 'Does My Master Mahmoud love me?' I rebuked her: 'What nonsense is that, girl? If you talk like that again, I'll throw you out on to the street!' She laughed and said, 'You're right, Master Mahmoud. Nonsense.' And she buried her head in my chest, repeating in the midst of her laughter, 'What nonsense!'" (87). Niʿma will only be treated as a full-fledged individual with human rights. Preferring to wrest her own freedom at any risk at the age of sixteen, she withdraws from Mahmoud's life. He finally recognizes her as an individual when he remembers her confident action in response to his threat, "but then she went out on her own into the street and disappeared" (88).

Nineteenth-century Egyptian streets were inhospitable sites for the dark-complexioned, as indicated by both Walz and Liat Kozma. Emancipated slaves had to carry their manumission documents at all times. Otherwise, they risked arrest, imprisonment, and an ill-fated trip to the slave market to be reentered into bondage.[49] Runaway slaves were found and captured, their owners usually accusing them of stealing as a ploy.[50] Local police and street watchmen made sure that Black people had reasons legitimating their presence in unusual locales. This, Walz notes, accounted for miraculous apprehensions of fugitive slaves, located many months following their disappearance in as far-flung locations as Upper Egypt, by masters and slave merchants operating from Cairo. Such measures made it very hard for the enslaved to escape.[51] For Niʿma, this means that she would have had a hard time evading the police. Obtaining freedom did not always lead to happiness either. If we accept Baer's theory, the absence of a free labor market in Egypt made it difficult for many slaves to find jobs. Many women became prostitutes, and many men became gang robbers, while many others chose to go back to slavery, preferring the safety of food and shelter to the insecurity of freedom.[52] This is why Mahmoud looks for Niʿma in hospitals, police stations, prisons, and brothels.

Lying on the margins of the story but ever present in Mahmoud's consciousness, Niʿma's character critiques both Egypt's colonizing efforts in Sudan and a nationalist vision whose shape has expanded only modestly since the nineteenth century. Mahmoud's ill-fated response to her question referred to earlier on marks his participation in an exclusionary ideology that has made an Other out of Egypt's minorities. Far from fraternal or familial, their interaction preserves the class structure that is itself built on the civilizational hierarchy to which, as noted earlier on, many Egyptian nationalists subscribed. Although a life-long companion, Niʿma still addresses Mahmoud as "*sayyidi*" (my master)[53] while he threatens to strip her of the "fictive-kin relationship" formed with his family, to use Ehud Toledano's term.[54] Her disappearance at the dawn of the Urabi Revolution and the subsequent British occupation of 1882 points to the fissures in the national imaginary as it foresees Egypt's "loss" of Sudan. Even after her departure, Niʿma insists on inserting herself in the narrative through Mahmoud's dreams.

(In)Formative Dreams

Dreams in Muslim worldview, and particularly in Sufism, the mystical branch of Islam, are accorded more importance than secular and Western frameworks grant them. More than just a jumbled world of suppressed subconscious desires, they are considered a " 'communicative technology' between the living and the dead," where sleepers may receive truths through communication with the deceased.[55] In much of the Muslim world, Sufi or not, dreams are part of the social and cultural aspects of life and are seen as an important part in cosmology. This manifests in the popularity of dream interpretation shows and websites on which many dreamers rely for the interpretation of their dreams.[56] Unlike their position in secular logic, dreams from a Muslim standpoint are more connected to daily life and sometimes to major life decisions.[57] In fact, one method of decision-making takes the form of *istikhāra*, a prayer invoking God for guidance, after which some Muslims believe that their answer will be delivered in a dream.[58]

However, because not all dreams are regarded equally in Islam, they fall into three types. First, *ru'ya* (pl. *ru'a*), which in Sufi tradition serves an "epistemic function, namely communicating knowledge not readily available otherwise,"[59] is a veridic dream where sleepers see the prophet, Sufi saints, or other dead people with a message to deliver. These visions may be revelatory, validatory, advisory, or cautionary and the message may be relayed directly or symbolically.[60] Second, *hulm* (pl. *ahlam*, also referred to as *adghath ahlam*); a dream may, in Freudian terms, reflect the memories, subconscious hopes and desires of the dreamer, and extend to include meaningless everyday dreams. Finally, occupying the lowest rung are false dreams inspired by the devil.[61] It is the first type, *ru'ya* or the true dream, that concerns us here owing to the epistemic qualities—real or perceived—that it shares with the bildungsroman.

Much in the same way that the bildungsroman is a medium for the protagonist's growth, *ru'ya* offers dreamers spiritual growth particularly to Sufis as they "integrate… such 'big' dreams into their journey towards their higher self."[62] Concerned with reaching knowledge and spiritual purity as a means of uniting with/annihilation in the Divine, Sufism relies on introspection, seen as a journey. Thus, in Sufism, and in the bildungsroman as well, an individual undertakes a journey—physical, spiritual, or both.[63] In this case, dreams providing guidance are instrumental to the Sufi journey of education and self-discovery as they are understood as "inner 'tastes' … of the divine."[64] For this reason, dream narratives abound in Sufism. Iain Edgar explains that in Sufism, as in Jungian psychology, veridic dreams are the "potential connection between the unconscious and the conscious mind. So, in Sufism the imagination and especially the true dream is the bridge between the sensible world and the archetypal intelligible world."[65] In order to achieve inner cleansing, Llewellyn Vaughan-Lee explains, travelers on the path toward God should be ready to explore the dark recesses of their consciousness, working through every little detail while showing willingness to shed all vestiges of material existence.[66]

Sufi attitudes toward dreams, however, are sometimes puzzlingly at odds with the significance of the medium in Islam and Sufism where a distinct line does not separate dreams from reality. In fact, according to Muslim worldview, dreaming and waking states ambiguously coexist and at times swap positions as evident in the oft-quoted saying that "people are asleep, and when they die, they awake."[67] Yet, in the same way that many Sufis either reject or embrace the moniker "Sufi," there are others who dismiss dreams as a way of solving problems even as they rely on them as a means of communication with a world beyond this material world, or what Amira Mittermaier calls "the Elsewhere"—in Muslim terms the *barzakh*; an in-between world where souls of the dead exist until the end of time.

On the other hand, some Sufi literature goes so far as to outline the process through which one can prepare oneself to receive *ru'ya*. *Dhikr* (invocation or remembrance of God), is one such method that is seen as a transformative process cleansing the heart and/or the spirit and clearing the way for *ru'ya*.[68] According to Sufi beliefs, farers on the path toward the Divine may receive messages through *ru'ya* delivered by inner guides either known to them in their waking world or in the world of dreams.[69] Although traditional dream literature tends to show *ru'ya* as the privilege of male figures of high religious and political stature, women, common people, and even the morally weak—and therefore Mahmoud—can have dream-visions.[70] Sufism provides the perfect vehicle for Taher—and other Arab writers, such as Naguib Mahfouz, Tayeb Salih, and Ibrahim al-Koni, whom Ziad Elmarsafy discusses—to evaluate political life and reflect on the novel and Arab identity.[71]

That Mahmoud has meaningful dreams once in Siwa is not surprising given his Sufi-tinged background as well as the region's own connection to Sufism. Mahmoud fondly remembers his father's weekly *dhikr* at the family house in which he fervently participated, and which no other *dhikr* event has surpassed. As Matthew Ellis explains, Siwa itself has a connection with Sufism through the Sanusiyya brotherhood, who, though settled in Libya, established several *zawaya* (sing. *zawya*; Sufi mosque), and whose power in the nineteenth century enabled them to play an intermediary role in Siwan affairs on behalf of the Egyptian government.[72]

Siwa's reputation for resisting invaders is germane to Mahmoud's self-quest. At the time of Mahmoud's official journey, Siwan dislike for strangers, their fierceness in the face of enemies, and their solidarity at times of war regardless of internal differences were no secret.[73] Indeed, Egypt's conquest of the region in 1820 did not put an end to the people's desire for sovereignty as Siwans stopped paying annual taxes to Cairo in 1829, 1839, 1844, 1852, and 1893, each time incurring the wrath of the Egyptian government.[74]

Thus, not only does Mahmoud grow up in a culture that values dreams, but he also embarks on a journey across the desert toward a destination with Sufi associations and a reputation for great warriorship, not to mention a firm dislike for foreign intrusion. Mahmoud is, therefore, in Siwa in his capacity as Sufi dreamer, renegade hero, cruel lover, as well as colonized colonizer. In Sufi understanding, his journey across the desert en route to Siwa is as much metaphorical as it is spatial/geographical. Mahmoud travels inward to explore his consciousness before he can reach knowledge about his several selves. One might say that by arriving in Siwa, he has reached the depths of his and Egypt's soul. In Youssef's words, Siwa becomes a "spatial emblem of self-quest, in which characters embark on journeys that … may or may not change their perspectives on themselves and others."[75] Nermin Haikal, who reads the novel through trauma theory, concludes that Mahmoud's journey across the desert brings him face to face with his past trauma, seen in his betrayal of the revolution.[76] Placed in the unfamiliar setting of Siwa, Mahmoud faces his self-alienation as he undergoes what Niʿma and the Siwans have experienced through linguistic and cultural estrangement. Such a position defamiliarizes his past life, granting him the opportunity to evaluate his own past from an outsider's perspective.

In this sense, his dreams are (in)formative. First, they are informative since, by letting Mahmoud recognize his agency for past actions, they disabuse the middle-aged protagonist of his self-created victim persona. Second, they are formative in that they afford him the opportunity to refashion himself into someone who takes responsibility for his actions. Consequently, Mahmoud's three dreams mark a progression on the path of self-examination. By prodding him to confront his personal and political disloyalty, they open up a space for critiquing the racial and patriarchal structures upon which Egyptian identity rests. At the same time, they pinpoint Egyptians' own incrimination in such exclusionary ideologies, which, as mentioned earlier on, presuppose "white," Arabic-speaking, Egyptian males as the norm. To evoke both Sufi dream terminology and bildungsroman narrative, Maleeka and Niʿma—the two marginalized women whom Mahmoud wrongs irreparably—alternately figure as his guides/mentors who reveal to him the truth about himself and, in the process, insert minority women's histories in the national narrative. It is these enlightening dreams that push Mahmoud toward his final act of suicide or self-martyrdom, as will be discussed further on.

Details from Mahmoud's waking and sleeping states converge to educate him about his true self. He dreams twice of Niʿma with an intervening dream of Maleeka. His constant soul-searching reveals four key moments that expose his dark side to himself and reflect his relationship with the bildungsroman and society: first, his rejection of Niʿma, which coincides with the revolution; second, his subsequent decision to condemn the revolution; third, his moment of hesitation when a huge stone falls from a temple ceiling, almost killing a Siwan boy; and, finally, his harsh treatment of Maleeka causing Catherine to shove her out of their house, exposing her to her people as the ghoul-woman. Niʿma's disappearance coincides with the end of the Urabi Revolution, which brings about the beginning of the British occupation, followed by Mahmoud's betrayal of the revolution. Thus, the personal is intertwined with the political and his hesitation during the boulder incident further prompts his Sufi introspection of previous as well as current stances, particularly his position as colonizer in Siwa and his failure to protect Maleeka.

The first dream, of which Mahmoud only remembers Niʿma's smiling face, occurs shortly after his arrival in Siwa and, thus, following his descent into the innermost corners of his consciousness. Besides inaugurating his recognition of guilt, this dream marks a shift in the way he views himself as he changes position from victim to perpetrator. He understands a little too late that he loves Niʿma, that he is only whole with her, and that he has known both love and pleasure only with her. Lamenting her loss on the heels of his rejection of her love, Mahmoud first brands her disappearance as betrayal before admitting his own agency: "I tell myself it was just another betrayal, but then I ask myself, 'And who, my dear Major Shahriyar, was the betrayer?'" (88). Mahmoud's sarcastic evocation of Shahriyar is an admission of his objectification of women in general and Niʿma in particular. Such admission of guilt denotes responsiveness to new evaluations of his past.

Along with dreams, the boulder incident acts as a stimulant that shocks Mahmoud out of his delusion. Lying between his first plunge into his consciousness after the first dream and his two subsequent dreams, the boulder accident precipitates his self-knowledge by triggering relentless introspection leading to full-on self-confrontation. It is this event that brings Mahmoud face to face with his agency in all past events. Paradoxically, it is an agency that has landed him in a state of stasis, arresting his development. Mahmoud recognizes his circular pattern—always backing down, submitting either to fear or authority or both, he ends where he started. His pattern in handling this incident mimics his role in the Urabi Revolution where initial enthusiasm is cut short by hesitation caused by fear for his life. Mahmoud rushes to save the Siwan boy, stops when he realizes he could die, then throws himself on top of his petty officer and the boy. This prompts him to evaluate his (in)action with reference to the revolution and Ni'ma.

In reassessing his role during the bombardment of Alexandria, Mahmoud interrogates concepts such as nationalism and heroism, exposing his false heroism and acknowledging as real heroes un-uniformed subaltern "men of the native population, wearing *gallabiyas*" and women who "climbed up to the forts and were wounded and never thought of themselves as heroines or martyrs" (135). Significant is his inclusion of acts of heroism by nonelite and gendered members of society in contrast to his trivial role "gallop[ing]" (135) in front of carts carrying the dead and the wounded. This gestures to an imminent maturity prompting him to re-draw the boundaries of Egyptian identity in a way that includes all of its fragments.

With newfound clarity, Mahmoud, delving deeper in his consciousness, begins to acknowledge his lie, concluding that his war heroism, like his false hero status after the stone incident, is just a sham. With unforgiving irony, he reflects on the grotesqueness of his injury—an injury not acquired on the battlefield but occurring casually. In revisiting the events, Mahmoud is confronted with his own agency, where, after the occupation, he makes the choice to bow down to the ruling powers to save his skin.

In this self-interrogation, Mahmoud realizes that it was not colonialism, his fellow officer's advice, or another's treason, but rather his own complicity in the conspiracy against Egypt that has caused his self-alienation and stunted his personal, professional, and political progress. Mahmoud's reconciliation with the sociopolitical order, seen as maturity in the traditional bildungsroman, in his case, becomes coterminous with treason. Mahmoud's self-reflection leads him to recognize his imprisonment in an eternal state of youth—his inability to mature as an individual and commit to a stance. He discovers that all four events point to his inability to pursue an action to the end: "The problem is precisely you, my dear major! It's no good in this world being half good and half bad, half a patriot and half a traitor, half brave and half a coward, half a believer and half a womanizer. Always in the middle. … Never was I one person, complete on the inside" (216). Mahmoud's cynicism, seen in the way he addresses himself as "my dear major," underscores his disillusionment with himself. As he locates his hesitance, he comes nearer to a critique of a conflicted Nile Valley identity whose discourse of inclusion is more exclusionary due to its hierarchical underpinnings. This lucidness leads to his second dream—a nightmare where Maleeka, as a frightful, red-eyed ghoul, tries to kill him. Qualifying as a dream from the devil, in Muslim and Sufi understanding, this nightmare is nevertheless significant since in acting as his double, Maleeka reveals to Mahmoud the darkness of his soul, spurring his growth.

Mahmoud's remorse toward Maleeka, his earlier acknowledgement of Niʿma's agency in staying with the family, then in leaving him, signal progress toward seeing both women—and therefore other minorities—as individuals. Gradually awakening to his own role as colonizer in Siwa, Mahmoud traces the overlap between the nationalist and colonialist paradigms as models that restrict plurality by positing a singular model for modernity. He begins to mature as he recognizes not only his agency in self-subjugation but also his colonizing role with the Siwans: "We didn't come to them as brothers, but as conquerors. We didn't treat them as though they were fellow citizens but as though they were a colonized people who had to pay their taxes to the conquerors, like it or not. … We practice the law of might here just as the British practice it there" (164). Mahmoud finally sees that the success of the nationalist project hinges on full inclusion of other groups as equals, not as lesser subjects in need of civilization, or subjects whose meager wealth is to be exploited. His education reflects a conviction among many contemporary writers, including Taher, that "difference is both a reality and a value in modern Egypt," to quote Youssef. This is demonstrated by their "desire to represent the historical and cultural experiences of the Nubian and Amazigh communities as integral parts of the larger whole of Egypt's complex culture and historical narrative."[77]

As Mahmoud recognizes himself as an agent in his and Egypt's subjugation, Egypt too emerges at once as victim and agent, colonized and colonizer. While Egypt was compelled to submit to the British occupation, corrupt government authorities and the Khedive made the country an agent in its own subjugation. Egypt, too, has forced its own policies on the Siwans, imposing exorbitant taxes and ignoring their conditions. Thus, while the British social order is presented as unjust and impervious to reason, the Egyptian government is equally incriminated.

Through the temple and other ruins, *Sunset Oasis* questions the various histories, or nationalist ideologies, that Egyptians have embraced at one point or another and finds them restrictive. As it does so, the novel foregrounds the fictionality of the past while it interrogates fictive notions of belonging. All of these fictive ethnicities prove inflexible, excluding certain ethnic groups and causing strife rather than harmony. For example, through Wasfi, the blond Circassian officer who refers to the ancient Egyptians as *his* ancestors, the novel interrogates Pharaonism and Ottomanism. The former, a short-lived form of nationalism popular at the end of the nineteenth century until the 1940s, acted as an inclusive Egyptian form of belonging that united Muslims and Christians by promoting pride in Egypt's ancient past and ancestry.[78] Although sympathetic to the Urabi Revolution, the novel also uses Wasfi to question Ottomanism as a national identity, which the revolution adopted. In fact, like several other Egyptian intellectuals, Taher believes the Ottomans to be partly responsible for the French and, later, British colonization of Egypt. In *Abnaa Rifa'a*, he adopts the view of Egyptian scholar and geographer Gamal Hamdan, presenting the Ottoman Empire as a religious colonialism, in which Turkey's suzerainties are colonies of the metropole. Instead of placing all blame on the West, Taher blames the Ottoman Empire for Egypt's intellectual stagnation, arguing that Turkey facilitated the West's domination of Egypt by neglecting education.[79]

Read in light of Mahmoud's denunciation of the Khedive as the real traitor, the novel rejects the revolution's Ottomanism.[80] Wasfi's interest in his so-called ancestors, however, prompts Mahmoud to reflect on Egyptian-Ottoman relations and finds in them an enactment of imperial relations; of the master-servant relation, concluding that Wasfi admires only the Pharaohs—the masters who ruled a community of Egyptian slaves. Finally, the novel critiques Egyptian nationalism, demonstrating how Egyptians themselves have assumed a colonial role in relation to Siwans. They do not understand the Siwan language—a fact that has engendered hatred toward Egyptians and created tensions between Siwan tribal leaders depending on whether they studied at al-Azhar Mosque in Egypt or at al-Zeitouna Mosque in Tunisia.

Sunset Oasis reflects a widespread disenchantment with the failure of the 1952 Revolution to live up to is promises. By refusing to share power, the post-1952 regime replicated the master-servant discourse about which Wasfi and Mahmoud disagree.[81] Comparing England and France to Egypt, Wasfi declares that a successful government is one that is run by strong politicians, not by the mob. Playing on the minor difference in Arabic between *al-sasa* (politicians) and *al-sada* (masters), Mahmoud sarcastically corrects him saying *al-sada*, "the masters" (268). Taher's disappointment with the 1952 legacy, represented in Mubarak's era, occasions his nostalgia for the Urabi era as the direct heir to the project of Egyptian enlightenment mapped out by nineteenth-century Egyptian intellectuals. According to al-Bahaa Hussein, Taher believed that the only successful project in Egypt was not Turcification, Westernization, or liberalism but that mapped out by intellectuals in the nineteenth century. In his view, this project succeeded because it provided national unity, national independence, social justice, and liberty for women. It was a vision planned by intellectuals, supported by society, and practiced by politicians at different times up until Nasser destroyed it by marginalizing the intellectuals.[82] Yet, the text's portrayal of the various peripheries of Egyptian society offers a critique of this project.

In spite of the death imagery, from a Muslim viewpoint Mahmoud's final vision carries auspicious symbols that promise relief, self-reconciliation, maturity, and a chance at a new life for him and for Egypt as well. This *ru'ya* is important as it acts as Mahmoud's final lesson initiating his action and his contradictory progress toward maturity through death. In keeping with Muslim traditions of dream interpretation, analysis of Mahmoud's dreams will bear in mind his specific gender, social, moral, marital, and professional contexts. In this final dream, Mahmoud sees himself receiving condolences at his own memorial service, except there are no guests and the sheikh who is supposed to recite the Quran is not reciting but laughing inaudibly. The funeral marquee, then, transforms into a lush garden with children at play and Mahmoud, carrying his own shroud, asks an elderly man the direction to the cemetery. Next he finds himself on the shore of a river with dangling ivy trees,[83] where he is holding hands with a beautiful girl who turns out to be Ni'ma sporting a new hair color. They get on a boat and Ni'ma, scared, points to a crocodile that is about to attack them. Together, they jump to the riverbank and, running over the water, end up safely in the marquee.

This vision promises happiness and self-reconciliation. The assurance of relief from a huge burden, brought about by dreaming of one's own memorial service, is supplemented by the safety that the cemetery provides to the anxious. Moving from an arid to a lush spot denotes a return to the right path, green also signifying happiness, reunion, and a happy future. Witnessing children at play foretells victory over hardships. Thus, Mahmoud is promised relief from the burden of betraying Ni'ma, Maleeka, and the revolution. His final actions, by returning him to his true self, will reduce anxiety over past decisions and bring him happiness through a reunion with himself and possibly with Ni'ma in a better world. Mahmoud's vision also suggests victory over personal and professional hardships since he is dealing with conspiracies at work, symbolized here by the menacing crocodile and the shroud that he carries. Immediately following the vision, Mahmoud discovers that Wasfi, the much younger Turkish officer sent by the pro-British government to aid him, is, in fact, spying on him. Unbeknownst to Mahmoud, and as per the British official's instructions, Wasfi is in cahoots with Sheikh Sabir, patriarch of the Eastern tribe, playing the game of divide and conquer. That Mahmoud dreams that he is riding a boat in clear water indicates good tidings, while jumping from the river to the bank implies protection from evil and victory over enemies. Finally, the act of walking on water in a river indicates good intentions and good faith. Although Mahmoud suspects that the sheikh in the marquee is Sheikh Sabir, the laughing reciter in the dream is a good omen.[84]

Bringing him lucidity, Mahmoud's vision materializes gradually through two incidents that usher in maturity: his confrontation with Wasfi and his final act of suicide. In a conversation with Wasfi about the British occupation and the Urabi Revolution, Mahmoud finally finds the courage to declare that Ahmed Urabi "had more honour [*sic*] than ten khedives put together" (285). Shortly after, he confesses that "it's twenty years too late to say that, my dear major! And you should have said it to someone other than Wasfi!" (285). A preliminary step toward maturity, Mahmoud's retort illustrates that he is finally taking a stance and defending it to the end. His suicide figures as the crowning moment of this newfound enlightenment, ironically occurring at the moment of his death. This final act is born out of annoyance with Catherine's insistence on finding evidence pointing to Alexander the Great's burial in Siwa. Catherine is so engrossed in presenting her findings to Mahmoud and her sister, Fiona, that she does not notice her sister dying.

It is useful to revisit two symbols from Mahmoud's vision: the shroud and the ivy trees lining the riverbank. First, besides signifying conspiracies at work, the image of Mahmoud carrying his own shroud bears two more meanings, one dream-related and the other cultural, both of which are relevant here. First, in indicating a leaning toward adultery the shroud may refer to Mahmoud's love for Fiona whose Irish folktale storytelling makes her Ni'ma's double. At a cultural level, carrying one's own shroud symbolizes intentional martyrdom, in which case it foreshadows Mahmoud's suicide reincarnated as a willingness to die for the nation. Mahmoud commits suicide by blowing up the Umm Ebeida temple while inside it. In addition to the ivy trees, which symbolize self-healing, by taking the conscious decision to sacrifice his own life for that of the nation, Mahmoud becomes an agent in his own self-healing. Therefore, from a literary perspective, Mahmoud taking condolences at his own funeral foretells his self-initiated death.

Mahmoud's final act of suicide is a resolution to carry out an act to the end and to do it in such a manner as to preclude further marginalization of groups and, thus, enable a future without a restricting past. Symbolically, his fragmented self and his inability to mature politically stand for the fragmentation of a nation whose ethnic and gender minorities are only partially included in its full mosaic. The Umm Ebeida temple plays a pivotal role in the novel. The site of Mahmoud's epiphany and burial as well as the location of Catherine's creative theory about Alexander the Great, it represents not only different pasts, and evaluations of the past, but also layers of subjugation of certain groups by others. It is an ancient Egyptian temple, assimilated under Greek rule, currently standing on Egyptian/Siwan territory surrounded by Siwans who do not glorify this part of Egypt's past because they view ancient Egyptians as infidels. In other words, the temple is the site of conflict over history/histories.

Noting the temple as the site where the personal converges with the political, Youssef states that Mahmoud's "failure to materialize his love signifies his impotence in resolving the predicament of colonial alienation and functions as a precursor to his end as a colonial subject. Mahmud's anguish and sense of defeat lead to his suicide at the temple of Amun, a site that symbolized foreign infatuation with Egypt, its treasures, and its history."[85] Mahmoud's suicide inspires hope since by destroying the temple, the subject of conflict over history and definitions of Egypt, he frees Egyptians to start defining themselves anew. He destroys two restrictive narratives: one which confines Egyptian greatness to the past, while claiming that contemporary Egyptians need to be civilized, and another corollary narrative that consoles Egyptians with their glorious past, almost excusing their current petrification. In his dying words Mahmoud declares, "We had to be done with all the stories of the ancestors if the descendants were to wake from their delusions of greatness and their false complacency. One day they'd thank me! They'd have to thank me!" (301). Evoking Walter Benjamin's reflections on the hidden barbarism in civilization, Hatem Hafez states that in destroying the temple Mahmoud destroys a despotic history even if that history is a civilizational landmark.[86] Benjamin notes that cultural treasures "owe their existence not only to the efforts of the great minds and talents who have created them, but also to the anonymous toil of their contemporaries." Barbarism, Benjamin continues, taints not only these treasures but also the manner of their transmission from one owner to another (258–9). To reappropriate Benjamin, Mahmoud's destruction of the temple is an attempt to "blast open the continuum of history" (264).

Congruent with Muslim belief that one enters the world of truth after death, and with Sufi epistemology where knowledge is equated with light,[87] Mahmoud's death, which marks the renunciation of his ego and his annihilation in the Divine, brings growth and self-reconciliation; "suddenly a light blazes up inside me. Yes, now I see everything, understand everything in life that I failed to grasp" (302). Mahmoud calls for the destruction of the past in its ruins, official histories, and unaccommodating narratives and genres.

Conclusion

Sunset Oasis refuses maturity as an inevitable outcome of the journey. As exemplified by Mahmoud, some people only find enlightenment and inner peace after death. The novel's use of Sufi dreams as a means for revising the past creates an avenue for a new modernity that includes all fragments of the nation where horizontal citizenship replaces hierarchical fraternity/paternity. The destruction of the temple is a call to destroy all restrictive identity narratives before forging a newer, more inclusive one. In this non-traditional bildgunsroman, the middle-aged protagonist reaches enlightenment after many detours. Ironically, he matures at the moment of death. Thus, *Sunset Oasis* both revises and refuses the formation narrative at the same time.

Conclusion

This study has analyzed twentieth- and twenty-first century Egyptian and British engagements with British civilizational narratives in four male-authored, male-centered texts. Whether directly or indirectly, the novels examined employ developmental narratives in their explorations of the legacy of Egypt's Urabi and 1919 revolutions. In spotlighting marginalized female narratives, *Female Voices and Egyptian Independence* has highlighted the impact of female characters on the respective journeys of male protagonists. These marginalized women shape the protagonists in ways that reflect the authors' understanding of (de)colonization and modernity as a bildungsroman, where the microcosmic journey of individuals reflects the larger progress of the nation toward political maturity. Ultimately, the authors craft narratives that show modernity to be a shifting concept that reflects their respective positioning on the question of Empire. The four novels included in this study are fictional predictions of reactions to the Queen's death stated in the Introduction, where denunciation of Britain's civilizational program by former colonies continues to be met by Britain's oblivion to its imperial history and failure to apologize for historical injustices.

Despite some ambivalence in Lawrence Durrell's *Mountolive*, and a revisionist strain prompting John Wilcox to imagine a feminist, anti-imperialist protagonist in *The Guns of El Kebir*, these two British accounts, published almost fifty years apart, exhibit a similar nostalgia in their narration of Egyptian resistance to British hegemony as their protagonists' maturity depends on their reconciliation with imperialist views. Lured at first by Egypt's exoticism and approaching Egypt and the Coptic Leila Hosnani mainly through colonial fantasy, Durrell's David Mountolive undergoes two maturations. The first, depicted in the novel as a reverse bildungsroman because it happens under

Leila's supervision/spell, occurs when she trains him as a cultured diplomat. The second, constituting his true maturity, occurs at the end of the novel when he discovers the Hosnani family's involvement in the Coptic conspiracy. The novel pronounces all Egyptians as irredeemably corrupt, regardless of religious affiliation. Mountolive's final growth is mirrored in his recognition of Egypt as a grotesque nation, incapable of political maturity.

The Guns of El Kebir merges the imperial romance with the romance of the archive. The former is an imperialist genre whose conventions require a fearless white male hero, a damsel in distress, and evil natives, while the latter is a twentieth-century revisionist genre that delivers postmodern depictions of British imperial past. In this genre merging, the imperial romance forces its conventions, overturning the author's modern-day attempt at depicting unconventional male and female protagonists. As a result, the novel undermines Alice Covington, the feminist journalist who serves as a British war correspondent, domesticating her and forcing on her the role of the vulnerable female while allowing Simon Fonthill, the male protagonist, to act as her male savior. *Guns* generates an imperialist narrative where both protagonists concede to the inevitability of Empire. Durrell's and Wilcox's texts reflect nostalgia generated by their immediate historical contexts. Their preoccupation with Britain's much diminished role on the world stage, added to depictions of chaos resulting from Egyptian resistance to British paternalism, serve as a defense of Empire. Both novels end with the positivism of the traditional bildungsroman with its the linear process of formation, positive closure, and confirmation of European models as the only path toward modernity. In both novels, Egypt poses as impervious to the civilizational mission.

Sugar Street and *Sunset Oasis*, also published almost fifty years apart, take a different stance on the bildungsroman, the former revising the genre to create an alternative Egyptian modernity and the latter rejecting the developmental model altogether. Both search for new tools that fit the specificities of their contemporary Egyptian society, resisting the bildungsroman's suppressive tendencies and its upholding of Enlightenment values that view the Other as an anachronism. In Mahfouz's novel, the new educated Egyptian woman and journalist, Sawsan Hammad, fights textual and social marginalization. Training Ahmed as a national intellectual, she helps him articulate a more inclusive Egyptian model for modernity. Although it follows a Western, Marxist framework in emphasizing the role of the proletariat, this model is flexible in its practice, allowing for constant revision to fit the moment. Whether intentionally or not, the novel also calls for a reimagined modernity that includes women as equal partners in nation-building. More precisely, Sawsan advocates for a genderless modernity in a postbourgeois social imaginary. While *Sugar Street* ends on a positive note, it does not mimic the traditional bildungsroman closure since Ahmed's selective adoption of Western and Egyptian structures and his dedication to constant revolution are at odds with British-endorsed visions of modernity. Ahmed crafts a new indigenous modernity that by nature is constantly evolving based on need.

Rather than rewrite the bildungsroman, Taher's *Sunset Oasis* rejects it as a philosophy. Portraying a male protagonist who takes a circuitous road toward progress and only matures at the moment of death, Taher contests the linearity and inevitability of growth. He takes issue with a narrowly defined Egyptian national identity that, replicating colonialist narrative, marginalizes its gender and ethnic minorities. It is thanks to the marginalized Siwan woman and the enslaved Sudanese woman in the narrative that Mahmoud Abd el Zahir recognizes his arrested development. The novel's Sufism subverts the European understanding of coming of age where maturity is uttered through the contradictory properties of individuality and submission to the social order. In contrast, Sufism locates growth and knowledge in the total annihilation of the individual self—where oneness with the bigger entity (God) is predicated upon integration with an amorphous, abstract force.

Mahmoud's suicide, which closes the novel, seen as a failure to mature in traditional developmental narratives, is an insistence on re-drawing the contours of Egyptian identity. It is an act of relinquishment of the individual self in the bigger entity that is represented in the diverse ethnic and gender components of Egypt since the nation is the sum of (dis)integrated fragments. Calling for a fresh new start, Mahmoud's moment of death becomes his moment of enlightenment. The most revolutionary in its resolution, *Sunset Oasis* calls for the destruction of narratives of acculturation in all their iterations, whether imperialist, nationalist, neo-imperialist, or generic. In so doing, it applies Ahmed's theory of constant revolution and an ever-changing modernity that shapes itself in answer to the exigencies of Egyptian society.

Notes

Introduction

1 On Irish reactions to the Queen's death, see Abrigail Williams, "Not Everyone Is Grieving Queen Elizabeth's Death: Here's Why Queen Elizabeth's Death Has Generated More Criticism Than Grief." *The GW Hatchet*, September 15, 2022. https://www.gwhatchet.com/2022/09/15/heres-why-queen-elizabeths-death-has-generated-more-criticism-than-grief/ (accessed November 27, 2022).

2 Steven Erlanger, "A Global Outpouring of Grief Mixes with Criticism of the Monarchy." *The New York Times*, updated September 9, 2022. https://indianexpress.com/article/world/queen-elizabeth-death-reactions-criticism-8140045/ (accessed November 27, 2022).

3 Emmanuel Felton and Meena Venkataramanan, "Black Americans See Complications in Adulation of Queen Elizabeth II." *The Washington Post*, September 13, 2022. https://www.washingtonpost.com/world/2022/09/13/queen-black-americans/ (accessed November 27, 2022).

4 Peter H. Hansen, "Coronation Everest: The Empire and Commonwealth in the 'Second Elizabethan Age.'" In *British Culture and the End of Empire*, ed. Stuart Ward (Manchester: Manchester University Press, 2001), 68.

5 See Frantz Fanon, *The Wretched of the Earth*, trans. Richard Philcox (New York: Grove Press, 2004) and Albert Memmi and Robert Bononno, *The Decolonization and the Decolonized* (Minneapolis: University of Minnesota Press, 2006).

6 Tobias Boes, *Formative Fictions: Nationalism, Cosmopolitanism, and the Bildungsroman* (New York: Cornell University Press, 2012).

7 Jed Esty, *Unseasonable Youth: Modernism, Colonialism, and the Fiction of Development* (New York: Oxford University Press, 2012).

8 Lisa Lowe, *Immigrant Acts: On Asian American Cultural Politics* (Durham: Duke University Press, 1996).

9 Geta J. LeSeur, *Ten Is the Age of Darkness: The Black Bildungsroman* (Columbia: University of Missouri Press, 1995).

10 Elizabeth Abel, Marianne Hirsch, and Elizabeth Langland, *The Voyage in: Fictions of Female Development* (Hanover, NH: Published for Dartmouth College by University Press of New England, 1983).

11 Nedal M. al-Mousa, "The Arabic Bildungsroman: A Generic Appraisal." *International Journal of Middle East Studies*, 25.2 (1993): 223–40.
12 Jeff Shalan, "Writing the Nation: The Emergence of Egypt in the Modern Arabic Novel." *Journal of Arabic Literature*, 33.3 (2002): 211–47.
13 Muhsin al-Musawi, *The Postcolonial Arabic Novel: Debating Ambivalence* (Boston: Brill, 2003).
14 Muhsin al-Musawi. "Beyond the Modernity Complex: Abd Al-Hakim Qasim's Re-Writing of the Self-Narrative." *Journal of Arabic Literature*, 41 (2010): 22–45.
15 Ellen McLarney, "The Socialist Romance of the Postcolonial Arabic Novel." *Research in African Literatures: Official Journal of the African Literature Committee of the African Studies Association of America and the African Literatures Seminar of the Modern Language Association*, 40.3 (2009): 186–205.
16 Hoda El Sadda, *Gender, Nation, and the Arabic Novel: Egypt, 1892–2008* (Syracuse, NY: Syracuse University Press, 2012) and Christine Gilmore, "'A Minor Literature in a Major Voice': Narrating Nubian Identity in Contemporary Egypt." *Alif: Journal of Comparative Poetics*, 35 (2015): 42–74.
17 Mary Youssef, *Minorities in the Contemporary Egyptian Novel* (Edinburgh: Edinburgh University Press, 2020).
18 Dina Heshmat, *Egypt 1919: The Revolution in Literature and Film* (Edinburgh: Edinburgh University Press, 2022).
19 Nedal al-Mousa, "The Changing Image of the Heroine in the Arabic Female Bildungsromane." *Middle Eastern Literatures*, 9.3 (2006): 257–70 and A. Idrissi Alami, "Moroccan Nation-Building and the Bildungsroman in Abd Al-Karim Ghallab's Dafanna Al-Madi and Al-Muallim Ali." *Middle Eastern Literatures*, 16.1 (2013): 60–75.
20 Maria Elena Paniconi, *Bildungsroman and the Arab Novel: Egyptian Intersections* (Abingdon, Oxon: Routledge, 2023).
21 See Heshmat, *Egypt 1919*.
22 See Beth Baron, *The Women's Awakening in Egypt: Culture, Society, and the Press* (New Haven: Yale University Press, 1994).
23 Hibba Abugideiri, *Gender and the Making of Modern Medicine in Colonial Egypt* (Farnham: Ashgate, 2010), 1–52.
24 Egyptian nationalists were guilty of collaboration with the British to limit access to education. See Mona L. Russell, "Competing, Overlapping, and Contradictory Agendas: Egyptian Education Under British Occupation, 1882–1922." *Comparative Studies of South Asia, Africa and the Middle East*, 21.1 (2001): 50–60.
25 Ziad Fahmy, *Ordinary Egyptians: Creating the Modern Nation through Popular Culture* (Stanford, CA: Stanford University Press, 2011), 25–7.

26 Ibid., 39. On Egyptian mass culture, see 39–60. On the role of mass culture in mobilizing the masses during the Urabi Revolution and after the onset of the British occupation, see 61–95.

27 Ibid., 168–9.

28 Hoda A. Yousef, *Composing Egypt: Reading, Writing, and the Emergence of a Modern Nation, 1870–1930* (Stanford, CA: Stanford University Press, 2016), 20.

29 Hanan Kholoussy, *For Better, for Worse: The Marriage Crisis That Made Modern Egypt* (Stanford, CA: Stanford University Press, 2010), 13–14.

30 Yousef, *Composing Egypt*, 20.

31 Baron, *The Women's Awakening in Egypt*, 39.

32 Bahaa Taher, *Abnaa Rifa'a: Al-thaqafa wa al-hurriyya* (Cairo: Dar al-Hilal, 1993), 42. Khedive is a Turkish title meaning Viceroy.

33 Kholoussy, *For Better, for Worse*, 13–14.

34 Ibid.

35 Fahmy, *Ordinary Egyptians*, 24.

36 Yousef, *Composing Egypt*, 39.

37 Kholoussy, *For Better, for Worse*, 13–14; Fahmy, *Ordinary Egyptians*, 24, 32–3. For the uses and circulation of literacy among the illiterate in Egypt, see Yousef, *Composing Egypt*.

38 Kholoussy, *For Better, for Worse,* 13–14.

39 Fahmy, *Ordinary Egyptians*, 32–3.

40 Kholoussy, *For Better, for Worse,* 13–14.

41 Fahmy, *Ordinary Egyptians*, 33–6.

42 While *Katatib* provided education for boys and girls alike, elite and upper-class families hired tutors for their daughters at home. For a history of the education of women in the nineteenth and twentieth centuries, see Mona L. Russell, *Creating the New Egyptian Woman: Consumerism, Education and National Identity 1863–1922* (New York: Palgrave Macmillan, 2004).

43 On these debates and on modernizing the nation through the family, see Lisa Pollard, *Nurturing the Nation: The Family Politics of Modernizing, Colonizing and Liberating Egypt, 1805–1923* (Berkeley: University of California Press, 2005).

44 Afaf Lutfi Sayyid-Marsot, *Egypt and Cromer: A Study in Anglo-Egyptian Relations* (New York: Praeger, 1969), 1. For details on the changes to the committee, see H. L. Wesseling, *Divide and Rule: The Partition of Africa, 1880–1914*, trans. Arnold J. Pomerans (Westport, CT: Praeger, 1996), 45–6.

45 'Abd al-Rahman al-Rafi'i, *Al-thawra al-Urabiya wa-al-ihtilal al-Injilizi* (Cairo: Dar al-Qawmiyah li al-Tiba'ah wa al-Nashr, 1966), 49.

46 Peter Mansfield, *The British in Egypt* (London: Weidenfeld and Nicolson, 1971), 14–21 and 27, and Rafi'i, *al-Thawra al-Urabiya wa-al-ihtilal al-Injilizi*, 134–5 and 46–7.

47 Mansfield, *The British in Egypt*, 14–21.

48 Thomas Pakenham, *The Scramble for Africa, 1876–1912* (New York: Random House, 1991), 130 and Rafi'i, *al-Thawra al-Urabiya wa-al-ihtilal al-Injilizi*, 82.

49 For a full account of the political, economic, and social reasons behind the Urabi Revolution, see Rafi'i, *al-Thawra al-Urabiya wa-al-ihtilal al-Injilizi*, 75–87.

50 Ibid., 71–5.

51 'Abd al-Rahman al Rafi'i attributes the European Powers' deposition of Ismail to their fear of the threat to their interests that an approved constitution and a flourishing Egyptian democracy might pose. See Rafi'i, *Al-thawra al-Urabiya wa al-ihtilal al-Injilizi*, 31–3.

52 Ibid., 135.

53 See Afaf Lutfi Sayyid-Marsot, *Egypt's Liberal Experiment, 1922–1936* (Berkeley: University of California Press, 1977).

54 Rafi'i, *al-Thawra al-Urabiya wa-al-ihtilal al-Injilizi*, 134–5 and 46–7.

55 Ibid., 137–50. For a detailed account of the two phases of the Urabi Revolution, see also 97–142.

56 M. E. Chamberlain, "The Alexandria Massacre of 11 June 1882 and the British Occupation of Egypt." *Middle Eastern Studies*, 13.1 (1977): 14 and "Egyptian Crisis: The Fatal Rioting at Alexandria, Official Report, Great Excitement at Cairo, Policy of Italy." *The Daily Telegraph*, June 13, 1882, issue no. 8, p. 436, col. 5, E-H.

57 Sayyid-Marsot, *Egypt and Cromer*, 21–2.

58 C. W. R. Long, *British Pro-Consuls in Egypt, 1914–1929: The Challenge of Nationalism* (London: Routledge Curzon, 2005), 1 and Michael V. Diboll, *Lawrence Durrell's "Alexandria Quartet" in Its Egyptian Contexts* (Lewiston, NY: Edwin Mellen Press, 2004), 159. Michael Barthorp on the other hand mentions only 2000. See Michael Barthorp, *War on the Nile: Britain, Egypt, and the Sudan, 1882–1898* (Poole, Dorset: Blandford Press, 1984), 69. This figure is consistent with Rafi'i who estimates Egyptian losses at 1,500 to 2,000 dead. Rafi'i quotes Wilfrid Scawen Blunt whose *Secret History of the English Occupation of Egypt* lists 10,000 dead and wounded based on a communication from Urabi's accompanying servant. Blunt, however, adds that he doubts the reliability of this figure (qtd in Rafi'i, *al-Thawra al-Urabiya wa-al-ihtilal al-Injilizi*, 491).

59 Mahmoud al-Khafif, *Ahmad 'Urabi al-za'im al-muftara 'alayh* (Cairo: Dar al-Hilal, 1971), volume 2, 80–5.

60 Afaf Lutfi Sayyid-Marsot, "Preface." In *Egypt and Cromer: A Study in Anglo-Egyptian Relations* (New York: Praeger, 1968), XI.

61 For revisionist account of 1919 inspired by reflections on the 2011 Revolution, see Heshmat, *Egypt 1919*, 182–203.

62 See Israel Gershoni and James P. Jankowski, *Egypt, Islam, and the Arabs: The Search for Egyptian Nationhood, 1900–1930* (New York: Oxford University Press, 1986).

63 ʿAbd al-Rahman al-Rafiʿi, *Thawrat sanat 1919: Tarikh Misr al-qawmi min sanat 1914 ila sanat 1921*, volume 2 (Cairo: Maktabat al-Nahda al-Misriyya, 1946), 27–38.

64 Sayyid-Marsot, *Egypt's Liberal Experiment*, 46–9.

65 Sayyid-Marsot, *Egypt's Liberal Experiment*, 49. On Copts in the *Wafd*, see Janice J. Terry, *The Wafd, 1919–1952: Cornerstone of Egyptian Political Power* (London: Third World Centre for Research and Publication, 1982). To this day the *Wafd* Party includes prominent Coptic figures, an example of which is Mounir Fakhry Abdel Nour, former Minister of Industry, Trade and Investment.

66 Sayyid-Marsot, *Egypt's Liberal Experiment*, 49–50.

67 For an Egyptian account of the revolution, see Rafiʿi, *Thawrat Sanat 1919*, 39–68. See also Sayyid-Marsot, *Egypt's Liberal Experiment*, 50.

68 For details of the demonstrations and the violent police response to it, see Sayyid-Marsot, *Egypt's Liberal Experiment*, 50–1. On the role of Egypt's female elite in the 1919 Revolution, see Beth Baron, *Egypt as a Woman: Nationalism, Gender, and Politics* (Berkeley: University of California Press, 2005), 105–213. For a brief, albeit orientalist, account of the contribution of females from various social classes, elite, *fallahat* (peasant-women), lower class courtesans, and schoolgirls, see Valentine Chirol, *The Egyptian Problem* (London: Macmillan, 1920, 177–89 and 167–9).

69 Sayyid-Marsot, *Egypt's Liberal Experiment*, 51–2.

70 ʿAbd al-Rahman al-Rafiʿi, *Fi aʿqab al-thawra al-misriyya* (Cairo: Maktabat al-Nahda al-Misriyya, volume 2, 1947), 174–202.

71 ʿAbd al-Rahman al-Rafiʿi, *Fi aʿqab al-thawra al-misriyya* (Cairo: Maktabat al-Nahda al-Misriyya, volume 3, 1947), 101–20. For details on the continued negotiations between 1920 and 1922, see Sayyid-Marsot, *Egypt's Liberal Experiment*, 55–64.

72 For the full text of the 1936 treaty, see Sayyid-Marsot, *Egypt's Liberal Experiment*, 253–67.

73 Ibid., 57.

74 See Heshmat, *Egypt 1919*, 38–58.

75 Paniconi, *Bildungsroman and the Arab Novel*, 65–86.

76 See Heshmat, *Egypt 1919*, 59–78.

77 Rasheed Enany, *Naguib Mahfouz: The Pursuit of Meaning* (London: Routledge, 1993), 4.

78 Paniconi, *Bildungsroman and the Arab Novel*, 67.

1 Egypt the Grotesque: Breaking Leila's Shackle in Lawrence Durrell's *Mountolive*

1 Hala Halim, *Alexandrian Cosmopolitanism: An Archive* (New York: Fordham University Press, 2013). While poor foreigners shared the straitened means of indigenous Egyptians, many held comfort in the "privilege" of belonging to an allegedly superior community.

2 For a *Quartet* chronology, see Donald Kaczvinsky, "When Was Darley in Alexandria? A Chronology for 'The Alexandria Quartet.'" *Journal of Modern Literature*, 17.4 (Spring 1991): 591–4.

3 Diboll, *Lawrence Durrell's "Alexandria Quartet,"* 2.

4 Diboll, *Lawrence Durrell's "Alexandria Quartet,"* 2, and Anna Lillios, "Introduction." In *Lawrence Durrell and the Greek World*, ed. Anna Lillios (Selinsgrove: Susquehanna University Press, 2004), 19 and 27.

5 Alan Warren Friedman, "Chronology." In *Lawrence Durrell and The Alexandria Quartet: Art for Love's Sake* (Norman: University of Oklahoma Press, 1970), XX.

6 Alan Warren Friedman, "Introduction." In *Critical Essays on Lawrence Durrell* (Boston, MA: G.K. Hall, 1987), 1.

7 Diboll, *Lawrence Durrell's "Alexandria Quartet,"* 3, 93.

8 Bonamy Dobrée, "Durrell's Alexandrian Series." *The Sewanee Review*, 69.1 (1961): 61–79.

9 Jack Stewart, "Soundscapes, Smellscapes, and Cityscapes in *The Alexandria Quartet*." In *Lawrence Durrell and the Greek World*, ed. Anna Lillios (Selinsgrove: Susquehanna University Press, 2004), 129–42.

10 Patrick Quinn, "'More Than a Fascination with the Divine Marquis': John Fowles's *The Magus* and Lawrence Durrell's *The Alexandria Quartet*." In *Lawrence Durrell and the Greek World*, ed. Anna Lillios (Selinsgrove: Susquehanna University Press, 2004), 270–81.

11 See Harry T. Moore, *The World of Lawrence Durrell* (Carbondale: Southern Illinois University Press, 1962). See also Alan Warren Friedman, ed., *Critical Essays on Lawrence Durrell* (Boston, MA: G.K. Hall, 1987).

12 See G. Creed Walter, *The Muse of Science and the Alexandria Quartet* (Norwood, PA: Norwood Library Editions, 1977).

13 See, for example, John M. Rose, "Multiple Truths and Multiple Narratives: Nietzsche's Perspectivism and the Narrative Structure of *The Alexandria Quartet*." In *Lawrence Durrell and the Greek World*, ed. Anna Lillios (Selinsgrove: Susquehanna University Press, 2004), 215–38.

14 See Carl Bode, "Durrell's Way to Alexandria." In *Critical Essays on Lawrence Durrell*, ed. Alan Friedman (Boston, MA: G.K. Hall, 1987), 135–44.

15 See David M. Woods, "Love and Meaning in *The Alexandria Quartet*: Some Tantric Perspectives." In *On Miracle Ground: Essays on the Fiction of Lawrence Durrell*, ed. Michael H. Begnal (Lewisburg: Bucknell University Press, 1990), 93–112.

16 Mahmoud Manzaloui, "Curate's Egg: An Alexandrian Opinion of Durrell's Quartet." In *Critical Essays on Lawrence Durrell*, ed. Alan Friedman (Boston, MA: G.K. Hall, 1987), 144–57.

17 William Leigh Godshalk, "Some Sources of Durrell's Alexandria Quartet." In *Critical Essays on Lawrence Durrell*, ed. Alan Friedman (Boston, MA: G.K. Hall, 1987), 158–71. For the sources Durrell consulted while writing the *Quartet*, see Diboll, *Lawrence Durrell's "Alexandria Quartet,"* 95.

18 Providing a romanticized description of Greek geography, Lillios writes that for Durrell, "After Greece, Egypt was a bitter disappointment." See Lillios, "Introduction," 20.

19 Rosalind Gwynne, "Islam and Muslims" in *The Alexandria Quartet. Deus Loci. The Lawrence Durrell Journal.* NS5 (1997): 92–102.

20 Alfred Kazin, "Lawrence Durrell's Rosy-Finger'd Egypt." In *Critical Essays on Lawrence Durrell*, ed. Alan Friedman (Boston, MA: G.K. Hall, 1987), 30–3.

21 Amani Tawfik, "The Motif of Mutilation of Character and Setting in *The Alexandria Quartet*." In *Durrell in Alexandria: On Miracle Ground 9, Conference Proceedings, Alexandria Egypt, June 1996*, ed. Shelly Ekhtiar (Baltimore, MD: International Lawrence Durrell Society, 2005), 70–80.

22 Mohamed Yehia Mohamed Hasan, "Images of the 'Other' in *The Alexandria Quartet*: Encounters and Self-Explorations." In *Durrell in Alexandria: On Miracle Ground 9, Conference Proceedings, Alexandria Egypt, June 1996*, ed. Shelly Ekhtiar (Baltimore, MD: International Lawrence Durrell Society, 2005), 312–22.

23 Michael Diboll, *Lawrence Durrell's "Alexandria Quartet."*

24 Donald Kaczvinsky, "Memlik's House and Mountolive's Uniform: Orientalism, Ornamentalism, and *The Alexandria Quartet*." *Contemporary Literature*, 48.1 (2007): 93–118.

25 Joseph A. Boone, "Vacation Cruises; or the Homoerotics of Orientalism." In *Feminist Postcolonial Theory: A Reader* ed. Reina Lewis and Sara Mills (New York: Routledge, 2003), 460–86.

26 Halim, *Alexandrian Cosmopolitanism*. For Durrell's depiction of Christian Egyptians, see Sahar Hamouda, "The Figure of the Copt in Lawrence Durrell's *Alexandria Quartet* and Edwar Al-Kharrat's *City of Saffron* and *Girls of Alexandria*." In *Durrell in Alexandria: On Miracle Ground 9, Conference Proceedings, Alexandria Egypt, June 1996*, ed. Shelly Ekhtiar (Baltimore, MD: International Lawrence Durrell Society, 2005), 100–10. For an examination of the orientalist depiction of Egyptians in relation to Europeans, see Mona

Mones, "The Egyptian People in Lawrence Durrell's *The Alexandria Quartet*." In *Durrell in Alexandria: On Miracle Ground 9, Conference Proceedings, Alexandria Egypt, June 1996*, ed. Shelly Ekhtiar (Baltimore, MD: International Lawrence Durrell Society, 2005), 112–22. Mones also analyzes character interactions between English and other European characters and Egyptian ones. For other critiques, see Roger Bowen, "Closing the 'Toybox': Orientalism and Empire in the Alexandria Quartet." *Studies in the Literary Imagination*, 24 (1991): 9–18.

27 Gordon Bowker, *Through the Dark Labyrinth: A Biography of Lawrence Durrell* (New York: St. Martin's Press, 1997), 151–2.

28 Lawrence Durrell, "Introduction." In E. M. Forster *Alexandria: A History and a Guide* (London, England: M. Haag, 1982), XI–XII.

29 Bode, "Durrell's Way to Alexandria," 136.

30 Fletcher Markle, "Teaching Your Characters That They're More or Less Free." In *Lawrence Durrell: Conversations*, ed. Earl G. Ingersoll (Madison: Fairleigh Dickinson University Press, 1998), 100.

31 Ian S. MacNiven, *Lawrence Durrell: A Biography* (London: Faber and Faber, 1998), 252.

32 Lillios, "Introduction," 22–3.

33 Boone, "Vacation Cruises; or the Homoerotics of Orientalism," 466.

34 Lillios, "Introduction," 22–3.

35 Ibid.

36 Boone, "Vacation Cruises; or the Homoerotics of Orientalism," 468.

37 See the Introduction to this study.

38 Diboll, *Lawrence Durrell's "Alexandria Quartet,"* 185.

39 Friedman, "Introduction," 1 and Lillios, "Introduction," 25.

40 Harry T. Moore, "Introduction." In *The World of Lawrence Durrell* (Carbondale: Southern Illinois University Press, 1962), X.

41 Lillios, "Introduction," 26.

42 Pinchin, *Alexandria Still: Forster, Durrell, and Cavafy* (Princeton, NJ: Princeton University Press, 1977), 159 and 162.

43 Sahar Hamouda, "The Figure of the Copt," 104.

44 Fahmy, *Ordinary Egyptians*, 2–27 and Baron, *The Women's Awakening in Egypt*, 73.

45 Baron, *The Women's Awakening in Egypt*, 13–39.

46 For the number of titles, authors, private and public presses, and printed books in Egypt between 1820 and 1899, see Fahmy, *Ordinary Egyptians*, 32.

47 Baron, *The Women's Awakening in Egypt*, 99. See 80–100 for literary tastes and reading habits.

48 See Introduction to this study.

49 Fahmy, *Ordinary Egyptians*, 27.

50 Yousef, *Composing Egypt*, 81–2. For a history of women's education in modern Egypt, see Russell, *Creating the New Egyptian Woman*.

51 Lawrence Durrell, *Mountolive* (New York: E. P. Dutton, 1961), 24. Subsequent page numbers in text.

52 Fu'ad University, later Cairo University, welcomed the first class of female students in 1929. See Laura Bier, *Revolutionary Womanhood: Feminisms, Modernity, and the State in Nasser's Egypt* (Stanford, CA: Stanford University Press, 2011), 45.

53 On girls' and women's education in nineteenth-century Britain, see Judith Flanders, *The Victorian House* (London: Harper, 2003), 47–59.

54 Judith Flanders, *The Victorian House*, 177–214.

55 Quoted in Russell, *Creating the New Egyptian Woman*, 154.

56 See Halim, *Alexandrian Cosmopolitanism*, for a richly informative study of the nature of Alexandria's cosmopolitanism in the early twentieth century. For an interesting history of the Greek community, Egypt's largest foreign community in the nineteenth and twentieth centuries, see Alexander Kitroeff, *The Greeks and the Making of Modern Egypt* (Cairo: The American University in Cairo Press, 2019). For a comparative study of the ways in which Egyptians and Jewish Egyptians remember and/or understand Egyptian cosmopolitanism from the mid-nineteenth into the twentieth centuries, see Deborah Starr, *Remembering Cosmopolitan Egypt: Literature, Culture, and Empire* (London: Routledge, 2009).

57 Lawrence Durrell, *Balthazar* (New York: Dutton, 1960), 77.

58 Ibid.

59 Lawrence Durrell, *Clea* (New York: Dutton, 1960), 311–13 and 312.

60 Durrell, *Balthazar*, 76.

61 For Halim's reading of Alexandria in the *Quartet* as fantastic and uncanny, see Halim, *Alexandrian Cosmopolitanism*, 191–212.

62 On the integration of Egyptian Muslims, Christians, and Jews in Egyptian sociopolitical life under Muhammad Ali (r. 1805–48) and until the British occupation, see Rabihah Sulayman, *Al-wihda al-wataniyya wa al-fitna al-ta'ifiyya, 1882–1919* (Cairo: Misr al-'Arabiyah li al-Nashr wa al-Tawzi', 2009), 13–19. For the role of Copts and Jews in the 1881–2 Urabi Revolution, see 35–7.

63 Sulayman, *Al-wihda al-wataniyya*, 32–41. On the Copts in Egyptian society from 1805 to 1954, see Vivian Ibrahim, *The Copts of Egypt: The Challenges of Modernisation and Identity* (London: I.B. Tauris, 2013).

64 Ibrahim, *The Copts of Egypt*, 44–5.

65 For the *Wafd*'s relation with Christian Egyptians see Terry, *The Wafd*. See also Sulayman, *Al-wihda al-wataniyya*, 283–352 for the role of Christian and Muslim intellectuals in fostering religious unity.

66 Jed Esty, *A Shrinking Island: Modernism and National Culture in England* (Princeton, NJ: Princeton University Press, 2004), 37–8.
67 Michael Diboll, "The Secret History of Lawrence Durrell's *The Alexandria Quartet*: The Mountolive-Hosnani Affair, Britain, and the *Wafd*." In *Lawrence Durrell and the Greek World*, ed. Anna Lillios (Selinsgrove: Susquehanna University Press, 2004), 92.
68 Homi Bhabha, *The Location of Culture* (London: Routledge, 1994), 82–9. Emphasis in original.
69 On hybridity, see ibid., 36–9.
70 See Bhabha's explanation of sly civility in Bhabha, ibid., 93–101.
71 Halim, *Alexandrian Cosmopolitanism*, 202–3.
72 Diboll, *Lawrence Durrell's "Alexandria Quartet,"* 127.
73 Halim, *Alexandrian Cosmopolitanism*, 183.
74 Hasan, "Images of the 'Other' in *The Alexandria Quartet*."
75 John Ruskin, *Lectures on Art* (London: G. Allen, 1910), 1–40.
76 See Diboll, "The Secret History," 92 and Hasan, "Images of the 'Other' in *The Alexandria Quartet*," 312–22.
77 Diboll, "The Secret History," 90–8.
78 Diboll, *Lawrence Durrell's "Alexandria Quartet,"* 203.
79 Kaczvinsky, "Memlik's House and Mountolive's Uniform," 114.
80 See Tawfik, "The Motif of Mutilation."
81 Kaczvinsky, "Memlik's House and Mountolive's Uniform," 114.
82 Diboll, *Lawrence Durrell's "Alexandria Quartet,"* 180–1.
83 Kaczvinsky, "When Was Darley in Alexandria?"
84 Anne R. Zahlan, "The Destruction of the Imperial Self in Lawrence Durrell's the Alexandria Quartet." *Perspectives on Contemporary Literature*, 12 (1986): 10.
85 On religious feeling as a sign of delayed evolution in imperialist historiography of the "Other," see Dipesh Chakrabarty, *Provincializing Europe: Postcolonial Thought and Historical Difference* (New Jersey: Princeton University Press, 2000), 97–113.
86 On Memlik Pasha as the Egyptian Sidqi Pasha, prime minister of Egypt from 1930 to 1935, see Kaczvinsky, "Memlik's House and Mountolive's Uniform," 93–118.
87 Halim, *Alexandrian Cosmopolitanism*, 212–25.
88 Kenneth Rexroth, "Lawrence Durrell." In *Critical Essays on Lawrence Durrell*, ed. Alan Friedman (Boston, MA: G.K. Hall, 1987), 24.
89 'Abd al-Rahman al-Rafi'i, *Fi a'qab al-thawra al-misriyya* (Cairo: Maktabat al-Nahda al-Misriyya, 1947, volume 3), 101–20.
90 Azza Kararah, "Introduction." In *Sophia Poole. The Englishwoman in Egypt: Letters from Cairo Written during a Residence There in 1842–46*

(Cairo: American University in Cairo Press, 2003), IX. For an interesting study of cross-cultural dressing in the life of nineteenth-century female European travelers to the Middle East, see Reina Lewis, "On Veiling, Vision, and Voyage: Cross-Cultural Dressing and Narratives of Identity." In *Feminist Postcolonial Theory: A Reader*, ed. Reina Lewis and Sara Mills (Edinburgh: Edinburgh University Press, 2003), 520–41.

91 Incidentally, Ziad Fahmy mentions a Coptic priest whose speeches during the 1919 Revolution were violent. On the fraternization of Muslims and Copts and use of religious spaces as public spaces to discuss nationalism and independence during 1919, see Fahmy, *Ordinary Egyptians*, 147–9.

92 One such instance took place in 1942 when the British surrounded the Egyptian King's palace with tanks in order to force him to appoint a pro-British prime minister. See Rafi'i, *Fi a'qab al-thawra al-misriyya*, volume 3, 101–20.

93 Diboll, "The Secret History," 95.

94 Bowker, *Through the Dark Labyrinth*, 143.

95 Taher, *Abnaa Rifa'a*, 54–6. See also Evelyn Baring Cromer, *Modern Egypt* (New York: Macmillan, 1908).

96 Halim, *Alexandrian Cosmopolitanism*, 203.

2 Lessons in Modernity: Naguib Mahfouz's *Sugar Street* and the Female National Intellectual

1 The *Cairo Trilogy* is comprised of *Palace Walk* (1956), *Palace of Desire* (1957), and *Sugar Street* (1957).

2 Al-Sayyid is an Arabic title meaning Master.

3 On the *Nahda*, see the Introduction to this study.

4 For a discussion of Kamal's journey and his love for Aïda as a reflection of his imprisonment in both European and native forms, see Rania Mahmoud, "Towards an Egyptian *Bildungsroman*: The National Intellectual after the 1919 Revolution in Naguib Mahfouz's *Sugar Street: Arab Studies Quarterly*, 41.4 (2019): 298–316.

5 Samia Mehrez, *Egypt's Culture Wars: Politics and Practice* (London: Routledge, 2008), 9.

6 Diboll, *Lawrence Durrell's "Alexandria Quartet,"* 93.

7 Roger Allen, *Naguib Mahfouz: A Retrospective* (Seattle, WA: Dept. of Near Eastern Languages and Civilization, University of Washington, 2004), 18.

8 Enany, *Naguib Mahfouz: The Pursuit of Meaning*, 3–4.

9 See Mahfouz and 'Abdel 'Aziz I, *Asatidhati* (Cairo: Mirit li al-Nashr wa al-Ma'lumat, 2002) and Enany, *Naguib Mahfouz: The Pursuit of Meaning*, 27 and 30.
10 Enany, *Naguib Mahfouz: The Pursuit of Meaning*, 30.
11 Ibid., 225–6.
12 For the 1952 Revolution and the ensuing political context, see Joel Gordon, *Nasser's Blessed Movement: Egypt's Free Officers and the July Revolution* (Cairo: The American University in Cairo Press, 2016).
13 See Enany, Naguib Mahfouz, *The Pursuit of Meaning*, 25 and Gamal al-Ghitani, *Al-majalis al-Mahfouziyya* (Cairo: Dar al-Shuruq, 2006), 211.
14 Allen, *Naguib Mahfouz*, 11–12.
15 Enany, *Naguib Mahfouz: The Pursuit of Meaning*, 25.
16 Allen, *Naguib Mahfouz*, 11–12.
17 Enany, *Naguib Mahfouz: The Pursuit of Meaning*, 4.
18 Quoted in Menahem Milson, *Najib Mahfuz: The Novelist-Philosopher of Cairo* (New York: St. Martin's Press, 1998), 29–30. Milson identifies this as the influence of French thinker Gustave Le Bon (1841–1931). One also detects a similarity with Saad Zaghloul who, in his prerevolutionary era, did not believe in revolution. See Sayyid-Marsot, *Egypt's Liberal Experiment*, 46–8.
19 Naguib Mahfouz and Fathi 'Ashri, *Hawla al-taharrur wa al-taqaddum* (Cairo: al-Dar al-Misryiya al-Lubnaniya, 1996), 27–8.
20 Mahfouz and 'Ashri, *Hawla al-taharrur*, 23–4 and Milson, *Najib Mahfuz*, 29–30.
21 Naguib Mahfouz, *Atahaddath ilaykum* (Beirut: Dar al-Awdah, 1977), 23–4.
22 Abd al-Muhsin Badr, *Al-ru'ya wa al-'ada: Naguib Mahfouz* (Cairo: Dar al-Ma'aref, 1984), 28.
23 Mahfouz, *Atahaddath*, 95, 106–7 and 162. See also Naguib Mahfouz and Raga' al-Naqqash, *Naguib Mahfouz: Safahat min mudhakkiratih wa-'adwa jadida 'ala 'adabih wa-hayatih* (Cairo: Markaz al-Ahram li al-Tarjamah wa al-Nashr, 1998), 336.
24 Badr, *Al-ru'ya wa al-'ada*, 64; Gamal al-Ghitani, *Al-majalis al-Mahfouziyya* (Cairo: Dar al-Shuruq, 2006), 148–50; Mahfouz and Naqqash, *Najib Mahfuz: Safahat*, 53; and Milson, *Najib Mahfuz*. On the Absurd in Mahfouz's fiction after the *Trilogy*, see Ahmad 'Atiyya, *Ma'a Naguib Mahfouz* (Beirut: Dar al-Jil, 1977), 99–112. Milson explains that despite the existence of Arabic fictional narrative works, such as the *One Thousand and One Nights*, these works were not considered literature due to their raunchiness and their use of the vernacular rather than classical Arabic. The emergence of the Arabic novel and short stories are indebted to Western literature; see Milson, *Najib Mahfuz*, 6–8. On the emergence of the novel in Egypt, see Sasson Somekh, *The Changing Rhythm: A Study of Najib Mahfuz's Novels* (Leiden: Brill, 1973), 1–34.

25 Ibrahim 'Awad, *Sitt riwayat misriyya muthira li al-jadal* (Cairo: Maktabat Jazirat al-Ward, 2011), 355–62 and Mahfouz, *Atahaddath ilaykum*, 51–2. For 'Awad's reading of the *Trilogy* as a naturalistic work, see 'Awad, *Sitt riwayat*, 365–73. Ghali Shukri argues that Mahfouz combines different modes. For this reason, it could be said that Mahfouz had always been pioneering and experimental. See Ghali Shukri, *Al-muntami: Dirasa fi adab Naguib Mahfouz* (Beirut: Dar al Afaq al Jadida, 1982), 6–16. Like Mahfouz, Mahmoud Amin El Alem and Somekh refuse to classify the *Trilogy* as a naturalistic work. See Mahmoud Amin El Alem, *Ta'ammulat fi 'alam Naguib Mahfouz* (Cairo: al-Hay'a al-Misriyya al-'Ammah li al-Ta'lif wa al-Nashr, 1970), 58–9 and Somekh, *The Changing Rhythm*, 108–10.

26 Mahfouz and Naqqash, *Naguib Mahfouz: Safahat*, 57–8 and 178 and Mahfouz, *Atahaddath*, 63.

27 Laura Bier, *Revolutionary Womanhood: Feminisms, Modernity, and the State in Nasser's Egypt* (Stanford, CA: Stanford University Press, 2011), 40.

28 El Sadda, *Gender, Nation, and the Arabic Novel*, 95.

29 Naguib Mahfouz, *Sugar Street*, trans. William M. Hutchins and Angele Botros Samaan (New York: Anchor Books, 1992), 242. Subsequent page numbers in text.

30 For the discourses on modern and traditional gender relations in the *Trilogy*, see El Sadda, *Gender, Nation, and the Arabic Novel*, 77–96.

31 Fanon, *The Wretched of the Earth*, 158–9.

32 Ibid., 173.

33 M. M. Badawi, "Commitment in Contemporary Arabic Literature." In *Critical Perspectives on Modern Arabic Literature*, ed. Issa J. Boullata (Washington, DC: Three Continents, 1980), 23–44.

34 See Shukri, *Al-muntami*, 73.

35 Hussam Ahmed. *The Last Nahdawi: Taha Hussein and Institution Building in Egypt* (Redwood City: Stanford University Press, 2022), 169–70.

36 Baron, *The Women's Awakening in Egypt*, 167 and Bier, *Revolutionary Womanhood*, 63.

37 Yousef, *Composing Egypt*, 81–2. For a history of women's education in modern Egypt, see Russell, *Creating the New Egyptian Woman*.

38 Bier, *Revolutionary Womanhood*, 39–40.

39 Latifa al-Zayyat, *Min suwar al-mar'a fi al-qisas wa al-riwayat al-'arabiyya* (Cairo: Dar al-Thaqafa al-Jadida, 1989), 129–64. Al-Zayyat's analysis spans Mahfouz's literature between 1939 and 1973.

40 Bier, *Revolutionary Womanhood*, 19.

41 Paniconi, *Bildungsroman and the Arab Novel*, 2.

42 Bier, *Revolutionary Womanhood*, 104–6.

43 El Sadda, *Gender, Nation, and the Arabic Novel*, 95.

44 El Sadda, "Introduction," XXXI. For an informative study of the *effendiya*, men educated in a Western-style system and their relationship to old forms of patriarchy, see Lucie Ryzova, *The Age of the Efendiyya: Passages to Modernity in National-Colonial Egypt* (Oxford: Oxford University Press, 2014).
45 El Sadda, *Gender, Nation, and the Arabic Novel*, 96.
46 Ibid., 95.
47 El Alem, *Ta'ammulat fi 'alam Naguib Mahfouz*, 113 and Abdel-Rahman Abu Ouf, *Al-Ru'a al-mutaghayyira fi riwayat Naguib Mahfouz* (Cairo: al-Hay'a al-Misriyya al-'Amah li al-Kitab, 1991),143–8.
48 Enany, *Naguib Mahfouz: The Pursuit of Meaning*, 91.
49 Abdul JanMohamed, *Manichean Aesthetics: The Politics of Literature in Colonial Africa* (Amherst: University of Massachusetts Press, 1983), 1–15.
50 Mahfouz and 'Ashri, *Hawla al-taharrur*, 85–6; Ghitani, *al-majalis al-Mahfouziyya*, 82 and 85.
51 For a portrait of Salama Musa, see Mahfouz and 'Abd al-'Aziz, *Asatidhati*, 225–48.
52 For Mahfouz's views on literary independence, see Ghitani, *al-majalis al-Mahfouziyya*, 174–5.
53 Enany, *Naguib Mahfouz: The Pursuit of Meaning*, 23.
54 For a brief history of the Muslim Brothers in Egypt, see Kamal Helbawy, "The Muslim Brotherhood in Egypt: Historical Evolution and Future Prospects." In *Political Islam: Context versus Ideology*, ed. Khaled Hroub (London: London Middle East Institute at SOAS, 2010), 61–85.
55 For the history of communism and socialism in Egypt, see Tareq Y. Ismael and Rifa'at el-Sa'id, *The Communist Movement in Egypt, 1920–1988* (Syracuse, NY: Syracuse University Press, 1990).
56 Naguib Mahfouz and Fathi 'Ashri, *Hawla al-din wa al-dimuqratiyya* (Cairo: al-Dar al-Misriyya al-Lubnaniyya, 1990).
57 Naguib Mahfouz and Fathi 'Ashri, *Hawla al-tadayyun wa al-tatarruf* (Cairo: al-Dar al-Misriyya al-Lubnaniyya, 1996).
58 See Jean Said Makdisi, Noha Bayoumi, and Rafif Rida Sidawi, ed. *Arab Feminisms: Gender and Equality in the Middle East* (London: I.B. Tauris Publishers in association with the Centre for Arab Unity Studies, Lebanese Association of Women Researchers, 2014), 3–168.
59 Mervat Hatem, "Class and Patriarchy as Competing Paradigms for the Study of Middle Eastern Women." *Society for Comparative Studies in Society and History*, 29.4 (1987): 811–18.
60 Joan Scott. "Feminism's Difference Problem." In *Arab Feminisms: Gender and Equality in the Middle East*, ed. Jean Said Makdisi, Noha Bayoumi, and Rafif

Riffa Sidawi (London: I.B. Tauris Publishers in association with the Centre for Arab Unity Studies, Lebanese Association of Women Researchers, 2014), 157–63.

61 Somekh, *The Changing Rhythm*, 122–3.

62 Naguib Mahfouz and Mahmoud Fawzi, *I'tirafat Naguib Mahfouz* (Cairo: Dar al-Shabab al-'Arabi, 1990), 63–4.

63 On the Copts in the *Wafd*, see Terry, *The Wafd, 1919-1952*. To this day, prominent Copts, such as former Minister of Industry, Trade and Investment, Mounir Fakhry Abdel Nour, continue to be part of the *Wafd* Party.

64 For a comprehensive history of events from 1937 to 1944, see Raf'i, *Fi a'qab al-thawra al-misriyya*, volume 2, 174–221 and volume 3, 44–138.

65 Starr, *Remembering Cosmopolitan Egypt*, 107.

66 Gudrun Krämer, "Political Participation of the Jews in Egypt between World War I and the 1952 Revolution." In *The Jews of Egypt: A Mediterranean Society in Modern Times*, ed. Shimon Shamir (London: Routledge, 2019), 68–82.

67 Krämer, "Political Participation," 74. On Jewish participation in the 1919 Revolution, see Fahmy, *Ordinary Egyptians*, 141 and 147.

68 Krämer, "Political Participation," 74.

69 Ibid., 79.

70 Ibid., 79 and 74.

71 Ahmad Muhammad 'Atiyya, *'Adwa' jadida 'ala al-thaqafa al-'Arabiyya: Ahadith 'Arabiyya* (Cairo: Ra' li al-Taba'a wa al-Nashr, 1980), 57–9. For the revolution in *Palace Walk* and the various attitudes of the Abd al-Jawad bourgeois family toward the events, see 'Atiyya, *Ma'a Naguib Mahfouz*, 51–70.

72 Ismael and el-Sa'id, *Communist Movement in Egypt*, 26.

73 Mahfouz and Fawzi, *I'tirafat Naguib Mahfouz*, 63–4.

74 Naguib Mahfouz and 'Abd Al-'Aziz, *Asatidhati*, 229–30.

75 On the poetry of *al-hubb al-'udhri*, see Shawqi Dayf, *Al-hubb al-'udhri 'inda al-'arab* (Cairo: al-Dar al-Misriya al-Lubnaniya, 1999), 19–27 and Yusuf Yusuf, *Al-ghazal al-'udhri: dirasa fi al-hubb al-Maqmu'* (Damascus: Manshurat Ittihad al-Kuttab al-'Arab, 1978), 34–69.

76 'Atiyya, *Ma'a Naguib Mahfouz*, 41.

77 Roger Allen, *The Arabic Novel: An Historical and Critical Introduction* (NY: Syracuse University Press, 1982), 56 and Ghitani, 151–2.

78 Abu Ouf names Mahfouz the writer who most understood and best analyzed what Abu Ouf terms the bourgeoisie's utilitarian cleverness, seen in its interaction with, and oscillation between loyalty to the high bourgeoisie, on the one hand, and laborers and peasants, on the other hand, Abdel-Rahman Abu Ouf, *Fusul fi al-naqd wa al-adab* (Cairo: al-Hay'a al-Misriyya al-'Amma li al-Kitab, 1996), 69.

79 Abdel-Azim Anis and Mahmoud Amin, *Fi al-thaqafa al-misriyya*, 2nd ed. (Rabat: Dar al-Aman, 1988), 31–4. See also 'Atiyya, *Ma'a Naguib Mahfouz*, 37.

80 'Atiyya remarks that the radical hero in Mahfouz's fiction belongs to the middle bourgeoisie, not the proletariat, and notes the absence of laborers and peasants, see 'Atiyya, *Ma'a Naguib Mahfouz*, 37.
81 Anis and Amin, *Fi al-thaqafa*, 111–16.
82 Anis and Amin, *Fi al-thaqafa*, 123–4. Anis' critique seems to accurately describe Mahfouz's vision who professed " 'bias' for the small bourgeoisie, which he viewed as *the candidate for the salvation of humanity*," Rasheed Enany, *Naguib Mahfouz: His Life and Times* (Cairo: The American University in Cairo Press, 2007), 31–2, emphasis in original.
83 Shukri, *Al-muntami*, 21–2. On *al-muntami* between faith and socialism in Mahfouz's work, see 206–94.
84 Ibid., 206–94.
85 Paniconi, *Bildungsroman and the Arab Novel*, 65–86.
86 'Atiyya, *Ma'a Naguib Mahfouz*, 37. Abu Ouf adds that the experiences of Mahfouz's communist characters, which mix Fabian socialism with Marxist thought, are unrelated to the experiences of leftist activists. See Abu Ouf, *Al-ru'a al-mutaghayyira*, 111–22 on the leftist intellectual in Mahfouz.
87 Anis and Amin, *Fi al-thaqafa*, 118–19.
88 Mahfouz, *Atahaddath ilaykum*, 45.
89 Shukri, *Al-Muntami*, 228–30.

3 Alice in Wonderland: Egypt and the Benevolent Empire in *The Guns of El Kebir*

1 John Wilcox, personal communication with the author of this study. For the narrative of voluntary decolonization as well as the preoccupation with Empire in British popular culture, see Stuart Ward, ed. *British Culture and the End of Empire* (Manchester: Manchester University Press, 2001).
2 John Wilcox, *Bombs and Betty Grable* (Warwickshire: Brewin Books, 2010), 13.
3 Wilcox, personal communication.
4 Wilcox explains that subs' boys ran errands for the subs, such as bringing them tea and lunch. Wilcox, *Bombs and Betty Grable*, 80, 71.
5 Ibid., 91–8.
6 John Wilcox, personal website (http://www.johnwilcoxauthor.co.uk/?fbclid=IwAR2uM5GAspw4J6P90KpP_4NHzGX34eNJ9nzYjycMXTUCESbzR8TU0tEvSc8). For the especially strong image of Uncle Alf, the uncle who won the Victoria Cross, see John Wilcox, *Bombs and Betty Grable*, 2–11.
7 Wilcox, personal communication.

8 John Wilcox, *The Guns of El Kebir (Guns)* back cover. Sharpe and Hornblower are protagonists in two series of twentieth-century novels written respectively by Bernard Cornwell and C. S. Forester and set during the Napoleonic wars and beyond.
9 John Wilcox, *Guns*, inside jacket.
10 Wilcox, personal communication.
11 Ibid.
12 See Kate Mitchell, *History and Cultural Memory in Neo-Victorian Fiction: Victorian Afterimages* (Basingstoke: Palgrave Macmillan, 2010).
13 Dana Shiller, "The Redemptive Past in the Neo-Victorian Novel." *Studies in the Novel*, 29.4 (1997): 558.
14 See Louisa Hadley, *Neo-victorian Fiction and Historical Narrative: The Victorians and Us* (Houndmills, Basingstoke, Hampshire: Palgrave Macmillan, 2010) and Shiller "The Redemptive Past."
15 Martin Green, *Dreams of Adventure, Deeds of Empire* (New York: Basic Books, 1979), 37. For an analysis of select Western adventure fictions from the seventeenth century and after, see Martin Green, *Seven Types of Adventure Tale: An Etiology of a Major Genre* (University Park: Pennsylvania State University Press, 1991).
16 John McClure, *Late Imperial Romance* (London: Verso, 1994), 2.
17 For elements of the imperial romance, see Linda Dryden, *Joseph Conrad and Imperial Romance* (Houndmills: Palgrave, 2000), 36–41.
18 Suzanne Keen, *Romances of the Archive in Contemporary British Fiction* (Toronto: University of Toronto Press, 2001), 3–27.
19 Esty, *Unseasonable Youth*.
20 John Wilcox, *The Guns of El Kebir* (London: Headline, 2007), 94. Subsequent page references in text.
21 Afaf Lutfi Sayyid-Marsot, "Entrepreneurial Women in Egypt." In *Feminism and Islam: Legal and Literary Perspectives*, ed. Mai Yamani (New York: New York University Press), 1996, 33–47.
22 Yousef, *Composing Egypt*, 81–2.
23 For views on women's work, see Baron, *The Women's Awakening in Egypt*, 144–67.
24 Mieke Bal, "The Point of Narratology." *Poetics Today*, 11.4 (1990): 731–2.
25 John Tosh, *A Man's Place: Masculinity and the Middle-Class Home in Victorian England* (New Haven, CT: 2007), 151–3. See also John Tosh, *Manliness and Masculinities in Nineteenth-Century Britain: Essays on Gender, Family, and Empire* (New York: Pearson Longman, 2005), 117–18.

26 Billie Melman, *Women's Orients: English Women and the Middle East, 1718–1918: Sexuality, Religion and Work* (London: Macmillan, 1992), 255. See 254–305 for women and Egyptology and ethnography.
27 Flanders, *The Victorian House*, 177–214.
28 Dryden, *Joseph Conrad and Imperial Romance*, 3–4.
29 Keen, *Romances of the Archive in Contemporary British Fiction*, 35.
30 For characteristics of romances of the archive, see Keen, *Romances of the Archive in Contemporary British Fiction*, 3–27.
31 For prolepsis, see David Herman on "Limits of Order: Toward a Theory of Polychronic Narration." *Narrative*, 6.1 (1998): 74.
32 Stuart Ward. "Introduction." In *British Culture and the End of Empire* (Manchester: Manchester University Press, 2001), 8.
33 John M. MacKenzie, "The Persistence of Empire in Metropolitan Culture." In *British Culture and the End of Empire*, ed. Stuart Ward (Manchester: Manchester University Press, 2001), 22.
34 For a history of Britain's dwindling power on the world stage, see Alasdair Blair, *Britain and the World Since 1945* (London: Routledge/Taylor & Francis Group, 2015), 49–54 and 118–59.
35 Mahmoud al-Khafif records that Admiral Seymour received instructions from the British government to use force against the Egyptian forts. On the situation in Egypt and specifically in Alexandria between the Alexandria massacre and the bombardment, see al-Khafif, *Ahmad Urabi al-za'im al-muftara 'alayh*, volume 2), 13–62.
36 See Alun Munslow, *Deconstructing History* (London: Routledge, 1997), 33 and 34.
37 Urabi's memoirs, Khafif and Rafi'i all mention general destruction visited upon the whole city without singling out either European or native residences as more tragically affected. Khafif contrasts 2,000 Egyptians killed in Alexandria, in addition to the wounded, to five fatalities among British soldiers and 19 wounded (Khafif, *Ahmad Urabi al-za'im al-Muftara 'alayh*, volume 2, 80).
38 For an analysis of the way the imperial romance forces its conventions even as twentieth-century authors attempt to subvert it, causing the traditionalist strain to triumph over the revisionist strain, see David Medalie, "A Century Later: New Fictional Representations of the Boer War." *Journal of Southern African Studies*, 30.2 (2004): 377–92.
39 On repetition and retardation, see Kathryn Hume, "Narrative Speed in Contemporary Fiction." *Narrative*, 13.2 (2005): 105–24.
40 Bal, "The Point of Narratology," 733.
41 Manfred Jahn, "Frames, Preferences, and the Reading of Third-Person Narratives: Towards a Cognitive Narratology." *Poetics Today*, 18.4 (1997): 445.

42 Michael Denning, *Cover Stories: Narrative and Ideology in the British Spy Thriller* (London: Routledge and K. Paul, 1987).
43 For how Edwardian spy novels reconciled ideas of gentlemanliness and espionage, see David Stafford "Spies and Gentlemen: The Birth of the British Spy Novel, 1893–1914." *Victorian Studies*, 24.4 (1981): 506–7.
44 Rafi'i, *Al-thawra al-urabiyya wa al-ihtilal al-Injilizi*, 114–21. See also Gershoni and Jankowski, *Egypt, Islam, and the Arabs*, 5–8.
45 Peter Mansfield, "Foreword." In *The British in Egypt* (London: Weidenfeld and Nicolson, 1971), XI.
46 Wilcox, personal communication.
47 Ibid.
48 Mansfield, *The British in Egypt*, 21–2.
49 See Pollard, *Nurturing the Nation*.
50 See the Introduction to this study.
51 Khafif, *Ahmad Urabi al-za'im al-Muftara 'alayh*, volume 1, 303–28.
52 David Herman on "Limits of Order," 73.
53 Keen, *Romances of the Archive in Contemporary British Fiction*, 3–27.

4 The Women of Mahmoud's Dreams: Bahaa Taher's *Sunset Oasis* and the National Mosaic

1 For a detailed study of the new-consciousness novel, see Youssef, *Minorities in the Contemporary Egyptian Novel*. The term "new-consciousness novel" is Youssef's.
2 On how Taher and other Arab writers use Sufism to process political life and reflect on the novel and Arab identity, see Ziad Elmarsafy, *Sufism in the Contemporary Arabic Novel* (Edinburgh: Edinburgh University Press, 2012).
3 Ahmed Fakhry, *Siwa Oasis* (Cairo: The American University in Cairo Press, 1973), 168–70.
4 Ibid., 97 and 105–6.
5 al-Bahaa Hussein, *Qariban min Baha' Taher:Muhawarat wa malameh* (Cairo: al-Majlis al-A'la li al-Thaqafa, 2004), 62–3.
6 Youssef, *Minorities in the Contemporary Egyptian Novel*, 57–63.
7 Hatem Hafez, "Iradat al-kalam fi al-riwaya 'ala hamish 'Wahat al-ghurub.'" In *Riwayat Baha' Tahir wa al-naqd al-misri* (Cairo: al-Hay'a al-'Amma li Qusur al-Thaqafa, 2008), 173–9.
8 Mustafa al-Dab', "Mustawayat al-qira'a fi Wahat al-ghurub." In *Riwayat Baha Taher wa al-naqd al-misri* (Cairo: al-Hay'a al 'Amma li Qusur al-Thaqafa, *kitab al-thaqafa al-jadida* 29. 214, 2008), 161–72.

9 Youssef, *Minorities in the Contemporary Egyptian Novel*, 61.

10 On the marginalization of Siwan cultural and political rights see Youssef, *Minorities in the Contemporary Egyptian Novel*, 43.

11 According to Fakhry, marriage between two males was common in Siwa until 1928. Even though it became a punishable crime, same-sex marriage continued to happen until the end of the Second World War, though without a contract. Fakhry does not speak to female same-sex relationships. See Fakhry, *Siwa Oasis*.

12 Youssef, *Minorities in the Contemporary Egyptian Novel*, 32.

13 On Egyptians as colonized colonizers, especially their construction of themselves as white vis-à-vis Nubians and Sudanese, see Eve Powell, *A Different Shade of Colonialism: Egypt, Great Britain, and the Mastery of the Sudan* (Berkeley: University of California Press, 2003).

14 Youssef, *Minorities in the Contemporary Egyptian Novel*, 62.

15 Boone, "Vacation Cruises; or the Homoerotics of Orientalism," 460–86.

16 For the imperial romance, see Green, *Dreams of Adventure, Deeds of Empire*; McClure, *Late Imperial Romance*); and Dryden, *Joseph Conrad and Imperial Romance*.

17 See Fakhry, *Siwa Oasis*.

18 Bahaa Taher, *Sunset Oasis*, trans. Humphrey T. Davies (London: Sceptre, 2009), 152. Subsequent page references in text.

19 'Awad, *Sitt riwayat misriyya muthira li al-jadal*, 239–76.

20 Gayle Rubin, "The Traffic in Women: Notes on the 'Political Economy' of Sex." In *Toward and Anthropology of Women*, ed. Rayna R. Reiter (New York: Monthly Review Press, 1975), 157–210.

21 For the grievances of contemporary Nubians and Siwans, see Youssef, *Minorities in the Contemporary Egyptian Novel*, 43.

22 John Hunwick, "Introduction: The Same but Different: Africans in Slavery in the Mediterranean Muslim World." In *The African Diaspora in the Mediterranean Lands of Islam*, ed. Hunwick, John O and Eve T. Powell (Princeton, NJ: Markus Wiener Publishers, 2002), XXI. For different types of responsibilities assigned to slaves based on their color, see Terence Walz, "Black Slavery in Egypt During the Nineteenth Century as Reflected in the Mahkama Archives of Cairo." In *Slaves and Slavery in Muslim Africa*, volume 2, *The Servile Estate*, ed. John R. Willis (Abingdon: Routledge, 2016), 137–60.

23 Eve T. Powell, *Tell This in My Memory: Stories of Enslavement from Egypt, Sudan, and the Ottoman Empire* (Stanford, CA: Stanford University Press, 2013), 27–8.

24 John Hunwick and Eve T. Powell, ed. *The African Diaspora in the Mediterranean Lands of Islam* (Princeton, NJ: Markus Wiener Publishers, 2002), 53.

25 Walz, "Black Slavery in Egypt," especially 151.

26 Terence Walz, "Sudanese, Habasha, Takarna, and Barabira: Trans-Saharan Africans in Cairo as Shown in the 1848 Census." In *Race and Slavery in the Middle East: Histories of Trans-Saharan Africans in Nineteenth-Century Egypt, Sudan, and the Ottoman Mediterranean*, ed. Terence Walz and Kenneth M. Cuno (Cairo: The American University in Cairo, 2010), 67.

27 Bahaa Taher, *Wahat al-ghurub*. Cairo: Dar al-Hilal, 2006, 83 (my translation).

28 Ibid., my translation.

29 Walz, "Black Slavery in Egypt," 140.

30 Kenneth Cuno, "African Slaves in Nineteenth-Century Rural Egypt: A Preliminary Assessment." In *Race and Slavery in the Middle East: Histories of Trans-Saharan Africans in Nineteenth-Century Egypt, Sudan, and the Ottoman Mediterranean*, ed. Terence Walz and Kenneth M. Cuno. Cairo: The American University in Cairo, 2010), 84.

31 Powell, *A Different Shade of Colonialism*, 26–63.

32 Hunwick, "Introduction," XVIII–IX.

33 Ahmad Sikainga, "Slavery and Social Life in Nineteenth-Century Turco-Egyptian Khartoum." In *Race and Slavery in the Middle East: Histories of Trans-Saharan Africans in Nineteenth-Century Egypt, Sudan, and the Ottoman Mediterranean*, ed. Terence Walz and Kenneth M. Cuno (Cairo: The American University in Cairo, 2010), 7–8.

34 Jay Spaulding, "'Slaves of the King?': Rhetoric and Reality in the Nubian State Tradition." In *African Systems of Slavery*, ed. Jay Spaulding and Stephanie Beswick (Trenton, NJ: Africa World Press, 2010), 247–65.

35 Powell, *A Different Shade of Colonialism*, 6–7.

36 Eve Powell, "Slaves or Siblings? Abdallah al-Nadim's Dialogues about the Family." In *Histories of the Modern Middle East: New Directions*, ed. I. Gershoni, Y. H. Erdem, and Ursula Woköck (Boulder, CO: Lynne Rienner, 2002), 155–65.

37 Powell, *A Different Shade of Colonialism*, 2–3 and 161–2. For 'Abdallah al-Nadim's—political activist and famous orator of the Urabi Revolution—portrayal of freed Sudanese slaves in writing and on stage, see Powell, "Slaves or Siblings?" 155–65. For the portrayal of Sudanese in Egyptian popular culture between the First World War and 1925 and on stage, including Egyptians in blackface, see Powell, *A Different Shade of Colonialism*, 168–216. See also Powell, "Burnt-Cork Nationalism: Race and Identity in the Theater of 'Ali al-Kassar," In *Colors of Enchantment: Theater, Dance, Music, and the Visual Arts of the Middle East* ed. Sherifa Zuhur (Cairo: American University in Cairo Press, 2001), 27–38. On the continued exoticization of the Sudanese and other Africans in Nasserist cinema, see Joel Gordon. "River Blindness: Black and White Identity in Early Nasserist Cinema." In *Narrating the Nile: Politics, Cultures, Identities*, ed.

I. Gershoni, Meir Hatina, and Ḥagai Erlikh (Boulder, CO: Lynne Rienner, 2008), 137–56.

38 Powell, *A Different Shade of Colonialism*, 6–7.

39 See, for example, Sister Bakhita Kwashe's story in Powell, *Tell This in My Memory*, 157–63.

40 See Hunwick and Powell, *The African Diaspora*, 65–81.

41 Ehud Toledano, *The Ottoman Slave Trade and Its Suppression, 1840–1890* (Princeton, NJ: Princeton University Press, 1982), 91.

42 See, for example, the story of Sister Mary Josephine Zeinab, a former slave adopted by Italian missionaries, see Powell, *Tell This in My Memory*, 163–5.

43 For slave names, see John Hunwick, "Black Africans in the Mediterranean World: Introduction to a Neglected Aspect of the African Diaspora." In *The Human Commodity: Perspectives on the Trans-Saharan Slave Trade*, ed. Elizabeth Savage (London: F. Cass, 1992), 13.

44 See Hunwick and Powell, *The African Diaspora*, 116–20.

45 Taher, *Wahat al-ghurub*, 84, my translation, emphasis added.

46 Ibid., my translation, emphasis added.

47 See Hunwick and Powell, *The African Diaspora*, 27–32.

48 For the concept of sly civility, see Bhabha, *The Location of Culture*, 93–101.

49 Walz, "Black Slavery in Egypt," 149. See also Liat Kozma, *Policing Egyptian Women: Sex, Law, and Medicine in Khedival Egypt* (Syracuse, NY: Syracuse University Press, 2011), 50–78 and Liat Kozma, "Black, Kinless, and Hungry: Manumitted Female Slaves in Khedival Egypt." In *Race and Slavery in the Middle East: Histories of Trans-Saharan Africans in Nineteenth-Century Egypt, Sudan, and the Ottoman Mediterranean*, ed. Terence Walz and Kenneth M. Cuno (Cairo: The American University in Cairo, 2010), 197–215.

50 Gabriel Baer, "Slavery in Nineteenth Century Egypt." *Journal of African History*, 8.3 (1967): 437.

51 Walz, "Black Slavery in Egypt," 146.

52 Baer, "Slavery in Nineteenth Century Egypt," 438.

53 Taher, *Wahat al-ghurub*, 85, my translation.

54 Ehud R. Toledano, "The Concept of Slavery in Ottoman and Other Muslim Societies: Dichotomy or Continuum?" In *Slave Elites in the Middle East and Africa: A Comparative Study*, ed. Toru Miura and John Edward Philips (London: Kegan Paul International, 2000), 172.

55 Ian Edgar, "Preface to the Paperback Edition: The Dreams of Islamic State." In *The Dream in Islam: From Qur'anic Tradition to Jihadist Inspiration* (New York: Berghahn Books, 2016), XIX.

56 For different dream interpretation media, see Amira Mittermaier's fascinating anthropological study of dreams: Amira Mittermaier, *Dreams That*

Matter: Egyptian Landscapes of the Imagination (Berkeley: University of California Press, 2011).

57 El-Sayed el-Aswad, "Dreams and the Construction of Reality: Symbolic Transformations of the Seen and the Unseen in the Egyptian Imagination," *Anthropos*, 105 (2010): 441–53.

58 On the importance of dreams in Islam and Sufism and on *istikhāra*, see Imran Hosein, *The Strategic Importance of Dreams and Visions in Islam: Eschatological and Epistemological Implications of True Dreams and Visions, A View from Islam* (Ajax, Ontario, Canada: Ironheart Publishing House, 2019), Elizabeth Sirriyeh, *Dreams and Visions in the World of Islam: A History of Muslim Dreaming and Foreknowing* (London: I.B. Tauris, 2018) and Özgen Felek and Alexander Knysh, eds. *Dreams and Visions in Islamic Societies* (Albany: State University of New York Press, 2012).

59 Erik Ohlander, "Behind the Veil of the Unseen: Dreams and Dreaming in the Classical and Medieval Sufi Tradition." In *Dreams and Visions in Islamic Societies*, ed. Özgen Felek and Alexander Knysh (Albany: State University of New York Press, 2012), 206.

60 Edgar, "Preface," XII, Mittermaier, *Dreams That Matter*, 100–2, and Ohlander, "Behind the Veil of the Unseen," 199–213.

61 Edgar, "Preface," XII, and Mittermaier, *Dreams That Matter*, 100–2, 184–5 and 189.

62 Ian Edgar, *The Dream in Islam: From Qur'anic Tradition to Jihadist Inspiration* (New York: Berghahn Books, 2016), 56.

63 See Edgar, *The Dream in Islam*, 56, and Franco Moretti, *The Way of the World: The Bildungsroman in European Culture* (London: Verso, 2000).

64 Edgar, *The Dream in Islam*, 56.

65 Ibid.

66 See Llewellyn Vaughan-Lee, *Catching the Thread: Sufism, Dreamwork & Jungian Psychology* (Inverness, CA: Golden Sufi Center, 1998), 1–104.

67 Mittermaier, *Dreams That Matter*, 239 and Özgen Felek and Alexander Knysh, "Introduction." In *Dreams and Visions in Islamic Societies* (Albany: State University of New York Press, 2012), 1–11. While some erroneously believe the saying to be a *hadith* (saying) by the prophet, the saying actually is Imam Ali's.

68 Mittermaier, *Dreams That Matter*, 100–2.

69 Edgar, *The Dream in Islam*, 54.

70 See Sirriyeh, *Dreams and Visions in the World of Islam*.

71 Elmarsafy, *Sufism in the Contemporary Arabic Novel*.

72 Matthew Ellis, *Desert Borderland: The Making of Modern Egypt and Libya* (California: Stanford University Press, 2018), 40–60.

73 On general Siwan history, see Fakhry, *Siwa Oasis*, 17–43 and Ellis, *Desert Borderland*, 17–21.
74 Fakhry, *Siwa Oasis*, 105–6.
75 Youssef, *Minorities in the Contemporary Egyptian Novel*, 57.
76 Nermin Ahmed Haikal, "Fight-or-Flight Response: A Study of Bahaa Taher's *Sunset Oasis* with Reference to Trauma Theory." *Majallat al-Bahth al-'Ilmi fi al-Adaab*, 20.2 (2019): 593–617.
77 Youssef, *Minorities in the Contemporary Egyptian Novel*, 44.
78 For a discussion of Pharaonism in general and in Egyptian literature in particular, see Elliott Colla, "The Stuff of Egypt: The Nation, the State, and Their Proper Objects." *New Formations: A Journal of Culture/ Theory/ Politics*, 45 (2001–2): 72–90 and Elliott Colla, *Conflicted Antiquities: Egyptology, Egyptomania, Egyptian Modernity* (Durham, NC: Duke University Press, 2007).
79 Taher, *Abnaa Rifa'a*, 22–4. For the image of the West in Taher's narrative, see Lorenzo Casini, "Beyond Occidentalism: Europe and the Self in Present-day Arabic Narrative Discourse." EUI working papers, 2008/30. San Domenico (FI): European University Institute (EUI), Robert Schuman Centre for Advanced Studies, 2008, 1–21.
80 Sayyid-Marsot corroborates this view. She pronounces Khedive Tawfiq as the real traitor, explaining that he supported a Cabinet decision to resist the British; then, to protect his throne, he asked the British to bombard Alexandria and occupy Egypt. See Sayyid-Marsot, *Egypt and Cromer*, 31.
81 For a review of political life in Egypt from the 1952 Revolution until the present day, see John Bradley, *Inside Egypt: The Land of the Pharaohs on the Brink of a Revolution* (New York: Palgrave Macmillan, 2008).
82 Hussein, *Qariban min Bahaa Taher*, 133.
83 In the English translation he sees willow trees.
84 In interpreting Mahmoud's dream, I have consulted Ibn Sirin, considered an authority on dream interpretation, in addition to https://tafsiralahlam.com/ and https://www.shmlool.com/dream/ (both accessed April 7, 2021).
85 Youssef, *Minorities in the Contemporary Egyptian Novel*, 62.
86 See Walter Benjamin, *Illuminations. "Theses on the Philosophy of History,"* trans. Henry Zohn (New York: Harcourt, Brace & World, 1955), 255–66 and Hafez, "Iradat al-kalam," 178.
87 Hosein, *The Strategic Importance of Dreams*, 72.

Bibliography

El Alem, Mahmoud A. *Ta'ammulat fi 'alam Naguib Mahfouz*. Cairo: al-Hay'a al-Misriyya al-'Amma li al-ta'lif wa al-Nashr, 1970.

El-Aswad, el-Sayed. "Dreams and the Construction of Reality: Symbolic Transformations of the Seen and the Unseen in the Egyptian Imagination," *Anthropos*, 105 (2010): 441–53.

'Atiyya, Ahmad Muhammad. *'Adwa' jadida 'ala al-thaqafa al-'arabiyya: ahadith 'arabiyya*. Cairo: Ra' li al-tiba'a wa al-nashr, 1980.

'Atiyya, Ahmad Muhammad. *Ma'a Naguib Mahfouz*. Beirut: Dar al-Jil, 1977.

'Awad, Ibrahim M. *Sitt riwayat misriyya muthira li al-jadal*. Cairo: Maktabat Jazirat al-Ward, 2011.

Abel, Elizabeth, Marianne Hirsch, and Elizabeth Langland. *The Voyage in: Fictions of Female Development*. Hanover, NH: Published for Dartmouth College by University Press of New England, 1983.

Abu Ouf, Abdel-Rahman. *Al-Ru'a al-mutaghayyira fi riwayat Naguib Mahfouz*. Cairo: al-Hay'a al-Misriyya al-'Amma li al-Kitab, 1991.

Abu Ouf, Abdel-Rahman. *Fusul fi al-naqd wa al-adab*. Cairo: al-Hay'a al-Misriyya al-'Amma li al-Kitab, 1996.

Abugideiri, Hibba. *Gender and the Making of Modern Medicine in Colonial Egypt*. Farnham, Surrey, UK: Ashgate, 2010.

Ahmed, Hussam R. *The Last Nahdawi: Taha Hussein and Institution Building in Egypt*. Redwood City: Stanford University Press, 2022.

Alami, A. Idrissi. "Moroccan Nation-Building and the Bildungsroman in Abd Al-Karim Ghallab's Dafanna Al-Madi and Al-Muallim Ali." *Middle Eastern Literatures*, 16.1 (2013): 60–75.

Allen, Roger M. A. *The Arabic Novel: An Historical and Critical Introduction*. New York: Syracuse University Press, 1982.

Allen, Roger M. A. *Naguib Mahfouz: A Retrospective*. Seattle: Department of Near Eastern Languages and Civilization, University of Washington, 2004.

Anis, Abdel-Azim, and Mahmoud Amin. *Fi al-thaqafa al-misriyya*, 2nd edition, Rabat: Dar al-Aman, 1988.

Badawi, M. M. "Commitment in Contemporary Arabic Literature." In *Critical Perspectives on Modern Arabic Literature*, ed. Issa J. Boullata. Washington, DC: Three Continents, 1980, 23–44.

Badr, Abd al-Muhsin Taha. *Al-ru'ya wa al-'ada: Naguib Mahfouz*. Cairo: Dar al-Ma'aref, 1984.

Baer, Gabriel. "Slavery in Nineteenth Century Egypt." *Journal of African History*, 8.3 (1967): 417–41.

Bal, Mieke. "The Point of Narratology." *Poetics Today*, 11.4 (1990): 727–53.

Baron, Beth. *Egypt as a Woman: Nationalism, Gender, and Politics*. Berkeley: University of California Press, 2005.

Baron, Beth. *The Women's Awakening in Egypt: Culture, Society, and the Press*. New Haven, CT: Yale University Press, 1994.

Barthorp, Michael. *War on the Nile: Britain, Egypt, and the Sudan, 1882–1898*. Poole, Dorset: Blandford Press, 1984.

Benjamin, Walter. *Illuminations. "Theses on the Philosophy of History,"* trans. Henry Zohn. New York: Harcourt, Brace & World, 1955, 255–66.

Bhabha, Homi K. *The Location of Culture*. London: Routledge, 1994.

Bier, Laura. *Revolutionary Womanhood: Feminisms, Modernity, and the State in Nasser's Egypt*. Stanford, CA: Stanford University Press, 2011.

Blair, Alasdair. Britain and the World Since 1945. London: Routledge/Taylor & Francis Group, 2015.

Blunt, Wilfrid Scawen. *Secret History of the English Occupation of Egypt: Being a Personal Narrative of Events*. New York: A. A. Knopf, 1922.

Bode, Carl. "Durrell's Way to Alexandria." In *Critical Essays on Lawrence Durrell*, ed. Alan Friedman. Boston, MA: G.K. Hall, 1987, 135–44.

Boes, Tobias. *Formative Fictions: Nationalism, Cosmopolitanism, and the Bildungsroman*. New York: Cornell University Press, 2012.

Boone, Joseph A. "Vacation Cruises; or the Homoerotics of Orientalism." In *Feminist Postcolonial Theory: A Reader*, ed. Reina Lewis and Sara Mills. New York: Routledge, 2003, 460–86.

Bowen, Roger. "Closing the 'Toybox': Orientalism and Empire in the Alexandria Quartet." *Studies in the Literary Imagination*, 24 (1991): 9–18.

Bowker, Gordon. *Through the Dark Labyrinth: A Biography of Lawrence Durrell*. New York: St. Martin's Press, 1997.

Bradley, John. R. *Inside Egypt: The Land of the Pharaohs on the Brink of a Revolution*. New York: Palgrave Macmillan, 2008.

Casini, Lorenzo. "Beyond Occidentalism: Europe and the Self in Present-Day Arabic Narrative Discourse." EUI working papers, 2008. San Domenico (FI),

Italy: European University Institute (EUI). Robert Schuman Centre for Advanced Studies, 2008. 1–21.

Chakrabarty, Dipesh. *Provincializing Europe: Postcolonial Thought and Historical Difference*. Princeton, NJ: Princeton University Press, 2000.

Chamberlain, M. E. "The Alexandria Massacre of 11 June 1882 and the British Occupation of Egypt." *Middle Eastern Studies*, 13.1 (1977): 14–39.

Chirol, Valentine. *The Egyptian Problem*. London: Macmillan, 1920.

Colla, Elliott. *Conflicted Antiquities: Egyptology, Egyptomania, Egyptian Modernity*. Durham, NC: Duke University Press, 2007.

Colla, Elliott. "The Stuff of Egypt: the Nation, the State, and their Proper Objects." *New Formations: A Journal of Culture/Theory/Politics*, 45 (2001–2): 72–90.

Creed, Walter, G. *The Muse of Science and the Alexandria Quartet*. Alexandria, Egypt: Norwood, 1977.

Cromer, Evelyn Baring. *Modern Egypt*. New York: Macmillan, 1908.

Cuno, Kenneth M. "African Slaves in Nineteenth-Century Rural Egypt: A Preliminary Assessment." In *Race and Slavery in the Middle East: Histories of Trans-Saharan Africans in Nineteenth-Century Egypt, Sudan, and the Ottoman Mediterranean*, ed. Terence Walz and Kenneth M. Cuno. Cairo: The American University in Cairo, 2010, 77–98.

Al-Dabe', Mustafa. "Mustawayat al qira'a fi Wahat al-ghurub." *Riwayat Baha Taher wa al-naqd al-misri*. Cairo: al-Hay'a al-'Amma li Qusur al-Thaqafa, *kitab al-thaqafa al-jadida*, 29.214, 2008, 161–72.

Dayf, Shawqi. *Al-hubb al-'udhri 'inda al-'arab*. Cairo: al-Dar al-Misriyya al-Lubnaniya, 1999.

Denning, Michael. *Cover Stories: Narrative and Ideology in the British Spy Thriller*. London: Routledge and K. Paul, 1987.

Diboll, Michael V. *Lawrence Durrell's "Alexandria Quartet" in Its Egyptian Contexts*. Lewiston, NY: Edwin Mellen Press, 2004.

Diboll, Michael V. "The Secret History of Lawrence Durrell's *the Alexandria Quartet*: The Mountolive-Hosnani Affair, Britain, and the *Wafd*." In *Lawrence Durrell and the Greek World*, ed. Anna Lillios. Selinsgrove: Susquehanna University Press, 2004, 79–105.

Dobrée, Bonamy. "Durrell's Alexandrian Series." *The Sewanee Review*, 69.1 (1961): 61–79.

Dryden, Linda. *Joseph Conrad and Imperial Romance*. Houndmills: Palgrave, 2000.

Durrell. *Clea*. New York: Dutton, 1960.

Durrell, Lawrence. "Introduction." In *Alexandria: A History and a Guide*, ed. E. M. Forster. London, England: M. Haag, 1982, IX–XIV.

Durrell, Lawrence. *Mountolive*. New York: E. P. Dutton, 1961.

Edgar, Iain R. *The Dream in Islam: From Qur'anic Tradition to Jihadist Inspiration*. New York: Berghahn Books, 2016.

Edgar, Iain R. "Preface to the Paperback Edition: The Dreams of Islamic State." In *The Dream in Islam: From Qur'anic Tradition to Jihadist Inspiration*. New York: Berghahn Books, 2016, XI–XXIX.

Ellis, Matthew H. *Desert Borderland: The Making of Modern Egypt and Libya*. Stanford, CA: Stanford University Press, 2018.

Elmarsafy, Ziad. *Sufism in the Contemporary Arabic Novel*. Edinburgh: Edinburgh University Press, 2012.

Enany, Rasheed. *Naguib Mahfouz: His Life and Times*, Cairo: The American University in Cairo Press, 2007.

Enany, Rasheed. *Naguib Mahfouz: The Pursuit of Meaning*. London: Routledge, 1993.

Erlanger, Steven. "A Global Outpouring of Grief Mixes with Criticism of the Monarchy." *The New York Times*. Updated September 9, 2022. https://indianexpress.com/article/world/queen-elizabeth-death-reactions-criticism-8140045/ (accessed online November 27, 2022.)

Esty, Jed. *A Shrinking Island: Modernism and National Culture in England*. Princeton, NJ: Princeton University Press, 2004.

Esty, Jed. *Unseasonable Youth: Modernism, Colonialism, and the Fiction of Development*. New York: Oxford University Press, 2012.

Fahmy, Ziad. *Ordinary Egyptians: Creating the Modern Nation through Popular Culture, 1870–1919*. Cairo: The American University in Cairo Press, 2011.

Fakhry, Ahmed. *Siwa Oasis*. Cairo: The American University in Cairo Press, 1973.

Fanon, Frantz. *The Wretched of the Earth*, trans. Richard Philcox. New York: Grove Press, 2004.

Felek, Ozgen, and Alexander Knysh, eds. *Dreams and Visions in Islamic Societies*. Albany: State University of New York Press, 2012.

Felek, Ozgen, and Alexander Knysh. "Introduction." In *Dreams and Visions in Islamic Societies*. Albany: State University of New York Press, 2012, 1–11.

Felton, Emmanuel, and Meena Venkataramanan. "Black Americans See Complications in Adulation of Queen Elizabeth II." *The Washington Post*, September 13, 2022, 3:47 p.m. EDT. .https://www.washingtonpost.com/world/2022/09/13/queen-black-americans/ (accessed online November 27, 2022.)

Flanders, Judith. *The Victorian House*. London: Harper, 2003.

Friedman, Alan Warren. "Chronology." In *Lawrence Durrell and the Alexandria Quartet: Art for Love's Sake*. Norman: University of Oklahoma Press, 1970, XIX–XXII.

Friedman, Alan Warren, ed. *Critical Essays on Lawrence Durrell*. Boston, MA: G.K. Hall, 1987.

Friedman, Alan Warren. "Introduction." In *Critical Essays on Lawrence Durrell*, ed. Alan Friedman. Boston, MA: G.K. Hall, 1987, 1–14.

Gershoni, I., and James P. Jankowski. *Egypt, Islam, and the Arabs: The Search for Egyptian Nationhood, 1900–1930*. New York: Oxford University Press, 1986.

Al-Ghitani, Gamal. *Al-majalis al-mahfouziyya*. Cairo: Dar al-Shuruq, 2006.

Gilmore, Christine. "'A Minor Literature in a Major Voice': Narrating Nubian Identity in Contemporary Egypt." *Alif: Journal of Comparative Poetics*, 35 (2015), 42–74.

Godshalk, William Leigh. "Some Sources of Durrell's Alexandria Quartet." In *Critical Essays on Lawrence Durrell*, ed. Alan Friedman. Boston, MA: G.K. Hall, 1987, 158–71.

Gordon, Joel. *Nasser's Blessed Movement: Egypt's Free Officers and the July Revolution*. Cairo: The American University in Cairo Press, 2016.

Gordon, Joel. "River Blindness: Black and White Identity in Early Nasserist Cinema." In *Narrating the Nile: Politics, Cultures, Identities*, ed. I. Gershoni, Meir Hatina, and Ḥagai Erlikh. Boulder, CO: Lynne Rienner, 2008, 137–56.

Green, Martin. *Dreams of Adventure, Deeds of Empire*. New York: Basic Books, 1979.

Green, Martin. *Seven Types of Adventure Tale: An Etiology of a Major Genre*. University Park: Pennsylvania State University Press, 1991.

Gwynne, Rosalind. "Islam and Muslims in *the Alexandria Quartet. Deus Loci*." *The Lawrence Durrell Journal*, NS5 (1997): 92–102.

Hadley, Louisa. *Neo-victorian Fiction and Historical Narrative: The Victorians and Us*. Houndmills, Basingstoke, Hampshire: Palgrave Macmillan, 2010.

Hafez, Hatem. "Iradat al-kalam fi al-riwaya 'ala hamish 'Wahat al-ghurub.'" In *Riwayat Bahaa Taher wa al naqd al-misri*. Cairo: al-Hay'a al-'Amma li Qusur al-Thaqafa, 2008, 173–9.

Haikal, Nermin Ahmed. "Fight-or-Flight Response: A Study of Bahaa Taher's *Sunset Oasis* with Reference to Trauma Theory." *Majallat al-Bahth al-'Ilmi fi al-Adaab*, 20.2 (2019): 593–617.

Halim, Hala. *Alexandrian Cosmopolitanism: An Archive*. New York: Fordham University Press, 2013.

Hamouda, Sahar. "The Figure of the Copt in Lawrence Durrell's *Alexandria Quartet* and Edwar Al-Kharrat's *City of Saffron* and *Girls of Alexandria*." In *Durrell in Alexandria: On Miracle Ground 9, Conference Proceedings, Alexandria Egypt, June 1996*, ed. Shelly Ekhtiar. Baltimore, MD: International Lawrence Durrell Society, 2005, 100–10.

Hansen, Peter H. "Coronation Everest: The Empire and Commonwealth in the 'Second Elizabethan Age.'" In *British Culture and the End of Empire*, ed. Stuart Ward. Manchester: Manchester University Press, 2001, 57–72.

Hasan, Mohamed Yehia Mohamed. "Images of the 'Other' in *the Alexandria Quartet*: Encounters and Self-Explorations." In Durrell in Alexandria: On Miracle Ground 9 Conference Proceedings, Alexandria, Egypt, June 1996, ed. Shelly Ekhtiar. Baltimore, MD: International Lawrence Durrell Society, 2005, 312–22.

Hatem, Mervat. "Class and Patriarchy as Competing Paradigms for the Study of Middle Eastern Women." *Society for Comparative Studies in Society and History*, 29.4 (1987): 811–18.

Helbawy, Kamal. "The Muslim Brotherhood in Egypt: Historical Evolution and Future Prospects." In *Political Islam: Context versus Ideology*, ed. Khaled Hroub. London: London Middle East Institute at SOAS, 2010, 61–85.

Herman, David. "Limits of Order: Toward a Theory of Polychronic Narration." *Narrative*, 6.1 (1998): 72–95.

Heshmat, Dina. *Egypt 1919: The Revolution in Literature and Film*. Edinburgh: Edinburgh University Press, 2022.

Hosein, Imran N. *The Strategic Importance of Dreams and Visions in Islam: Eschatological and Epistemological Implications of True Dreams and Visions, A View from Islam*. Ajax, Ontario, Canada: Ironheart Publishing House, 2019.

Hume, Kathryn. "Narrative Speed in Contemporary Fiction." *Narrative*, 13.2 (2005): 105–24.

Hunwick, John. "Black Africans in the Mediterranean World: Introduction to a Neglected Aspect of the African Diaspora." In *The Human Commodity: Perspectives on the Trans-Saharan Slave Trade*, ed. Elizabeth Savage. London: F. Cass, 1992, 5–38.

Hunwick, John O. "Introduction: The Same but Different: Africans in Slavery in the Mediterranean Muslim World." In *The African Diaspora in the Mediterranean Lands of Islam*, ed. John O. Hunwick and Eve T. Powell. Princeton, NJ: Markus Wiener, 2002, IX–XXIV.

Hunwick, John O., and Eve T. Powell. *The African Diaspora in the Mediterranean Lands of Islam*. Princeton, NJ: Markus Wiener, 2002.

Hussein, Al Bahaa. *Qariban min Baha Taher: Muhawarat wa malameh*. Cairo: al Majlis al 'A'ala li al-Thaqafa, 2004.

Ibrahim, Vivian. *The Copts of Egypt: The Challenges of Modernisation and Identity*. London: I.B. Tauris, 2013.

Ismael, Tareq Y., and Rifa'at el-Sa'id. *The Communist Movement in Egypt, 1920–1988*. Syracuse, NY: Syracuse University Press, 1990.

Jahn, Manfred. "Frames, Preferences, and the Reading of Third-Person Narratives: Towards a Cognitive Narratology." *Poetics Today*, 18.4 (1997): 441–68.

JanMohamed, Abdul R. *Manichean Aesthetics: The Politics of Literature in Colonial Africa*. Amherst: University of Massachusetts Press, 1983.

Kaczvinsky, Donald P. "Introduction." In *Lawrence Durrell's Major Novels: Or, the Kingdom of the Imagination*. Selinsgrove: Susquehanna University Press, 1997, 15–19.

Kaczvinsky, Donald P. "Memlik's House and Mountolive's Uniform: Orientalism, Ornamentalism, and *the Alexandria Quartet*." *Contemporary Literature*, 48.1 (2007): 93–118.

Kaczvinsky, Donald P. "When Was Darley in Alexandria? A Chronology for 'the Alexandria Quartet.'" Web. *Journal of Modern Literature*, 17.4 (Spring 1991): 591–94.

Kararah, Azza. "Introduction." In *Sophia Poole. The Englishwoman in Egypt: Letters from Cairo Written during a residence there in 1842–46*, ed. Azza Kararah. Cairo: AUC Press, 2003, VII–XIX.

Kazin, Alfred. "Lawrence Durrell's Rosy-Finger'd Egypt." In *Critical Essays on Lawrence Durrell*, ed. Alan Friedman. Boston, MA: G.K. Hall, 1987, 30–3.

Keen, Suzanne. *Romances of the Archive in Contemporary British Fiction*. Toronto: University of Toronto Press, 2001.

Al-Khafif, Mahmoud. *Ahmad Urabi al-za'im al-muftara 'alayh*. Cairo: Dar al-Hilal, 1971, volume 2.

Kholoussy, Hanan. *For Better, for Worse: The Marriage Crisis That Made Modern Egypt*. Stanford, CA: Stanford University Press, 2010.

Kitroeff, Alexander. *The Greeks and the Making of Modern Egypt*. Cairo: The American University in Cairo Press, 2019.

Kozma, Liat. "Black, Kinless, and Hungry: Manumitted Female Slaves in Khedival Egypt." In *Race and Slavery in the Middle East: Histories of Trans-Saharan Africans in Nineteenth-Century Egypt, Sudan, and the Ottoman Mediterranean*, ed. Terence Walz and Kenneth M. Cuno. Cairo: The American University in Cairo, 2010, 197–215.

Kozma, Liat. *Policing Egyptian Women: Sex, Law, and Medicine in Khedival Egypt*, Syracuse, NY: Syracuse University Press, 2011.

Krämer, Gudrun. "Political Participation of the Jews in Egypt between World War I and the 1952 Revolution." In *The Jews of Egypt: A Mediterranean Society in Modern Times*, ed. Shimon Shamir. London: Routledge, 2019, 68–82.

Lane, Edward W. *Manners and Customs of the Modern Egyptians.* London: Dent, 1954.

LeSeur, Geta J. *Ten Is the Age of Darkness: The Black Bildungsroman.* Columbia: University of Missouri Press, 1995.

Lewis, Reina. "On Veiling, Vision, and Voyage: Cross-Cultural Dressing and Narratives of Identity." In *Feminist Postcolonial Theory: A Reader*, ed. Reina Lewis and Sara Mills. Edinburgh: Edinburgh University Press, 2003. 520–41.

Lillios, Anna. "Introduction." In *Lawrence Durrell and the Greek World*, ed. Anna Lillios. Selinsgrove: Susquehanna University Press, 2004, 13–29.

Long, C. W. R. *British Pro-Consuls in Egypt, 1914–1929: The Challenge of Nationalism*. London: Routledge Curzon, 2005.

Lowe, Lisa. *Immigrant Acts: On Asian American Cultural Politics*. Durham: Duke University Press, 1996.

MacKenzie, John M. "The Persistence of Empire in Metropolitan Culture." In *British Culture and the End of Empire*, ed. Stuart Ward. Manchester: Manchester University Press, 2001, 21–36.

MacNiven, Ian S. *Lawrence Durrell: A Biography*. London: Faber and Faber, 1998.

Mahfouz, Naguib. *Al-sukkariya*. Cairo: Maktabat Misr, 1962.

Mahfouz, Naguib. *Atahaddath ilaykum*. Beirut: Dar al-Awdah, 1977.

Mahfouz, Naguib. *Sugar Street*, trans. William M Hutchins and Angele Botros Samaan. New York: Anchor Books, 1992.

Mahfouz, Naguib, and ʿAbdel ʿAziz I. *Asatidhati*. Cairo: Mirit li al-Nashr wa al-Maʿlumat, 2002.

Mahfouz, Naguib, and Fathi ʿAshri. *Hawla al-din wa al-dimuqratiyya*. Cairo: al-Dar al-Misryiya al-Lubnaniya, 1990.

Mahfouz, Naguib, and Fathi ʿAshri. *Hawla al-tadayyun wa al-tatarruf.* Cairo: al-Dar al- Misryiya al-Lubnaniya, 1996.

Mahfouz, Naguib, and Fathi ʿAshri. *Hawla al-taharrur wa al-taqaddum*. Cairo: al-Dar al-Misryiyya al-Lubnaniyya, 1996.

Mahfouz, Naguib, and Mahmoud Fawzi. *Iʿtirafat Naguib Mahfouz*. Cairo: Dar al-Shabab al-ʿArabi, 1990.

Mahfouz, Naguib, and Ragaʾ al-Naqqash. *Naguib Mahfouz: Safahat min mudhakkiratih wa adwaʾ jadida ʿala adabih wa hayatih*. Cairo: Markaz al-Ahram li al-Tarjama wa al-Nashr, 1998.

Mahmoud, Rania. "Towards an Egyptian *Bildungsroman*: The National Intellectual after the 1919 Revolution in Naguib Mahfouz's *Sugar Street*." *Arab Studies Quarterly*, 41.4 (2019): 298–316.

Makdisi, Jean Said. Noha Bayoumi, and Rafif Rida Sidawi, eds. *Arab Feminisms: Gender and Equality in the Middle East*. London: I.B. Tauris Publishers in association with the Centre for Arab Unity Studies, Lebanese Association of Women Researchers, 2014.

Mansfield, Peter. *The British in Egypt*. London: Weidenfeld and Nicolson, 1971.

Mansfield, Peter. "Foreword." In *The British in Egypt*, ed. Peter Mansfield. London: Weidenfeld and Nicolson, 1971, IX–XII.

Manzaloui, Mahmoud. "Curate's Egg: An Alexandrian Opinion of Durrell's Quartet." In *Critical Essays on Lawrence Durrell*, ed. Alan Friedman. Boston, MA: G.K. Hall, 1987, 144–57.

Markle, Fletcher. "Teaching Your Characters That They're more or Less Free." In *Lawrence Durrell: Conversations*, ed. Earl G. Ingersoll. Madison: Fairleigh Dickinson University Press, 1998, 99–104.

McClure, John. *Late Imperial Romance*. London: Verso, 1994.

McLarney, Ellen. "The Socialist Romance of the Postcolonial Arabic Novel." *Research in African Literatures: Official Journal of the African Literature Committee of the African Studies Association of America and the African Literatures Seminar of the Modern Language Association*, 40.3 (2009): 186–205.

Medalie, David. "A Century Later: New Fictional Representations of the Boer War." *Journal of Southern African Studies*, 30.2 (2004): 377–92.

Mehrez, Samia. *Egypt's Culture Wars: Politics and Practice*. London: Routledge, 2008.

Melman, Billie. *Women's Orients: English Women and the Middle East, 1718–1918*. London: Macmillan, 1992.

Memmi, Albert, and Robert Bononno. *The Decolonization and the Decolonized*. Minneapolis, University of Minnesota Press, 2006.

Milson, Menahem. *Najib Mahfuz: The Novelist-Philosopher of Cairo*. New York: St. Martin's Press, 1998.

Mitchell, Kate. *History and Cultural Memory in Neo-Victorian Fiction: Victorian Afterimages*. Basingstoke, Hampshire: Palgrave Macmillan, 2010.

Mittermaier, Amira. *Dreams That Matter: Egyptian Landscapes of the Imagination*. Berkeley: University of California Press, 2011.

Mones, Mona. "The Egyptian People in Lawrence Durrell's *the Alexandria Quartet*." In Durrell in Alexandria: On Miracle Ground 9 Conference Proceedings, Alexandria, Egypt, June 1996, ed. Shelly Ekhtiar. Baltimore, MD: International Lawrence Durrell Society, 2005, 112–22.

Moore, Harry T. "Introduction." *The World of Lawrence Durrell*, ed. Harry T. Moore. Carbondale: Southern Illinois University Press, 1962, IX–XIX.

Moore, Harry T. *The World of Lawrence Durrell*. Carbondale: Southern Illinois University Press, 1962.

Moretti, Franco. *The Way of the World: The Bildungsroman in European Culture*. London: Verso, 2000.

Al-Mousa, Nedal M. "The Arabic Bildungsroman: A Generic Appraisal." *International Journal of Middle East Studies*, 25.2 (1993): 223–40.

Al-Mousa, Nedal M. "The Changing Image of the Heroine in the Arabic Female Bildungsromane." *Middle Eastern Literatures*, 9.3 (2006): 257–70.

Munslow, Alun. *Deconstructing History*. London: Routledge, 1997.

Al-Musawi, Muhsin. "Beyond the Modernity Complex: Abd Al-Hakim Qasim's Re-Writing of the Self-Narrative." *Journal of Arabic Literature*, 41 (2010): 22–45.

Al-Musawi, Muhsin. *The Postcolonial Arabic Novel: Debating Ambivalence*. Boston, MA: Brill, 2003.

Ohlander, Erik S. "Behind the Veil of the Unseen: Dreams and Dreaming in the Classical and Medieval Sufi Tradition." In Felek, Ozgen, and Alexander Knysh. *Dreams and Visions in Islamic Societies*, ed. Ozgen Felek and Alexander Knysh. Albany: State University of New York Press, 2012, 199–213.

Pakenham, Thomas. *The Scramble for Africa, 1876–1912*. New York: Random House, 1991.

Paniconi, Maria Elena. *Bildungsroman and the Arab Novel: Egyptian Intersections*. Abingdon, Oxon: Routledge, 2023.

Pinchin, Jane L. *Alexandria Still: Forster, Durrell, and Cavafy*. Princeton, NJ: Princeton University Press, 1977.

Pollard, Lisa. *Nurturing the Nation: The Family Politics of Modernizing, Colonizing and Liberating Egypt (1805–1923)*. Berkeley: University of California Press, 2005.

Powell, Eve M. T. "Burnt-Cork Nationalism: Race and Identity in the Theater of 'Ali al-Kassar." In *Colors of Enchantment: Theater, Dance, Music, and the Visual Arts of the Middle East*, ed. Sherifa Zuhur. Cairo: American University in Cairo Press, 2001, 27–38.

Powell, Eve M. T. *A Different Shade of Colonialism: Egypt, Great Britain, and the Mastery of the Sudan*. Berkeley: University of California Press, 2003.

Powell, Eve M. T. "Slaves or Siblings? Abdallah al-Nadim's Dialogues about the Family." In *Histories of the Modern Middle East: New Directions*. Boulder, CO: Lynne Rienner Publishers, 2002, 155–65.

Powell, Eve M. T. *Tell This in My Memory: Stories of Enslavement from Egypt, Sudan, and the Ottoman Empire*. Stanford, CA: Stanford University Press, 2013.

Quinn, Patrick. "'More than a Fascination with the Divine Marquis': John Fowles's *The Magus* and Lawrence Durrell's *the Alexandria Quartet*." In *Lawrence Durrell and the Greek World*, ed. Anna Lillios. Selinsgrove: Susquehanna University Press, 2004, 270–81.

Al-Rafi'i, 'Abd al-Rahman. *Al-thawra al-Urabiya wa al-ihtilal al-Injilizi*. Cairo: Dar al-Qawmiyya li al-Tiba'a wa al-Nashr, 1966.

Al-Rafi'i, 'Abd al-Rahman. *Fi a'qab al-thawra al-misriyya*. Cairo: Maktabat al-Nahda al-Misriyya, volume 1, 1947

Al-Rafi'i, 'Abd al-Rahman. *Fi a'qab al-thawra al-misriyya*. Cairo: Maktabat al-Nahda al-Misriyya, volume 2, 1947.

Al-Rafi'i, 'Abd al-Rahman. *Fi a'qab al-thawra al-misriyya*. Cairo: Maktabat al-Nahda al-Misriyya, volume 3, 1947.

Al-Rafi'i, 'Abd al-Rahman. *Thawrat sanat 1919: Tarikh Misr al-qawmi min sanat 1914 ila sanat 1921*. Cairo: Maktabat al-Nahda al-Misriyya, volume 1, 1946.

Al-Rafi'i, 'Abd al-Rahman. *Thawrat sanat 1919: Tarikh Misr al-qawmi min sanat 1914 ila sanat 1921*. Cairo: Maktabat al-Nahda al-Misriyya, volume 2, 1946.

Rexroth, Kenneth. "Lawrence Durrell." In *Critical Essays on Lawrence Durrell*, ed. Alan Friedman. Boston, MA: G.K. Hall, 1987, 22–30.

Rose, John M. "Multiple Truths and Multiple Narratives: Nietzsche's Perspectivism and the Narrative Structure of *the Alexandria Quartet*." In *Lawrence Durrell and the Greek World*, ed. Anna Lillios. Selinsgrove: Susquehanna University Press, 2004, 215–38.

Rubin, Gayle. "The Traffic in Women: Notes on the 'Political Economy' of Sex. In *Toward an Anthropology of Women*, ed. Rayna R. Reiter. New York: Monthly Review Press, 1975, 157–210.

Ruskin, John. *Lectures on Art*. London: G. Allen, 1910, 1–40.

Russell, Mona L. "Competing, Overlapping, and Contradictory Agendas: Egyptian Education Under British Occupation, 1882–1922." *Comparative Studies of South Asia, Africa and the Middle East*, 21.1 (2001): 50–60.

Russell, Mona L. *Creating the New Egyptian Woman: Consumerism, Education, and National Identity, 1863–1922*. New York: Palgrave Macmillan, 2004.

Ryzova, Lucie. *The Age of the Efendiyya: Passages to Modernity in National-Colonial Egypt*, Oxford: Oxford University Press, 2014.

El Sadda, Hoda. *Gender, Nation, and the Arabic Novel: Egypt, 1892–2008*. Syracuse, NY: Syracuse University Press, 2012.

El Sadda, Hoda. "Introduction." In *Gender, Nation, and the Arabic Novel: Egypt, 1892–2008*. Syracuse, NY: Syracuse University Press, 2012, XIII–XLII.

Sayyid-Marsot, Afaf Lutfi. *Egypt and Cromer: A Study in Anglo-Egyptian Relations*. New York: Praeger, 1969.

Sayyid-Marsot, Afaf Lutfi. *Egypt's Liberal Experiment, 1922–1936*. Berkeley: University of California Press, 1977.

Sayyid-Marsot, Afaf Lutfi. "Entrepreneurial Women in Egypt." In *Feminism and Islam: Legal and Literary Perspectives*, ed. Mai Yamani. New York: New York University Press, 1996, 33–47.

Sayyid-Marsot, Afaf Lutfi. "Preface," *Egypt and Cromer: A Study in Anglo-Egyptian Relations*. New York: Praeger, 1969.

Scott, Joan. "Feminism's Difference Problem." In *Arab Feminisms: Gender and Equality in the Middle East*, ed. Jean Said Makdisi, Noha Bayoumi, and Rafif Riffa Sidawi. London: I.B. Tauris Publishers in association with the Centre for Arab Unity Studies, Lebanese Association of Women Researchers, 2014, 157–63.

Shalan, Jeff. "Writing the Nation: The Emergence of Egypt in the Modern Arabic Novel." *Journal of Arabic Literature*, 33.3 (2002): 211–47.

Shiller, Dana. "The Redemptive Past in the Neo-Victorian Novel." *Studies in the Novel*, 29.4 (1997): 538–60.

Shukri, Ghali. "Preface." *Al-muntami: Dirasa fi adab Naguib Mahfouz*. Beirut: Dar al-Afaq al-Jadida, 1982.

Sikainga, Ahmad Alawad. "Slavery and Social Life in Nineteenth-Century Turco-Egyptian Khartoum." In *Race and Slavery in the Middle East: Histories of Trans-Saharan Africans in Nineteenth-Century Egypt, Sudan, and the Ottoman Mediterranean*, ed. Terence Walz and Kenneth M. Cuno. Cairo: The American University in Cairo, 2010, 147–70.

Sirriyeh, Elizabeth. *Dreams and Visions in the World of Islam: A History of Muslim Dreaming and Foreknowing*. London: I.B. Tauris, 2018.

Somekh, Sasson. *The Changing Rhythm: A Study of Najib Mahfuz's Novels*. Leiden: Brill, 1973.

Spaulding, Jay. "'Slaves of the King?': Rhetoric and Reality in the Nubian State Tradition." In *African Systems of Slavery*, ed. Jay Spaulding and Stephanie Beswick. Trenton, NJ: Africa World Press, 2010, 247–65.

Stafford, David A.T. "Spies and Gentlemen: The Birth of the British Spy Novel, 1893–1914." *Victorian Studies*, 24.4 (1981): 489–509.

Starr, Deborah A. *Remembering Cosmopolitan Egypt: Literature, Culture, and Empire*. London: Routledge, 2009.

Stewart, Jack. "Soundscapes, Smellscapes, and Cityscapes in *the Alexandria Quartet*." In *Lawrence Durrell and the Greek World*, ed. Anna Lillios. Selinsgrove: Susquehanna University Press, 2004, 129–42.

Sulayman, Rabihah I. *Al-wihda al-wataniyya wa al-fitna al-ta'ifiyya, 1882–1919*. Cairo: Misr al-'Arabiyya li al-Nashr wa-al-Tawzi', 2009.

Taher, Bahaa. *Abnaa Rifa'a: Al-thaqafa wa al-hurriyya*. Cairo: Dar al-Hilal, 1993.

Taher, Bahaa. *Sunset Oasis*, trans. Humphrey T. Davies. London: Sceptre, 2009.

Taher, Bahaa. *Wahat al-ghurub*. Cairo: Dar al-Hilal, 2006.

Tawfik, Amani. "The Motif of Mutilation of Character and Setting in *the Alexandria Quartet*." In *Durrell in Alexandria: On Miracle Ground 9, Conference Proceedings, Alexandria Egypt, June 1996*, ed. Shelly Ekhtiar. Baltimore, MD: International Lawrence Durrell Society, 2005, 70–80.

"Egyptian Crisis: The Fatal Rioting at Alexandria, Official Report, Great Excitement at Cairo, Policy of Italy." *The Daily Telegraph*, June 13, 1882, issue no. 8, p. 436, col. 5, E-H.

Terry, Janice J. *The Wafd, 1919–1952: Cornerstone of Egyptian Political Power*, London: Third World Centre for Research and Publication, 1982.

Toledano, Ehud R. "The Concept of Slavery in Ottoman and Other Muslim Societies: Dichotomy or Continuum?" In *Slave Elites in the Middle East and Africa: A Comparative Study*, ed. Toru Miura and John Edward Philips. London: Kegan Paul International, 2000, 159–75.

Toledano, Ehud R. *The Ottoman Slave Trade and Its Suppression, 1840–1890*, Princeton, NJ: Princeton University Press, 1982.

Tosh, John. *Manliness and Masculinities in Nineteenth-Century Britain: Essays on Gender, Family, and Empire*. Harlow: Pearson Longman, 2005.

Tosh, John. *A Man's Place: Masculinity and the Middle-Class Home in Victorian England*. New Haven, CT: 2007.

Vaughan-Lee, Llewellyn. *Catching the Thread: Sufism, Dreamwork & Jungian Psychology*. Inverness, California: Golden Sufi Center, 1998.

Walz, Terence. "Black Slavery in Egypt during the Nineteenth Century as Reflected in the Mahkama Archives of Cairo." In *Slaves and Slavery in Muslim Africa*, volume 2, *The Servile Estate*, ed. John R. Willis. Abingdon: Routledge, 2016, 137–60.

Walz, Terence. "Sudanese, Habasha, Takarna, and Barabira: Trans-Saharan Africans in Cairo as Shown in the 1848 Census." In *Race and Slavery in the Middle East: Histories of Trans-Saharan Africans in Nineteenth-Century Egypt, Sudan, and the Ottoman Mediterranean*, ed. Terence Walz and Kenneth M. Cuno. Cairo: The American University in Cairo, 2010, 43–76.

Ward, Stuart, ed. *British Culture and the End of Empire*. Manchester: Manchester University Press, 2001.

Ward, Stuart. "Introduction." In *British Culture and the End of Empire*, ed. Stuart Ward. Manchester: Manchester University Press, 2001, 1–20.

Wesseling, H. L. *Divide and Rule: The Partition of Africa, 1880–1914*, trans. Arnold J. Pomerans. Westport, CT: Praeger, 1996.

Wilcox, John. Author's Note. In *The Guns of El Kebir.* London: Headline, 2007, 432–5.

Wilcox, John. *Bombs and Betty Grable.* Warwickshire: Brewin Books, 2010.

Wilcox, John. *The Guns of El Kebir.* London: Headline, 2007.

Wilcox, John. http://www.johnwilcoxauthor.co.uk/questions.asp.

Williams, Abrigail. "Not Everyone Is Grieving Queen Elizabeth's Death: Here's Why Queen Elizabeth's Death Has Generated More Criticism than Grief." *The GW Hatchet*, September 15, 2022. https://www.gwhatchet.com/2022/09/15/heres-why-queen-elizabeths-death-has-generated-more-criticism-than-grief/ (accessed online November 27, 2022.)

Woods, David M. "Love and Meaning in *the Alexandria Quartet*: Some Tantric Perspectives." In *On Miracle Ground: Essays on the Fiction of Lawrence Durrell*, ed. Michael H. Begnal. Lewisburg: Bucknell University Press, 1990. 93–112.

Yousef, Hoda. *Composing Egypt: Reading, Writing, and the Emergence of a Modern Nation, 1870–1930.* Stanford, CA: Stanford University Press, 2016.

Youssef, Mary. *Minorities in the Contemporary Egyptian Novel.* Edinburgh: Edinburgh University Press, 2020.

Yusuf, Yusuf. *Al-ghazal al-'udhri: Dirasa fi al-hubb al-maqmu'.* Damascus: Manshurat Ittihad al-Kuttab al-'Arab, 1978.

Zahlan, Anne R. "The Destruction of the Imperial Self in Lawrence Durrell's the Alexandria Quartet." *Perspectives on Contemporary Literature*, 12 (1986): 3–12.

Al-Zayyat, Latifa. *Min suwar al-mar'a fi al-qisas wa al-riwayat al-'arabiyya.* Cairo: Dar al-Thaqafa al-Jadida, 1989.

Index

www.ingramcontent.com/pod-product-compliance
Lightning Source LLC
Chambersburg PA
CBHW070543100726
47907CB00004B/1238